SANDMANN

By

Glenna Jarvis

Dedicated in loving memory of
Terry Lynn Earls

You were a true friend with the most beautiful heart.

Chapter 1

Green eyes the color of moss growing on rocks. Nice. He liked them. No, *loved* them, had to have those eyes, watch as they turned into liquid pools of black and the soul seeped out of them and into *him*.

He couldn't see it happen but could *feel* it. That hot tendril of life pierced his chest and curled lazily in his gut. That's what happened with the first one, and oh it felt good—a sensation so tangible that, if he tried, he could reach out and snatch it from the air.

But he didn't want to taint her soul; to do so might lessen the effect and he wanted to experience every pulsating moment. Tightness spread through his groin. He breathed deeply, exhaled and stared at the woman on the splintered floor.

Kneeling, he pressed two fingers against her cool neck. He could barely feel life pulse through the latex glove.

Folds of her cream-colored dress tangled about her thighs, covered in pasty white stockings. Her hair—ratted, sprayed and stiff—resembled steel wool. The heavy makeup looked just as unnatural.

He returned to the bathroom with pull-chain toilet and enamel sink, cracked and loose from its pipe. A single flame from the grimy lamp sent shadows twisting over peeled wallpaper, fissures in the ceiling, and boarded-over windows through which weak shards of twilight seeped. He spread plastic over the rust-stained bathtub, tucked it into place, considered taping it down but why bother. She could no longer struggle. And there wouldn't be as much blood as there had been with the first one.

With his fists he pushed himself up, stepped into the front room and let his vision readjust to the dimness. He needed to collect the fragments hidden in three women's souls, the pieces that would blend into the single woman he'd lost years ago.

After this, all he required was one more. Already he'd found her. Tonight he would give her the gift of his reflection. Wherever she went, he would know. Whatever she felt, he would feel. And when it was time, he'd capture her eyes—those inquisitive, haunting green eyes.

Three Mason jars sat on a two-by-four brace between wooden supports, exposed where the sheetrock had been ripped away. One held milky orbs, slightly flattened, their color faded now that Stella's soul was gone. The other two waited to be filled.

"One more," he whispered as he set the battery operated CD player to repeat. Soothing music caressed the air.

He returned his attention to the woman on the floor, gripped beneath her arms and dragged her toward the bathroom. Her foot caught where age and moisture had rotted the wood. Sweat broke out across his upper lip. With a sharp tug he freed her foot. The force sent him crashing against the doorframe. Her head struck the floor. She moaned softly with a hint of vibrato. He hadn't made a mistake; she had an exquisite voice.

He reinforced his hold, pulled her into the bathroom, propped her on the tub's edge and rolled her inside.

She peered up at him. Her eyes, black framed by thin green rings, widened. Then the lids drooped. Still drowsy. He'd get her to open those eyes, but didn't want a fight. Didn't want to hit her.

There had been enough fighting in his life. After those long nights when Mom suffered the beatings and she screamed—oh, how she had screamed—she had taken him into her room. There, she played beautiful music and told him stories.

Love. Betrayal. Revenge. Triumph.

All those years ago, as a child huddled in fear against her breast, he'd made a pact with himself that he'd never hit a woman.

Killing them. That was different. It was what he *had* to do.

Chapter 2

Someone once told me flies die out in winter. Whoever it was hadn't considered green flies. Hoards now buzzed above the steel dumpster, small winged insects defying the frigid December air in order to lay eggs on the rancid snack.

At five-feet two, I had to rise on my toes to get a glimpse of the body two parking slots and a chain-link fence away. Not an easy task when perched on the trunk of my broken-down Corsica, and wearing Mary Jane flats. I really didn't *need* a look, but I wanted one. Morbid? Perhaps if I wasn't a reporter who savored those forensic tidbits that covering crime fed me. Not just anyone could hide his or her fascination under such an effective guise unless they were law enforcement.

"Hannah? What have you got?" Adam Grigsby, my managing editor, tilted his head of white hair toward the cops clustered around the trash bin. Rain fell at a slant, darkening his gray tie and creating transparent splotches in his shirt. "Well?"

"Not enough for a story." I returned my attention to the dumpster just beyond the fence separating the lot from the pressroom loading bays. No maggots on the body, but all I could really see was a leg covered in a tattered, white stocking. Still, the lack of larvae could mean the woman had been killed less than twelve hours ago.

"Well, get enough." Grigsby glared at me. "And *quick*. Our subscribers are angry they haven't gotten their papers."

The rain intensified, driving the flies beneath the cover of discarded newspapers. I dropped from the trunk, landed in a puddle and shook off my black leather shoe. Although soaked, I backed under the eaves framing the *Borden Gazette* to escape the downpour.

That morning my roommate, Ozrick, had dropped me off at seven, an hour before the janitor found the body. How crazy is that? I mean, I'd walked right past it, trudged into the newsroom without noticing a thing. Then again, that wasn't unusual. I needed at least three cups of coffee to get the mental gears going, especially after a gig. I played drums in a classic rock band from nine until two A.M., three nights a week, which made seven o'clock a real killer.

When the janitor came screaming inside, Grigsby went wild. It wasn't often someone handed us a headline. We'd get the scoop. Nothing else mattered. After nine years covering crime in my small, Central California town even I wasn't that calloused. I still have heart and soul, two essential elements Grigsby lacked.

I glanced at the half-dozen cars in the lot, and the three near the corner of Ponderosa and state Route 41. What time had the advertising crew arrived? The pressmen had been in the building since two A.M. Maybe they saw something. I posted a mental note to ask.

Poking my glasses into place, I noticed the detective, Sergeant Dan Morales, study something on the asphalt. Regardless of the rain, he pulled his poncho off over his head, bunched it up and tossed it over the wet, yellow crime scene tape. The rain gear was a distraction. Morales hated distractions.

He motioned to the department's Identification Technician and placed an upside down V-shaped marker on the ground. The IT, Esteves—who looked more like a scrawny monk than a crime scene investigator—snapped photos, sending bursts of light through the gloom.

Morales pinched open a small envelope and used tweezers to grasp—a thread? No, thicker, like a waterlogged carpet fiber. From the brown plastic tackle box, he took another marker and set it beside a cigarette butt.

"I'm scrapping the A section." Grigsby leaned against the building beside me and focused on the detectives. "We'll push the trial coverage to the rail and drop everything else below the fold. We need art," Grigsby shouted through the open door, and added under his breath, "Hell of a time for Jeremy to take leave."

"He's in the hospital," I reminded Grigsby.

"He should've been more careful getting shots of that crash."

I wanted to defend Jeremy—a rubber-necker struck him on state Route 99, the main artery through Madera County. "It wasn't like he jumped in front of the car."

"I've got a guy coming in this morning," Grigsby said. "He might shoot until Jeremy returns. It's going to bust my budget though."

No compassion, but that didn't surprise me. While everyone in the newsroom pooled in for a get-well card and an African violet, Grigsby had issued a warning to Jeremy via the phone that if he didn't get back soon he'd be out of a job. Guess I wasn't the only workaholic. But least I wasn't an ass about it. "Jeremy'll be back once the doctors release him."

"Until then I've got to find someone to catch this. As for the story, we've got to get the paper on the press by noon, Monakee. Not a minute after."

"Don't worry." Unmindful of the rain, I stepped closer to the sagging yellow tape, twisted in the fence's metal links. "You'll have your headline."

"Damn right I will," Grigsby muttered. "And it better be good."

Or what? You'll fire me? That wouldn't free up his budget. And this wasn't a good time to get smart-mouthed with my boss. I was already on Grigsby's shit list. The publisher had been served a lawsuit just before closing yesterday. When I left he and Grigsby were in a closed-door meeting. I bit my lower lip and returned my attention to Morales.

From beneath a fringe of black hair, Morales fixed his piercing gaze on me. Rain trickled down his face and jiggled on the tip of his nose. He swiped the drop away and stalked toward me, his arrogant swagger letting everyone know he packed a gun and wasn't afraid to use it. His shaggy hair and week-old beard stubble gave him a dark, dangerous appearance, one I still found attractive. It wasn't a look he intentionally went for. He neglected things like haircuts and shaving. He propped his fingers on the hips of his black Wranglers and shifted his attention between Grigsby and me.

"Ready to move the body. No shots once its lifted. Going to get photos? Get 'em now."

Grigsby ducked into the tan, green-trimmed Gazette building.

"Where's the coroner?" I asked.

"Came and left. No question. She's dead. Merry fuckin' Christmas," Morales muttered. "Almost made it a year without a murder. Now we've got two. The sonofabitch."

Along the road that ran behind the Gazette, brittle pine trees with clumps of tinsel lay in the gutter and shook as wind rocked them. Artificial snow clung to dingy windows beside doors with bare hooks where wreaths had been taken down for storage.

Yep. Murder had a way of putting a crunch on Christmas.

Grigsby returned with the company's Nikon.

"What can you give me?" I asked Morales.

"Not much."

"Is there a connection to last week's homicide?"

"Off the record?" He raised a brow, which disappeared beneath his rain-soaked hair.

"I'm working on a story, and I have less than an hour to finish." It wasn't like I'd asked him to reveal all the details of his case, just enough to know whether our citizens had a problem—like a serial killer. "She's not dismembered like the other?"

He gave me a hard stare.

"Okay, how about a duffle bag?"

He shook his head. Water droplets splashed over his black, police-issue jacket. "Not releasing details."

"A name? Can you give me that much?" I gripped my pen, stemming the hot ball of anger rising in my chest. Since I broke up with him, I suspected he withheld information out of spite. Now, I'm certain. He'd been a fantastic lover and great friend, but it was just sex. I wanted a certain amount of tenderness in a man. Morales only showed tenderness when cleaning his gun. "Let's not make this personal."

A grin played the corner of his thin lips. "Ongoing investigation."

"At least give me a description."

"Female, five-four, approximately two-thirty."

I scribbled the information on the notepad's damp page. "Age?"

"Mid forties."

"Is she local?"

"No ID. No personal belongings." He glanced back at the dumpster.

Esteves scrubbed his hands with a Wet Ones, donned a fresh pair of gloves and peered over the dumpster's rim. The canister of wipes, his constant companion, was wedged in his coat pocket. In bird-like motions, he peeked through the heavy-framed bifocals, over their tops, back through the glass.

"She's dressed odd," Morales added.

"Oh?" I poised my pen over the page. "Define *odd*."

"Theatrical."

"An actress?" We didn't have a performing arts center, but my roommate, Ozrick, intended to change that. He had big plans of restoring culture to the crime-ridden town. Anything would be better than its current title: Meth Capitol of the World.

If these murders continued, the town would acquire an even darker name. Two bodies inside a week weren't unusual if they were gang related. But these were grisly. Not something Borden, with its thirty-three thousand population, was used to seeing.

Borden was the kind of town where people locked their doors, but felt relatively safe walking to the Quick Mart after dark. An old town with all the character of a bullet-riddled, sun-faded billboard. The kind of place one passes without noticing, where chimes from the Catholic Church at the west edge of town were loud enough to haunt everyone's sleep.

Morales motioned toward the officers. "Called Fresno PD. Got them checking their missing list. That's their Commander." He jerked his head toward a man half hidden behind the dumpster. "Sure got here quick."

I added the information, set my pen and notepad on my Corsica's wet hood and faced Morales. "Off the record. What do you know?"

He pulled a Three Musketeers from his pocket, tore the wrapper down its seam and pried chocolate off the bar's end. "Not dismembered, no duffle bag. But, two pieces of evidence link the murders."

This time I raised my brow, waiting for details. "And they are?"

"Holdbacks." He popped the chocolate in his mouth.

That wasn't fair. I could voice my objection but it wouldn't change anything. He was as tight-lipped as any good detective, and dumping him only locked those lips tighter.

I'd call my contact at Borden Funeral Home, Carley Summers. She already told me the first victim hadn't been hacked up, but the amputations of her legs and arms were almost surgical. Also the woman's eyes had been gouged out. I'd be willing to bet a month's pay the woman in the dumpster was missing her eyes, too. I couldn't ask without risking my source, and if the information wasn't on the record, I couldn't publish it.

Two Emergency Medical Technicians climbed from a white, blue and red ambulance.

"Why are they here?" I asked.

"Funeral home's unavailable," Morales said, tilting his chin toward the EMTs. "Not supposed to transport the dead, but I've got no choice."

"Bending the rules?" That was shocking. Morales was a *by the book* guy.

"Least I'm not breakin' 'em," he said with a scowl.

Brushing the accusation aside, I scanned my notes. I needed more information, and wasn't getting it here, which gave me until five o'clock to dig up more details. I'd do a follow up for tomorrow's edition.

The first victim's funeral was set for tomorrow. Maybe a family member would talk. But I'd already tried to speak with Mr. De La Cruz, and he threatened to have me arrested.

Morales poked the rest of the candy bar in his mouth, wiped his fingers against his jeans and ducked back under the police tape.

Esteves, overseeing the EMTs' removal of the body, uttered instructions too soft to hear through the steady rain. But I could imagine his tone was jittery and filled with caution. The guy was a genius and a little high strung. No one was allowed in his lab unless he was there. Even then, he went *idiot savant* if someone touched something. I learned that the hard way.

Beneath protection of the building's eaves, I chewed my thumbnail, a nasty habit I couldn't shake. The older EMT, Kurkis, sent his trainee into the dumpster to do the dirty work. Once the rookie lifted the woman, Kurkis gripped the milky plastic in which she was wrapped. Though the plastic, I caught a fuzzy glimpse of her clothes. White stockings, ruffled dress. Red patches marked her cheeks. They placed her in a zippered body bag.

Rain pounded the asphalt. I retrieved my notepad and pen from the Corsica's hood, pulled open the door and sank onto the passenger seat. With a dead alternator the car wouldn't get me anywhere, but it could provide shelter.

On the dashboard lay a rose so dark it looked like a splotch of blood. I lifted its long stem and the bud tilted. It had been there long enough to wilt. The car died last night, which meant someone left the flower within the last fifteen hours.

Morales. It had to be. Over the past few months, he'd made attempts at reconciliation. But a rose? His style was to grab me around the waist, pull me hard against him and suggest we climb into the back of his Bronco.

Once the body had been placed in the ambulance, I caught Morales' attention and waved him over. He strode across the parking lot.

I held up the rose. "Rather inappropriate for a crime scene, don't you think?"

He froze mid-stride and his dark-eyed gaze melted with fear, a look that sent cold waves of panic surging through me.

"Sonofabitch," he shouted. "Drop it. Put it down and back the fuck away from the car."

My hand reflexively tightened, then I tossed the flower onto the driver's seat, scrambled out, laced my fingers behind my head and fought the urge to drop to my knees.

He lowered my arms. "Guilty conscience?"

I tugged my coat into place and glared at him. "That attorney filed a lawsuit over my story. I've been edgy, and I don't like getting yelled at."

I'd sifted through three trashcans to find documents to support that story. If Morales found out, he'd arrest me and probably enjoy every moment.

My fingers trembled, and I balled them into fists. "I take it you didn't leave the rose."

He motioned toward the rookie EMT and shouted, "Bring water."

The rookie dug a bottle from a pack in the ambulance and jogged toward my car. His olive skin and ebony hair lent him an exotic look that always sent a sensual flutter through me. Only now, blended with panic, the flutter came across as a mild bout of nausea. He flicked his gaze over me, twisted off the cap and handed the water to Morales who grabbed my arm and doused my hand.

"What are you doing?" I tried to pull away, but he dug his fingers hard against my wrist. "You're scaring me."

"Sedative." Using the hem of his jacket, he scrubbed my palm.

Hard as I tried, I couldn't make his word sink in. It was Friday, and I'd had a rough week. I didn't want to deal with this. Oh no. I just wanted to get through the day, go home, grab a cold Budweiser and soak in the tub. Maybe plug a mind-numbing movie I'd seen a hundred times into the DVD so I could curl up with a pillow and blanket and vegetate.

"Sedative?" Then the word sank in like cold sap oozing from a tree and I shivered. "Someone tried to drug me?"

I stared at the rose. The flower's stem was pinched like someone had snipped it with dull scissors. It had landed on a compact-sized mirror. The petals' reflection went from sharp to dull where they hit the mirror's silver frame.

"*That's* not mine."

Morales glanced past me, into the car. "The mirror? Sure about that?"

"Positive. The only one I owned is above my bathroom sink."

He approached the car, hand hovering above his Glock as though he'd find someone huddled inside. Kneeling, he tugged a pencil from his coat and used the eraser to carefully lift the thorny stem.

"Seen anyone hanging around lately?"

"No." I crammed my hand into my coat pocket to warm it. Cold air seeped through a hole and I posted a mental sticky-note to stitch it up.

"Any new employees?"

"You've seen this before, haven't you?"

"Answer me," he shouted, and I flinched. Man, he was stressed.

"No new employees, no one hanging around." I turned toward the ambulance just as Kurkis closed the doors, bringing two halves of the caduceus symbol together. "What's going on?"

"Whoever left this knows your car."

"You wouldn't turn cop on me because someone left a rose on my dashboard." Unless it connected to one of his cases. "You found a rose in that duffle bag, didn't you?"

Over his shoulder, he shouted, "Holmes, call a tow."

"Got it, Sarge."

Facing me, Morales asked, "This rose. Ever seen it before?"

"Ruth grows them. She has an elaborate garden."

"Your mom grows this rose?"

"I've asked you not to call her that," I said under my breath, and twisted the Celtic knot ring on my middle finger. After my brother, Richard's death more than twelve years ago I'd been instructed to use only her given name. In my opinion, I didn't have a mother. "She special ordered plants when I was a kid. They're in her greenhouse between *Deep Secret* and *Red Devil*."

"Does she sell them?"

"No. She prunes them, occasionally brings in a bouquet. She has more than a hundred varieties."

"Any significance?"

"It's known as the black rose. Black means vengeance," I said, although Ruth scolded me numerous times for calling it the black rose. *There is no such thing*, she would say, and the species name would roll off her tongue like a well-practiced line in one of her operas: *Barkarole*.

"Think that attorney's sending a message? Lance Parkston, right?"

"The story ran a week ago. His goon served the lawsuit last night. It doesn't make sense he'd threaten me now."

"What time did you get here?"

"Seven. But my car's been here all night."

"Broke down again?"

"Dad's sending a tow truck this afternoon." With my fifteen-year-old Chevy sporting close to two hundred thousand miles, Dad had the tow company on speed dial.

"What's Parkston suing for?" Morales shifted his attention from the rose, and used the pencil to rotate the mirror.

"He's demanding my notes, and he wants me to reveal my source."

"Gonna give him what he wants?"

"Of course not." My source would face federal charges just for talking to me. "I've got the Constitution in my corner."

"Didn't stop them in Texas."

"Or New York," I added, "but I'm still not talking."

"Willing to go to jail?"

A knot tightened my throat. Swallowing hard, I glanced at the cops. I imagined stainless steel locking my wrists. I'd rather die than go to jail. The closest I'd been to a cell was the visitor's side of a Plexiglas partition.

"Well?"

"I don't think it's him. He's going to fight his battle in court."

"Does he have lawsuits against anyone else?"

"He files a suit whenever someone pisses him off," I said. "He could be suing half the county."

Morales stood, fumbled in his pocket for a notepad and scribbled something down. I managed to read two words before he pocketed the book: De La Cruz and Parkston.

De La Cruz was the first victim, the dismembered body found in a duffle bag. "You think there's a connection between this and the murders?"

"Didn't say that."

"You're not saying anything." I pulled off my glasses and rubbed my eyes. I didn't need this. On top of the heat I was getting from Grigsby, I didn't need some psycho sending me drug-laced roses.

"The woman." I tilted my head toward the dumpster. "Brown hair, green eyes?"

Morales licked his lips and shifted his weight.

"Just like the first victim." I sighed. "And me."

He nodded.

"Have you tried to track down this flower?"

"Got Badorini on it. Nothing yet."

"That could take weeks." Something told me I didn't have weeks. Whoever left this rose wanted me dead and cold and, oh God, I didn't want to end up with my arms and legs tucked next to my torso in a cramped duffle bag.

I stared at my palm, red from his scrubbing. "You found roses with the other two women, didn't you? They had drugs on them. That's one of your holdbacks, isn't it?"

Morales slid his hand over my waist. "De La Cruz got one four days before her body was discovered. Found another in the duffle bag. Traces of a sedative on the second, but didn't want to take a chance this wasn't laced."

"And this woman?"

"Don't know."

"Four days," I muttered.

"Too early to establish a pattern," he said, but the slight twitch next to his eye told me he was thinking along the same lines.

Four days. And the only leads I had were a rose and mirror.

Chapter 3

A diesel truck, *Turner Towing* scrawled on its yellow door, pulled into the parking lot and groaned to a halt. Dad said the truck wouldn't come until late afternoon. Narrowing my eyes, I turned toward Morales.

"You're confiscating my car?"

"Evidence." He waved to the driver and jabbed the air above my Corsica.

"Take the mirror and rose. Don't take the *whole thing.*"

"Gotta check for trace, dust for prints—provided you haven't fucked them up," he grumbled.

"Without a warrant?" I chuckled. "I don't think so."

"Don't need one. Probable cause."

"Dad's supposed to fix it today." Knowing Morales, he'd keep my car until Esteves examined every discarded Starbucks bottle. I practically lived out of the broken-down Chevy. "I've got a gig tonight."

"Call someone to fill in."

"No one's sitting in for me." That was a C-note I couldn't afford to lose.

"Stayin' with me." With his knee, he knocked my car door closed.

"No I'm not."

"Not gonna argue."

"You think that's the answer?" I took several measured breaths, and in a carefully controlled voice, added, "Do you expect me to sit around and wait for this guy to kill me?"

"We'll catch him first."

"You're not hiding me away. If that's how you solve crimes, you might want to rethink your tactics."

"Protective custody. Gotta cuff you, I will."

"You can't do that," I said. "It's illegal."

"Fuck legal. Not going to let this sonofabitch kill you." He was a veteran officer, spent his rookie days in Compton, south of Los Angeles. A war zone. He'd come back a streetwise cop, played by the book, and sometimes interpreted that book by his own experience. *Legal* and *necessary* didn't always have the same meaning. But I wasn't playing the cop-wise game.

"I'm not sitting around while this guy tries to find me. I'll find him with or without your help."

"No choice," Morales shot back. His anger stemmed from fear. He didn't want me ending up like the woman on her way to the funeral home's autopsy room. I knew that. But he didn't have much more to go on than I did, and I had a better chance of gaining information. Law didn't bind me. Not that I was in the habit of breaking it, just bending a little when necessary.

They would take the latest victim to Carley's mortuary. Madera County was too small, and its budget too tight to afford its own coroner. We contracted with Fresno, and autopsies were performed in the funeral home of record. And I knew Morales envisioned me lying on the cold steel slab in Carley's preparation room.

"I'll borrow Dad's truck." I'd been reduced to using stubbornness as my only defense.

"Sonofabitch. This killer's one sick fuck. Chopped up a woman, strangled another. Not going to let that happen again. Got no problem arresting you."

"On what charge? Wanting to figure out who's trying to kill me? That's one I haven't found in the penal code."

"Fuckin' smart ass, know that?"

"So Grigsby tells me." I cupped Morales' cheek, forcing him to face me. "I know you want to protect me. But I can't sit around and do nothing. Respect that."

His scowl deepened. "Stick close to home. Anything suspicious, call my cell. You should carry one."

"Cells are a leash, and I don't like anyone yanking my chain." I started to lean away, but he slid his hand beneath my coat, hooked his finger in my jeans' belt loop. "Okay, I'll see if I can hold onto Ozrick's phone. Happy?"

"Be happy when this Sonofabitch is caught."

"Right now, I've got a story to write." Rising on my toes, I planted a quick kiss on his cheek.

"Not in front of the guys."

"They don't care. Makes you human."

"Whatever," he mumbled. Before I could plant another symbol of gratitude—of affection, I'd always had a sweet spot in my heart for Morales—he leaned away.

"Going to get Badorini to follow you," Morales whispered, referring to his senior detective. "Get you his cell number, too. We'll be watching—Ah, shit. Feel like we're using you as bait."

"Maybe that's not such a good idea." I gently tugged his arm, urging him to release me.

"Because it'll keep you from conducting your own investigation?" Morales shook his head. "Leave the job to me."

"Fine." I fought the urge to slide my hand into my coat pocket and cross my fingers.

"Giving up?" His mouth hardened into a tight grin. "You're a rotten liar. Anyone tell you that?"

I bit my lower lip.

"Not going to answer?" Morales' smile broadened. "Remember. We'll be watching."

He shifted his attention to the police rookie, tugging the waist of his too-large pants as he sauntered toward us. Holmes' utility belt sagged with the weight of his gun as it would on a kid playing cops and robbers. With his short cropped, strawberry hair and spatter of freckles he reminded of me of Opie from the *Andy Griffith Show*.

"Hey Ms. Monakee."

"Your boss is stealing my car."

"Securing evidence." Morales scowled. To Holmes, he said, "Get this to the station. No one touches it but Esteves."

"You got it, Sarge."

Turner dropped heavy chains on the pavement next to my car's bumper. Although the ambulance had pulled out ten minutes ago, the young EMT remained. He came through the chain-link gate and set a white plastic first-aid kit at his feet.

"Missed your ride," I said.

"The office is only a couple of blocks. Kurkis thought I ought to check you out before leaving."

"Drug's fast acting." Morales folded his arms and widened his stance. "She would've passed out by now."

I met the EMT's gaze, and that flutter returned. Heat flooded my cheeks.

"You might want to avoid driving," he said.

"That won't be a problem." I gestured toward Turner, who wiggled beneath the bumper and hooked chains to my Corsica's undercarriage.

The EMT pulled a card from the pocket of his blue satin jacket. I suddenly remembered who he reminded me of. That actor from an old Stephen King film. Rear Window? No, *Secret Window*. Johnny Depp.

I glanced at the card. Eddie Tolson. A golden ticket if he'd responded to the first murder. Morales wouldn't talk. Maybe Tolson would.

He retrieved his case. A silver chain looped through a white-gold band escaped his collar. He straightened, tucked the ring back into his shirt and smiled. "If you need a ride, I get off at four."

"Not going anywhere," Morales said.

"How about after work?" Tolson asked.

"I'll have transportation," I said.

"If you change your mind, let me know. Maybe I'll toss in dinner," he added, and flashed that heart-fluttering smile.

"Sounds intriguing."

"Christ," Morales uttered.

Flipping the card over, I scanned the writing on back. Tolson had added his phone and room number at the Inn.

He strolled across the lot, crossed Yosemite Drive and sank beyond the corner of the feed store.

"What the fuck was that?" Morales snagged the card. "The Inn? Guy's barely employed, stayin' at a fuckin' motel."

"*Hotel.*" I tugged the card from his fingers and slid it into my pocket.

"Guy's a fuckin' deadbeat."

Ah. The F-word three times in a row meant something had rattled his cage. "I guess news has hit the streets."

"What news?"

"That I'm an eligible woman."

"Getting too old for dating," he grumbled.

"I'm only thirty-one."

"Not you. Me."

In other words he wanted me back so he could abandon the hunt. Convenience wasn't about to become part of my vows. I was tired of speaking that foreign language, trying to explain the difference between romance and a nookie session. Part of me wanted to tell him not to worry, that he'd find someone. But he'd already chased off one wife, and still hadn't learned there's more to life than the job. No one could compete with a badge and gun. It was like sleeping with Dirty Harry.

"I have a story to write." I skirted a rain puddle and pushed open the Gazette's heavy steel door.

"Anything happens--"

"I'll call."

The morning's dismal gray followed me into the newsroom. An invisible veil of printers ink mingled with dusty scents of paper. Phones rang, keyboards clacked as reporters battled for quotes that would earn them front-page exposure.

I slipped into my cubicle where Post-It notes framed the computer monitor. I moved through life by way of notes-to-self scribbled on the brightly colored squares.

Call Dad about car.

I plucked it off and tossed it into the wastebasket.

Meet Keitz at eleven.

Damn. An appointment with the district attorney wasn't easy to score. I tossed that one, too, found the stack of blue sticky notes and jotted down: *Call Keitz and apologize—Reschedule.*

I had a story to write, but all I wanted was to get to the florists before they closed, get information on the flower and maybe who bought them.

I dropped my coat on the table beside my desk, settled in the wobbly chair and flipped through my notebook. After opening a *News Edit* document, I spent the next forty minutes composing the murder story. Then I moved it into the electronic folder where Grigsby would find it, sat back, folded my arms and rested them on my head.

One more story would fill my quota for the day. It wouldn't publish until tomorrow's edition, but two bylines was the general rule. If I could get one more in the queue, I could call it quits and focus on the rose.

Down the hall of threadbare carpet, I made my way to the fax machine. The probation department had conducted a sweep last night and officer Deorian promised me a press release. I'd follow up with phone calls; he never included enough details.

Maybe I could get Dad's truck and slip out early. I wanted to check every florist in town before heading for *The Dock*, where I'd be stuck behind a six-piece drum kit until two o'clock tomorrow morning.

The door was closed to Grigsby's office, what the staff called the fishbowl. Windows on three sides, he could swim around like a guppy in a drunken stupor while the grunts did all the work.

Through the blinds, I saw our publisher Leslie Vargas' head as he sat facing Grigsby, seated at his steel gray desk. In the chair beside Vargas sat a blond man, a full head taller and a good twenty years younger than the publisher. The four-by-four post separating the windows blocked the man's profile, so I couldn't be sure who he was. My guess was the company's lawyer—they were probably discussing the lawsuit.

I snagged pages from the fax machine and rifled through them, searching for the probation office's logo. Found it.

"*Monakee*." Even through the closed door, Grigsby's voice boomed and rattled what remained of my nerves. I pushed into his office and eased the door shut.

"I burned my notes and won't give up my source," I said before he could speak.

"I didn't call you in about the lawsuit," Grigsby said in a tone he reserved for me and any other pain-in-the-ass reporter. "This is Quint Rydell. He's heading up the County's Search and Rescue team," Grigsby continued, but I barely heard him. "He's a former Navy SEAL, big-wall climber, tracker. He's also a photographer. He's agreed to fill in until Jeremy gets back."

Everything beyond the name faded, became tinny as the words reached my ears. My chest ached as though a giant hand reached around me and crushed the air from my lungs.

Quint Rydell. My past had come back to haunt me.

Chapter 4

Quint Rydell. A name I hoped never to hear again. Oh, I didn't want to be here. If I could slip out, get back to my desk and write the story, everything would be okay. I moved toward the door.

"Hannah?" Turning, I peered at Grigsby, leaning over his desk. "Still with us?"

I should face Quint; it'd be the polite thing to do. But my legs locked, my feet froze and the breath caught in my lungs. Finally, I flicked my gaze briefly to his.

He stood to his full height of six-feet two. Slowly, I shifted my attention to shoulders broad enough to test the seams of his pale brown shirt. Something made in India. Hand stitched. And why the hell did that seem important? Why focus on his shirt?

To keep from looking into those soft, hazel eyes. I didn't need to see them. It wasn't like I'd ever forget them. I'd tried, oh God, how I'd tried. For twelve years I'd tried.

Instead of facing him, I studied the way his snug-fitting Levis hugged his trim hips, those muscular thighs—I let my gaze wander to his hands, slender fingers with neatly trimmed nails. No ring, not that it mattered. But there wasn't one, and somehow that seemed important.

"Hey, Monkey." That voice. I'd finally gotten it out of my head and there it was. Deeper, stronger, a sultry undertone, the way a too-perfect hero in a bodice-buster romance might sound. My knees weakened. I reached behind me and grasped the doorknob.

"Monkey?" Grigsby gave me a quizzical look.

"Monakee. Monkey." I glanced up at Quint. "It's what he called me when we were kids. We knew each other when . . . we were kids."

That evening more than twelve years ago flooded my mind; a hot summer night made even hotter in the tangled sheets of my twin-sized bed. The night after graduation. The night my brother Richard had died.

Quint lifted those too-long lashes and peered back. His eyes adopted the color of warm caramel. Then he grinned that crooked smile I'd always thought of as cocky. His golden-blond hair teased his shoulders in a style that revealed the hint of rebellion he'd possessed as a teenager, too long for a recent military discharge. A strip of silver trailed from the haphazard part as though someone dropped a piece of tinsel on his head.

Heart slamming against my ribs, I switched my attention to Grigsby. "The murder story is in the queue."

"Good." To Quint, he said, "I took photos. Not great, but they'll do. Could you adjust them and put them in the system? We've got to get this baby on the press."

"Sure."

"Hannah will show you Jeremy's station and where to place the art in the system." Grigsby's expression hardened as he glared my way. "We'll talk about that lawsuit later."

I slipped out of the office, fixed my attention on the narrow path between cubicles and the gap that marked my corner of the newsroom. If I could duck in there, close myself off awhile I'd be okay. Yep. I'd be fine. Everything would be just peachy-keen.

I hovered a moment beside that gap, glanced at my chair, the computer, the Post-It notes blooming from the monitor. All I wanted was to get my last story in the queue, get out of there and track down the rose. Instead I stepped past my cubicle, rounded the corner to the one beside mine where my first lover—who bolted from my life just as quickly as he had stolen my virginity—would be working.

I drew a deep breath, and gritted my teeth until I thought my jaw would crack. The pounding of my heart created a dull buzzing in my head.

"Photo station," I said, and sucked in another lungful of air. "Photos are--" I sat, booted up the computer and waited until the icons flickered into place. "Photos are in a folder marked with the edition's date. After they're adjusted--"

He crouched down and placed his hand over mine. "It's good to see you, Monkey."

I eased my hand from under his. How dare he? After he left, I waited for a phone call. Maybe a letter. Hell, an email with the entire message in the subject line would have sufficed. But no, I got nothing. Nada. Not a single word. And now I wanted to slap him. Hard. Very, very hard. He deserved that and so much more.

He cleared his throat and stared at the screen.

The job. Focus on the job. "The shots you need are dated today. Once they're corrected, copy them into the A-1 folder. Got it?"

"Yeah."

Shoving my glasses into place, I brushed past him. The warm, musky hint of sandalwood soap filled my senses. I remembered that scent, too, alluring and sensual.

Don't go there, girl. Keep those thoughts in the past where they belong. Focus on the rose. If the four-day timeline was correct, I didn't have time to think about Quint.

I returned to my desk, pulled my foot onto the chair and propped my chin on my knee. Slipping on my headphones, I scanned the clutter, found the *Hard Promises* CD, plugged it into the iMac and skipped to number seven. Following a fast, hard drum roll, Tom Petty's voice filled my head: *I'm not much on mystery.*

Stan Lynch was a hell of a drummer. Plugging in Petty always calmed me. He helped me let go and drift, mindlessly, for a while. As a kid I listened with headphones, played cassettes over and over until I could emulate Lynch's moves. He taught me to feel the rhythm, play with heart. Richard taught me to play from the soul.

I stared at my computer, the Tom Petty and the Heartbreakers screen saver fading, sharpening, fading again as images shifted and changed like reflections of my life, which until two hours ago was quasi normal. Odd. I could take a killer stalking me—as long as Morales was close by. But Quint and memories of my brother's death? I wasn't sure I could deal with both. I tugged the Celtic knot ring from my middle finger and read the inscription: *The Hollow Men.*

"Remember us—if at all—not as lost violent souls, but only as the Hollow Men," I whispered. "Miss you, big brother."

I had given Richard the ring on his sixteenth birthday. Dad gave it back to me after the mortician pried it from Richard's dead finger.

Almost thirteen years ago, while I stood over his grave and watched his casket lowered into the ground, I promised I'd find out what really happened. His image may have faded over the years, but not the desire to clear his name. He wasn't a junkie like the television media depicted. Beer, sometimes Jack Daniels, and a lot of pot—he and Quint loved weed—but never heroin. He left that night pissed off at the world—pissed off at me—but he was deathly afraid of needles. He'd never use one.

I glanced at the blue, cloth-covered partition. Only one person knew Richard better than I did. He'd been there when Richard and I got into a screaming match over Ruth. Wasn't my fault, but Richard had been right. I could have kept my smart mouth shut. Even Quint got mad at me that night. I had stormed inside my parent's house. He'd stayed in the driveway until Richard tore off in his Camaro and, later that night, died. What transpired while I was inside, fuming? Maybe I could use Quint's return to my advantage. Turn a negative into a positive.

Right now, I had to focus on the rose. There'd be plenty of time to pick Quint's brain since Jeremy wasn't expected back for eight to ten weeks.

The industrial-sized heater rumbled into action and spit ink-stained warmth over me. Suspended below the heater was the twenty-seven-inch television, always tuned to CNN. An image of the Sacramento fur king's widow, Emma Langtry, filled the screen above the message; *Langtry to file wrongful death suit.*

"Good luck," I muttered. I'd followed the case in high school journalism class. Mr. Langtry did time for embezzlement, fifteen years if memory served me, a rap that should have landed Emma Langtry behind bars. While incarcerated, he became ill and never fully recovered. He died three weeks ago. Why she wanted to clear his name after allowing him to soil it by covering for her didn't make sense. But I couldn't worry about that. Leave it to the Associated Press. Emma had local ties, so we'd run the AP article.

"Get focused, girl." I wasn't usually so scatter brained. This was Quint's fault. Once I had wanted him close. Now, his presence unnerved me. So I'd do what I always did when things got too personal: Work.

"Car and rose," I said, repeating the words as one would a mantra. Then I cradled the phone against my shoulder and jabbed in the number for the Shell station.

"Yosemite Shell," Dad answered after the fifth ring.

"Dad?" I said, although I recognized his voice.

"Hey there, Kiddo."

"Cancel the tow."

"Why? Did someone fix that car of yours?" he asked, fishing for a hint of a man in my life, no doubt. I couldn't help but smile.

"No. It's involved in an incident," I said. "Morales took it as evidence. Just my luck, huh?" I chewed my thumbnail. "Can I borrow the truck?"

"I'll need it tonight. Gonna help your Mom move some stuff. You need a ride home?"

"Yep. Come by at five?"

"Will do. Tell you what. I'll buy you dinner, too, if you got time for the old man," he added with a chuckle.

"Always have time for you, Dad." On my meager budget, I accepted all the freebies I could. And the times I spent with Dad were few and far between. I missed his company.

"You can have the truck tomorrow. Will that be soon enough?"

"That'd be great. Love you."

"Love you too, Kiddo." He hung up.

I returned the receiver, sat back and chewed my thumbnail, splintered and soft. So, I'd have a pickup in the morning, but I didn't want to wait. The rose and mirror—hadn't I seen that before? Perhaps read about it? I rubbed my temple, where a dull ache crept in. Beneath a stack of police dispatch reports I found the Borden phone book, rifled through and scribbled down addresses of the town's three florists.

I couldn't search for the rose until I'd met my quota, so I shuffled papers until I found the probation department's press release, punched in Deorian's number and waited.

"Monkey?"

On the phone, *Madera County Probation.*

"Officer Deorian, please."

"Hannah?" Quint folded his arms on top of the partition. I pointed to the receiver against my ear, and mouthed the words *I'm on the phone.*

"When you got a sec?"

"Whom are you holding for?" Another receptionist.

"Deorian—Assistant Chief," I said.

"When you're off, can you give me a hand?" Quint asked.

I waved him away, cradled the phone against my shoulder and searched for my notepad.

"It'd be easier to find stuff if you straightened up in here." Quint gave me that cocky grin.

"I know where everything is."

"Excuse me?"

"Not you," I said into the phone.

"You're holding for Officer Deorian?"

"Yes."

"And you are?"

"Hannah Monakee," I said. "Borden Gazette."

"He's away from his desk. Would you like his voicemail?"

Does he check it? I wanted to ask. Instead, I agreed, and she switched me over. "Got the press release. I need more info. Give me a call." I rattled off the number and hung up. "Okay, what do you need?"

"Those folders," Quint said, and I swear I detected a hint of amusement. "Where are they?"

"Electronic folders." Come on. He wasn't stupid.

"Yeah. Where do I find them?"

"Shared drive."

"Where's that?"

"Forget it," I ground out, sounding for a moment like Morales. I pushed off my chair and stalked around the partition. "I'll do it myself."

He dropped into the chair before I could slide on and wiggled the mouse, waking the computer. On the screen, I glimpsed the milky white plastic barely visible beyond the dumpster's wide mouth. A shape under the shroud caught my attention—something slender, undefined, with a black splotch at one end.

He minimized the photo. "Where's the drive?"

"Bring that back up."

He restored the photo. "Not my first choice, but the others show EMT ass. Not what people want with their Cheerios."

"As long as you don't show the body," I said, my attention glued to what could be—stretching the imagination—a rose tucked in the plastic. "Can you print that for me?"

"You have a color printer around here?"

"In the hall by the fax." I reached for the mouse, let my hand hover over his but he wasn't turning over control. "Before you send it—"

"Change the settings? I think I can handle that." Two-finger style, he tapped the keys, switched settings and regained command of the mouse. He clicked *OK* and the printer down the hall came to life. "Why do you need a print?"

None of his business, actually. "Curious." I tapped the screen. "On the desktop, open the shared drive. You'll see a folder with today's date, then folders inside. They're separated by page number and section."

"Thanks." Following my instructions, he found A-1 and saved the image. "So. Are you busy tonight?"

In my cubicle, the phone jangled. I straightened and headed around the five-foot wall.

"Are you gonna answer me?"

"Yes." I grabbed the receiver on the third ring. "Newsroom. Monakee speaking."

"Yes, you'll answer, or yes, you'll go out with me?"

"Cold day in Hell," I muttered.

"Bad day?" Morales said through the phone.

"Wasn't asking for Hell's forecast," Quint said through the cubicle wall.

"You have no idea," I said into the phone.

"Got some idea. Was there when you found the flower."

"What's up?" In other words, get to the point. I still had one story to write—if I could track Deorian down.

"That rose. Found another."

I stared at the clutter of notes tacked to my cubicle wall. "Inside the plastic?"

"Sonofabitch," Morales grumbled. "Got a fuckin' mole."

"No, you don't. The photo Grigsby took. I thought it showed something inside the wrapping."

"Good. 'Cause if someone in here talks, I'll can his ass."

"The rose?" I prompted.

"Yeah. Just like the others."

"Has Badorini tracked it down?" I shifted my attention to Tom Petty on the computer screen.

"Still lookin'. I'm gonna take over. Free him up to watch you."

"Let me know?"

"Yeah." Morales severed the call.

I replaced the phone, tapped my short-cropped nail against its plastic as though willing Deorian to call. I wanted to visit those florists before Badorini or Morales got to them and swore the owners to silence. I needed more information, and Morales was my sole source. He knew more than he was telling. Before Turner hauled off my car, Morales said he would be questioning someone. I wanted to know whom, but he clammed up.

Questioning the first victim's husband? De La Cruz had no connection to me, other than threatening to have me arrested when I tried to get an interview.

An image of gouged-out eyes filled my mind and I shuddered. Just the thought of someone removing them like some acid-trip version of the Sand Man made my skin crawl.

Normally Morales gave me enough off-the-record information it would grab the attention of the Pulitzer crowd, if I could use it. Occasionally, he slipped up after a few beers. Maybe I'd invite him to The Dock, buy him a couple, get him loosened up.

Yep. A few drinks should do it. I hoped it wouldn't take more than that. I wasn't willing to compromise my morals for a lead, and that was a game Morales liked to play.

Chapter 5

By five o'clock, my head throbbed. I donned my coat, hooked my purse strap over my arm and head so it crossed my chest and hurried out the side door. Deorian never called, so I was one story short. I'd hear about that in the morning, but right now I had to get out of here. Dinner first, then call the florists before getting ready for the gig. Dad said he'd pick me up after he closed shop, but I didn't want to wait inside. With Quint in the neighboring cubicle, and the unshakable feeling I was being watched, I couldn't focus on work. Four days. Less now. That had been this morning, and if the stalker counted the hours I'd better, too.

The building's wide eaves offered protection from the rain, which now fell in sheets. Quint slipped outside and crossed toward his vintage, navy blue Mustang. He motioned toward the car in an offer of a lift. I wanted to give him a single-finger response. Instead, I gave him a tight-lipped smile and shook my head.

Twelve and a half years ago I'd know what he was thinking. Now, he was a stranger. He'd turned thirty-four last October, four months younger than Richard would have been.

Quint still had that reserve he'd acquired shortly after his father died. That had been the first time he disappeared. The second was after Richard's funeral.

The first hadn't affected our friendship. The second destroyed it.

I resisted the urge to chew my thumbnail. While I had no interest in reinstating our friendship, the reporter in me was curious. Why was his hair long if he'd just been discharged? And if he'd been out a while, where had he been before returning? Why return to Borden after all these years? Most people who escaped never returned.

A police cruiser pulled into the lot, blocking Quint in. He propped his elbow on the Mustang's roof.

Holmes climbed out, hitched up his pants and readjusted his weighty belt. Nights I couldn't sleep I stared at reruns of *The Andy Griffith Show.* Yep. He was Opie all right, with that baby face and coltish build. In the heavily padded, blue jacket he looked oddly unbalanced like its weight would topple him at any moment. Through the rain's steady drone, I could barely make out his words.

"Quint Rydell?"

Quint flicked his gaze at me then back to Holmes. "Yeah."

"Sergeant Morales would like to speak with you."

"What about?" Quint asked.

Holmes opened the cruiser's rear door. "Please get in."

"I don't think so." Quint leaned against the Mustang and folded his arms. "If your boss wants to talk, he can call."

Forget trying to stay dry, this was getting interesting. I edged closer and pretended to check my reflection in the rain-streaked window of Grigsby's BMW.

"Sergeant Morales ordered me to bring you to the station." Holmes touched the butt of his service weapon. "You can comply and get into the vehicle, or—"

"Or what? You're going to shoot me?" That crooked grin spread across Quint's face. He pulled a Marlboro from the box in his leather jacket's pocket, cupped his Bic against the rain and blew a stream of gray into the gloomy air. "Borden's gotten that bad, huh?"

"Or I'll cuff you and force you in," Holmes said, his freckled face reddening.

"What's up?" I asked Holmes.

"It's . . . an ongoing investigation."

"Cut the crap. That's Morales' line."

Holmes shuffled his feet, kept his attention locked on Quint as though his would-be prisoner might bolt. Leaning toward me, he dropped his tone: "Sarge didn't say. He just ordered me to bring this guy in."

"I think I know." Quint pushed away from his car and plugged the key into the lock. "Tell your Sarge I'll talk. But I'm driving."

"I'll follow you." Despite the cold, sweat beaded across Holmes' upper lip. "You try anything, I'll shoot your tires out."

"What is he?" I asked. "Borden's most wanted?"

"Look," Holmes said, and again leaned toward me. "I goofed up. I do it again, Sarge is going to send me to dispatch."

Morales had little patience when it came to rookies. I'd seen him send an officer to the evidence locker after screwing up a report.

"I won't run." Quint slid into the Mustang.

I hurried to his car and caught the door before he could close it. "Why does Morales want to question you?"

Quint propped his arms on the over-sized steering wheel and looked up at me. "Have dinner with me and maybe I'll tell you."

"I danced with the devil once," I said.

"Suit yourself." He twisted the ignition. The engine started with a well-tuned roar. Classical music—Tchaikowsky, I recognized it from *The Nutcracker Suite*—drifted from speakers embedded in the dash.

"Maybe a drink." Oh, great. I was sacrificing my principles for a lead. Morales said he was questioning someone in connection to the murders. He wanted to talk to Quint. Seemed odd to me.

Besides, I had only four days before this sick freak came after me. Any tidbit I could grab might bring me closer to figuring out who the killer is. Morales wasn't going to share details. Maybe Quint would. Which meant seeing him again. Damn him, and my curiosity.

"I'm playing at The Dock," I said.

"Yeah. Kept the band together. I heard."

"Well? Are you going to be there?"

"Maybe." Quint tugged the door. I let go, and he closed himself inside. Before he pulled out he peered at me through the rain-streaked glass. His eyes adopted a vacant look that left me cold inside. Clutching my coat around me, I stepped away.

Holmes eased his car back. Once Quint cleared the lot and turned onto Yosemite Drive, Holmes practically hooked bumpers. The cars bounced over the railroad tracks and sank on the far side.

Dad's Eighties-model Ford eased to a stop at the curb. I jogged across the lot and climbed into the passenger seat. Rain dripped from my hair and soaked the cloth-covered bench.

"Kiddo? Why were you standing in the rain?" Worry creased his brow, shadowed by the bill of his Shell Station cap. Grease streaked his blue uniform. Black, half moons had wedged themselves beneath his nails. Scents of oil and gasoline wrapped me in familiar comfort, and I relaxed for the first time since finding the rose. "Are you okay?"

"I've had a rotten day." I wasn't about to burden him with the details. He looked haggard and old as though the weight of his own problems had aged him ten years in the past month.

He pulled away from the curb, turned north on Whilhite and cruised past the feed store's storage bay with its sun-faded, eight-foot rooster painted eons ago on the steel door.

"Strange seeing that old Mustang." Dad's way of broaching a subject he wasn't sure I wanted to discuss.

"Yes, it's Quint. He's back. God only knows why," I added under my breath.

"Town doesn't have much to offer. Usually when people get out they never come back."

"He's not too bright."

"I remember when you thought different."

"He tutored me in Algebra. Just because someone knows math doesn't mean he's intelligent." I yanked the seatbelt over my lap and jabbed the metal tongue into its slot.

"That wasn't math he was tutoring on the couch that night," Dad mumbled.

I couldn't help chuckling. Dad had snapped on the light, grabbed Quint by his shirt collar and dragged him into the kitchen. When Quint returned he was pale and shaky.

"I sure thought you two could make it. Still don't know why you didn't," Dad added.

I gripped my purse strap. It was one thing to joke about the past, another to mangle the memory into something I didn't want to discuss.

"What happened, anyhow?"

"He joined the Navy."

"What? You don't like sailors? My uniform won over your mother."

"Dad . . . "

"Really. What happened?"

"He left. I never heard from him. End of discussion."

Damn. No matter how I lied to myself, that was still a sore spot. Graduation, Richard's overdose, Quint walking out. In a matter of days my life had gone to shit.

But as I always did when life dished out an extra helping of rancid food, I purged myself much like a bulimic shoving her finger down her throat. Only I used a car and a few days holed up in a cabin high in the Sierra.

Dad brought the truck up the weed-lined ramp and merged with congested traffic on Route 99. On the shoulder, three CalTrans workers in bright orange coats patched another sinkhole that had taken half the right-hand lane. Patch and seal was a way of life in the Valley. State funds earmarked for upgrades usually fell into Los Angeles' hands. They had the voters.

"When's the last time you saw your mom?"

I searched my memory and frowned. I hadn't gone over for Christmas or Thanksgiving. She quit having family gatherings after Richard died. Last summer I stopped by so Dad could check a hose on my car. "August?"

"Have you driven by the house at all?"

"No. Why?"

"She put the place up for sale. Moving back to Texas in a week."

"Why are you guys going there? You hate Texas."

"I'm not going, Kiddo."

"You're divorcing her? Oh, shit," I muttered.

"She filed. And clean up that mouth. You didn't go to college to be a journalist so you could talk like that."

He'd never spent time in a newsroom. Foul language was almost a prerequisite.

"After all these years?" I wasn't stunned. Confused, yes. Ruth had never been easy to live with even before Richard died. *Glad you're not here to see this, Bro.* "Why now?"

"We saw a lawyer a couple months ago. I'll wrap things up so she can move on." He breathed deeply and uttered a long sigh. "I figured it was coming. Just don't know what took her so long."

He exited the freeway, pulled into Denny's parking lot and found an empty slot. Moisture glistened in his blue eyes, but didn't touch his leathery face. He'd never allow himself the luxury of crying.

"Where are you going to live?" It felt weird knowing I wouldn't see him relaxing in his recliner, watching old John Wayne movies anymore.

"I moved out last weekend," he said. "Got an apartment. You know where Live Oak Village is? Nice place."

Damn. I was so out of touch with life outside the newsroom, my own father could die and I wouldn't know until I read his obituary. I posted another mental note: *Visit Dad more often.*

Before he could pull the door handle, I clutched his neck and buried my face against his gasoline-scented shoulder. He slipped his arms around me and held me close. A knot tightened my throat. My chest grew heavy. My heart broke. Not for the loss of their relationship, but the pain I knew he suffered. I pulled away, only mildly surprised to feel warm tears on my cheeks.

"Okay. That's that," he said. "Come on, Kiddo. Let's get some food. You look like you haven't eaten in a week," he added, and grumbled, "Gettin' too skinny."

Chapter 6

I really wanted to check out those florists, but couldn't involve Dad in my drama. So I pushed the rose to the back of my mind and tried to enjoy our time together. Over bacon, lettuce and tomato sandwiches we chatted about San Francisco's chances for the Super Bowl, our jobs, whether or not the temperature would dip below freezing and damage the citrus crops. Anything but Ruth.

Then Dad broke the unspoken rule. "I'll be at the house Sunday. There's stuff to fix before the realtor can show it. You ought to drop by and see your mom before she leaves."

I brushed the not-so-subtle hint aside. "Is she flying?"

"Already got the ticket. The movers will be there in a few days. Anything you want, you'd better get."

"Can't pretend I'm sorry she's leaving. It's not like we've had a relationship. She's always been such a—" I bit back the word *bitch* and cradled the coffee mug in my hands.

What I also wouldn't say was that her leaving left me with a sense of relief and freedom I hadn't felt since my college days when I moved into the dorms at Fresno State.

"She's your Mom. I know she's been distant since Richard died, but she deserves respect."

"She's been distant since the day I was born," I shot back, caught the stern look in his eyes and softened my tone. "She just got worse."

"I know she don't show it, but she loves you," Dad said. "Don't doubt that."

"I wasn't what she expected." No, Ruth wanted a carbon copy of herself, a little debutante she could parade around in high-dollar dresses, one that said *Thank you*, and *Please, Yes Ma'am*. Not one in pigtails, Richard's outgrown jeans and scabs on her knees.

"I remember her takin' you to them plays in San Francisco. She loved those plays and stuff. She always wanted me to go, but I couldn't stand all that singing."

"Opera," I corrected him. "She berated me all the way home because I nodded off before the third act. *Cosi fan tutte*, the aria *Un Aura Amonsa*. A real snoozer."

I remember sitting there, mind-dead and body numb. Tom Petty and Beverly Sills were worlds apart. All I could think back then, while those heavily made-up women in elaborate costumes and high-piled hair sang words I couldn't understand, was how badly I wanted to sit behind my kit and pound out some old Beatles tune. Rolling Stones. Petty. *Anyone*. Those were truly some *God kill me now* moments.

"I've got to get going," I said, hoping to end the conversation. I had a freak wanting to kill me. Somehow even Ruth's prey on my psyche paled in comparison. And if I was going to figure out why the rose freak chose me, I needed to get to the bottom of this whole rose thing. The list of shops nestled in my purse might get me one step closer.

He reached across the table, clasped my hand and ran his thumb over my nails, bitten to the quick. "You nervous about something?"

My nails were worse than usual. I tried to tug away, but he tightened his hold.

"Kiddo? Something you're not telling me?"

"Work has been stressful," I lied, and offered him a smile.

"If you say so," he said, and I knew he didn't believe me. "Excuse me, Kiddo. Be right back. Then we'll leave." Dad folded his napkin onto his plate, and headed toward the men's room.

As he left I caught sight of the young EMT, Tolson, at the booth near the exit. Rain coursed down the window behind him, casting his face in rippling shadow. He lifted his ice tea in greeting.

I looked down at my few remaining fries half buried in ketchup. A moment later he slid into the chair Dad had vacated.

"Ed Tolson." He extended his hand over the dirty plates.

"I know. You gave me your card." I accepted the offer. "Hannah Monakee."

"That's why you were at the *Gazette*. You're the reporter, right?"

"Guilty as charged." I blotted my lips and tucked the napkin beneath the plate's rim.

"What's the story with the stabbing on the east side?"

"Today?" *Damn-it, Morales.*

Tolson held onto my hand longer than necessary. I gently tugged free. He smiled and rested his forearms on the table's edge.

"A kid of thirteen," he said. "I figured you knew about it."

"Probably another gang fight." Criminal street gangs were as prolific as cockroaches, and had direct ties to the Mexican drug cartel. They were behind most of the methamphetamine production in the San Joaquin Valley, a side business they killed each other for.

"They happen often here? Gang fights?" Tolson asked.

"They're probably having another turf war." I sipped the coffee, slightly bitter but warm and I needed the caffeine. I had a five-hour gig ahead of me. "You're not from around here, are you?"

"Sacramento."

"Why move here?"

"I can tell you're a reporter. Get right to the point. You're a strong woman. I like that."

"So? Why Borden?"

"Training as an EMT doesn't guarantee a position. I finished classes last summer, and it took three months to land this job." He glanced at my ring. "That's nice."

I twisted the Irish band around my finger. "It was my brother's."

"How about you? If Borden's so bad, why stay?"

"It gives me something to write about."

"You enjoy your work?"

"Never a dull moment." I glanced at the clock above the cashier's glass desk. The florist shops would close within the hour. I caught sight of the chain, barely visible under his collar. I'd first noticed it at the crime scene. Odd. Men don't usually wear rings on a chain. That was more a high school going steady thing.

"What's with your ring?" I indicated the chain around his neck. None of my business, but that never stopped me.

He toyed with the white gold band, and a sad smile leant a slight curve to his lips. "My mother. She died when I was young. It's all I have of her."

He must have been very young when she died, the ring didn't have so much as a scratch. "Sorry."

"No, I'm sorry. You probably think I'm . . ."

"Sensitive?" I leaned back and cradled the mug in my hands. "Nothing wrong with that."

"You're different," he said, and the smile turned into a grin. "I'd really like to see you sometime."

"You're seeing me now."

"Strike two. Better make the third try a grand slam, huh?" Apparently deciding to abandon the chase, he leaned over Dad's plate of toasted crust and the lettuce he'd pulled from the sandwich, lowered his voice and asked, "What's your take on that murder?"

I sipped more coffee, set the mug in its saucer and slid my finger over the too-small handle. "I don't know enough about the cases."

"*Cases?*"

I pushed the cup away and leaned back. "How long have you been here?"

He shrugged. "A month."

"You didn't work the first murder?"

"I started going on calls this week."

Great. So much for my *golden ticket*. Tolson knew less than I did.

"Well? There was a murder before this one?

I bit my thumbnail, glanced at the clock. *Come on, Dad.*

"Do you think they're connected?" Tolson persisted.

"We had a murder last week," I said, and sighed. "A young woman found in a dumpster."

"So they *are* connected?"

"It's possible."

"Any similarities the cops picked up on? Everyone says *you* get the inside information."

"Really?" I shrugged, although the comment flattered me.

"Yeah. So?"

"Nothing I can print, and nothing I can talk about."

"You're a good reporter." He glanced over his shoulder as Dad rounded the corner and wove through the scatter of tables. Standing, Tolson again offered his hand.

I accepted, again, and instead of shaking he bowed and touched his lips to my fingers. *"Au diable celui qui pleure pour deux beaux yeux."*

The only world I caught was *pleasure.* "French?"

"They say it's the most romantic." Tolson smiled. "You have my number. I'll buy you something better than a BLT."

"Sounds tempting." I tugged my hand away, knowing I'd never call. Men complicated life too much. Right now, I had all the complications I could deal with. A killer wanted to gouge my eyes out. Somehow a romantic dinner with a handsome medical technician didn't sound appealing.

He retreated to his dimly lit corner.

Dad tugged a twenty from his wallet and tossed it onto the table. He glanced at Tolson, returned his attention to me and grinned.

"Don't start," I said. "I barely know him."

"Dating is how you get to know him. Don't spend your life alone."

"When I'm ready, I'll find someone."

He tilted his head and frowned.

"Men don't want a woman who slips out at two in the morning to cover a homicide," I said. "It's a job hazard."

Besides, relationships started out like a walk on the beach at dusk, the sun's brilliant orb kissing the ocean, where I searched for that perfect seashell I could set on my fireplace mantle to remind me of that peaceful moment. But I always stepped on glass, plopped on that beach while blood flowed into the sand and wondered how the hell something so beautiful could turn ugly and painful.

I stood, let Dad help me with my coat and followed him into the drizzling rain. Fifteen minutes later, he dropped me off outside my two-story duplex and promised to bring the truck by in the morning.

I strolled toward the tan, stucco house. Boxwood framed the small porch where terracotta pots overflowed with oregano, rosemary, garlic, and dark green leaves of sweet bay.

My roommate, Ozrick, stepped out of the house and locked the door. He headed toward his lipstick-red Neon. Ducking past him, I started to dig out my keys, and remembered Morales had snagged the set. I dropped to my knees on the porch. Hidden by the boxwoods, taped under the railing, was the spare.

"Home a bit late aren't you, girlfriend?"

"Dinner with Dad. I don't have my key." I picked at one edge of the duct tape.

"Where's your car? Don't tell me," he said. "It broke down again, didn't it? You've simply got to get more reliable transportation."

"Confiscated, and I'll explain later." Having freed one side of the tape, I felt for the key.

"I'll let you in, but then I've got to run," Ozrick said in his singsong voice. "Got to pick up spinach for the quiche. My performing arts group is coming over. We've got so many details to tie up for the New Year's Gala and only three days." He started back toward the door and stopped. "Do you want to tag along? That boutique next to Sac and Save has got this lime green shirt I've been dying to get. You've got to see it girlfriend. It's so *yummy*."

The list of florists was still in my bag and I had two hours before the gig. "Could we run a couple errands?"

"Sure thing, sweetie." He made a swooping gesture toward his car, tossed the end of his pink wool scarf around his neck and pushed up the sleeves of his mauve colored coat. "I've got to get shots of the old opera house for the posters. Lance took some, but they're dark and grainy and oh, they just won't do. You don't mind?"

"No problem." I pressed the tape back over the key and stood. "But I have to be at the club before nine."

He slid into the driver's seat. I jogged around the car, pulled open the door and clambered in as he started the engine.

We got the spinach, his silk shirt and by the time we reached the last florist on my list sounds of Boy George singing "*Do You Really Want To Hurt Me*" had given me a piercing headache. It wasn't so much the music blaring through the speakers but Ozrick's off-key accompaniment. His notes landed smack in between pitches. God kill me if I ever sound that bad.

"That opera house has been vacant at least seventy years," I said, hoping to stop his singing.

"Closer to eighty," he said. "Back in the day it was the heart and soul of culture. Oh they had plays and vaudeville and operas and we're going to bring all that back to Borden."

"It'll cost a fortune."

"We got that grant. And the gala will bring in more funds. And," he tapped the blinker arm and turned into the shopping center's lot, "we're doing a fundraiser this spring. Shakespeare. *Taming of the Shrew*. Girlfriend, you've just got to see our production."

Men would play every role, no doubt.

"I hate to take advantage, you being with the newspaper and all, but do you think we could get some coverage?"

"No problem." A brief write up and listing in the community calendar should suffice. "When's the play?"

"*Production*. In March."

"Get me the details."

"You're an absolute doll."

He parked next to a flowerbed filled with waterlogged mums. The florist sat nestled between a jewelry store and Books and Bagels. I started to climb out when Ozrick touched my arm.

"May I come with you?" he asked. "I know the clerk."

"That's not necessary." I'd have to bring him into the loop, but the longer I could procrastinate the better. He'd freak out, and I didn't need a freaked-out gay man to deal with. Too many things to focus on, like finding the killer before he killed me.

"Maybe I can help. I do know flowers." He raised a neatly plucked brow and tilted his head like a cocker spaniel begging for attention. The pink spiked hair killed the image, but the pleading look was there.

I slumped in the seat. "Okay. But leave the questions to me."

"I won't say a word." He pretended to lock his lips and toss the key over his shoulder. Then he swooped out of the driver's seat before I could stand and ease the door closed. "Is this for one of your stories? Did someone here commit a crime?"

"Nothing like that."

Scents of gardenias and daisies hit me as I stepped into the store's cool dimness. In a glass-front refrigerator, various shades of roses stood on long stems in water-filled buckets. Beyond curtains separating the showroom from the workstation, a woman clipped satin ribbon and tucked it between lilies in a large casket spray.

She laid the ribbon aside, brushed her hands on her blue smock and stepped through the gap in the curtains. A black headband trapped her hair away from her small, round face. Strands cascaded down, flipped on her shoulders in a classic Sixties style. She briefly regarded me and shifted her attention to Ozrick.

"You buying flowers?"

"I wasn't going to but these are absolutely wonderful." He stroked the eucalyptus. "A bunch of these, a few sprigs of lavender—It'll really set off . . ." He waved the air as though dispelling his words. "I've been busy as a bee all day. Hannah has such a surprise waiting for her."

"I do?" I wasn't sure I wanted any more surprises. My heart could only handle so much in one day, and his surprises usually meant something of mine lay in the county landfill.

"Never mind me, girlfriend. I'll just gather these up." He pulled the eucalyptus from the container one stem at a time. "Go ahead. Ask your questions. She's working on a story," he added, and winked at the clerk.

"Oh?" Eyes narrowed, she peered at me with reserve and lightly tapped her sculptured nails against the counter. Apparently, she was one of those who believed *reporter* was synonymous with *leach*—we clung to people and sucked out every detail of their lives for the sake of a story.

"I'm looking for someone who may have special ordered this rose." I dug through my oversized purse, pushed a clump of ATM transactions aside and found a dog-eared Gazette card. I scrawled *Barkarole* across the back and handed it to her.

She studied the card, glanced at me and shrugged. "Yes, he ordered a dozen. I remember because it's rare someone walks in and asks for a specific variety. He paid in advance."

"Do you remember who ordered them? Did he pay with a credit card?" If there a paper trail I could step onto that might lead to the killer, I wanted to find it. I bit my thumbnail and held my breath.

She set the card on the counter. "Cash."

"What did he look like?" I glanced around, hoping to spot a security camera. None.

"He was about four feet tall, twelve or thirteen years old. He was paying for someone else. At least that's what he said."

"Can you be more specific?" Tracking the kid down would be a chore, but I didn't have any other choice.

"Dark hair, dark eyes. He carried a skateboard."

"Long hair? Short?"

"Unkempt, black and long. Kind of gothic," she said, and regarded Ozrick. "Finding everything?"

"Oh, these jonquils are yummy. They'd brighten up that drab old kitchen, don't you think?" He peered at me.

I didn't care about the flowers or the fact my kitchen was drab. I wanted to know about the kid who bought the roses.

"What did the skateboard look like?"

"Black. It had markings on it, but it was pretty scuffed up."

"Try to remember."

"I think there was a skull."

"How long ago?" Perspiration dampened my palms, and I rubbed them against my coat. "When did the flowers come in?"

"Sometime last week."

That could account for why the rose in my car had wilted. "Did the same boy pick them up?"

"Look, honey," she said, and toyed with a curl resting on her shoulder. "I already told all of this to the cops."

"When?"

"This afternoon."

Morales. He was a step ahead of me. "This is personal. It involves a friend."

"The one who was murdered?" She leaned closer. "That spray I've been working on? It's for her funeral."

Breathing deeply, I nodded. I didn't dare open my mouth. I've never been a good liar, and didn't want to get caught in one now. "Did the boy pick up the roses?"

"No one did."

"You still have them?"

She strolled toward the refrigerated unit and gestured to a cluster of dark red roses in back. Eleven left.

"One's missing."

"That's right. No one picked them up so that gives me the right to resell them. A gentleman bought one about fifteen minutes ago."

I spun around, scanned the parking lot, but he wouldn't be that easy to find. "You didn't get his name, did you?"

"He's local. Well, he recently returned." She smiled and toyed with her hair. I half expected her to twist the strands around one finger, start swaying like a love-struck adolescent.

"Well?" I prompted. I wanted a name.

She sighed and returned to her post behind the counter. "He didn't say I couldn't tell. You know him, everyone does. I sold it to Quint Rydell."

Chapter 7

Through the intermittent slap of windshield wipers, he watched Hannah beyond the flower shop's window. It was good seeing her again. He remembered her as a young, spunky girl. Kind of a geek with glasses and books and notepad she jotted everything in. Even then she'd been a nosey little bitch.

She'd gone inside with that roommate, but he didn't feel threatened by that company. That fruit, Ozzy or whatever his name was, wouldn't take her places like a man could. Places *he* would take her.

He chuckled. Dinner? A movie? A long, hard fuck?

Yeah. He'd take her places she'd never been, and she'd love every hot, ripping thrust inside her.

She'd scream. And the thought of those screams excited him. He hadn't wanted the others like he wanted Hannah. He *needed* her, and his need was great. He'd waited so long. Now, he was close to holding Stella in his arms.

Three more days. He could wait that long. Three days, and he'd give her the final symbol of his devotion. A rose so dark it looked black. The *Barkarole*.

His cock stiffened, testing the zipper of his jeans. He shifted uncomfortably against the recently upholstered seat. Although a voice in his head told him to leave, he let the car's powerful engine rumble and idle in the parking lot. He wouldn't get caught. She wouldn't see him. He wouldn't let her, and he had more power than she did. Besides, he'd kept far enough away he wouldn't be seen but close enough that, if he tried, if he breathed deeply enough, he could catch her scent. Sweet. Musky. Her warm, soft scent.

Part of him knew that was impossible. But the other part believed all things were possible. It wasn't like he had split personalities. He was gifted. Mom said he was, and she'd been right. Gifted with heightened awareness, heightened senses, heightened knowledge.

When he turned it on.

When he flipped that switch in his head, the one near the mental door Mom told him to hang a sign on that said *Do Not Touch*.

But he'd touched. After Mom died, he touched *a lot* and realized he liked living in the special world. He knew more, saw more, heard and tasted and felt more.

In that special world, trapped behind that door with the sign, he came *alive*.

That's where the music played.

That's where music always played.

That's where *he* played.

He'd had to shut and lock that door for years. They didn't take well to his games in the military, didn't like the way he switched on and off as he stepped through that door and back again. But those years of training helped him learn to control the switch in his brain. He owed a lot to the good ole' *U-S* of -*A*.

The switch wasn't like those that controlled lights. More like an electrical impulse, one that, when tripped, sent threads of living fire through him. Each tiny thread pulsed with life of its own, and when woven together showed him what he could do like movies projected on the empty backdrop of his mind.

And there was always the music.

He loved the music.

He punched the CD into the player, an addition he'd made although it didn't keep with the authenticity of the vintage car.

Mozart's *Cosi Fan Tutte* filled him with chilling tones, dark and dangerous. The swells of emotion matched those crashing inside him, reflected the shattered hopes he would set to rights during his quest. The cello vibrated deep inside him. Oh, how he loved music.

He lowered the window just an inch. Sharp needles of rain shot in with the wind and he breathed deeply. Ah. There. Her scent, musky and sweet and tinged with soap, just as he remembered. Hannah was different. Deceptive. Seductive. More dangerous and more beautiful than the others. And her eyes— green, beautiful, alive. He couldn't wait to capture them and feel the essence of Stella pour into him.

He would take his time with her. Test her. *Taste* her. It had been a long time and he didn't know if the plumbing would work with a real woman in his arms. But just the thought of Hannah's cool skin against his, her thighs wrapped tightly around him, that patch of wetness he would penetrate and the moans she would make because he would *make* her moan—*Oh, how he'd make her moan*—gave him the courage to try.

After all, it wasn't like she was a stranger. Part of her belonged to him already.

Chapter 8

Before leaving the florist, I got the clerk to agree to call if the boy returned. Ozrick had one more errand: Photos of the old opera house. He promised he'd get me home in time for a quick shower before the gig. I glanced at his watch, gold, the face trimmed with tiny diamonds. Seven P.M. We'd be cutting it close. I hoped his perusal of the old opera house wouldn't take more than an hour.

Heady scents of eucalyptus and lavender from the back seat choked me as he drove toward the theater. Dusk gathered in shades of gray, darkening the already gloomy sky. Headlights from an oncoming car sent needles through my head. I wanted to go home, spend what precious time I had before the gig gathering information on the rose. It was familiar somehow, and not just because Ruth grew them. I couldn't put my finger on it, and that irritated me. Normally, my mind was razor sharp. Guess a guy with a goal of killing me had a way of scrambling the brain.

I leaned back and gazed through the rain-streaked glass. Across the tracks, old-town Borden's east side consisted of a dozen buildings with boarded-over windows, crumbling stucco that left unsightly patches like inert forms of psoriasis. When Ozrick stopped, I stared through the water-splattered windshield.

The old theater was far beyond repair. Windows had been busted out. Steps were rotted. The cracked, weather-beaten door hung from one hinge. Perched on top of the building, the marquee held tattered remnants of posters. I could just make out the shape of a leg poking from beneath a frilly skirt.

I joined Ozrick on the weather-decayed steps, careful not to sink my foot into a spongy area. Glass fragments littered the porch. A soiled shirt and equally soiled condoms had been crammed into a crack in the octagon-shaped ticket booth. Odors of stale urine overwhelmed me as I followed him inside.

"This is your project?" I covered my mouth and drew short, shallow breaths. This place reeked of a cross between a convalescent hospital and neglected men's room.

"It's what we're working for." He flipped his wrist, gesturing toward the stairs leading to the balcony. "A few steps missing, but we'll fix that. She'll come alive again and who knows? We might start a whole *bring-back-Borden* effort. Wouldn't it be absolutely wonderful if we can chase off the druggies and reclaim history?"

All the Clorox in the state couldn't sanitize this place. "It might be better to bulldoze and rebuild."

"Where's your sense of adventure?" He waved my remark aside. "Oh it'll be a challenge, but me and my girlfriends aren't afraid of a challenge. Look at her. She's got so much potential."

Webs heavy with dust drooped from what remained of the crystal chandelier, clinging overhead by one cloth-covered wire. This place had all the potential of a corpse and it gave me the creeps.

I half listened to his litany on how Borden Carnegie Players would restore the velvet curtains, wainscoting, and the motif that once framed the expansive stage.

Ozrick led me to the green room that wasn't green but a putrid shade of brown. Used syringes, some with needles still attached, waited for their junkies to return. A candle and spoon rested on a two-by-four where sheetrock had been torn from the wall. A door led to dressing rooms and a dark, moldy-smelling bathroom.

"Just think of the creative minds that once gathered in this room. We're standing in history—the same air, the same floor beneath our feet."

"The same dirt?" I shook my head. "Sorry, I just don't see it."

A rat scratched along the floorboards and darted into a ragged hole, taking with him a scrap of pasty-white cloth.

From a pouch in his leather man-purse, Ozrick pulled out his digital Canon and snapped off several frames. Light flashed through the room, faded, and left specks staining my vision.

"I'm waiting in the car." Suddenly I didn't want to be there. The place unnerved me. Clutching my purse strap, I backed toward the doorway. An icy sensation, what my aunt called a ghost whisper, caressed my face, swirled around me, passed *through* me and I shivered. Whatever it was, it left me with an impression of familiarity that frightened me even more. "Let's get out of here."

"Simmer down, sweetie. A few more then we'll go." He raised the compact camera and focused on the bathroom.

A wide path in the dusty floor connected the bathroom to a splotch near the green room's entrance. Something had been dragged from the splotch to the bathroom; there was a forward sweep to the path's edges. Probably a drunk rolling another for the half-bottle of vodka stashed in his coat. Such a horrible lifestyle. I couldn't imagine being so hard up I'd rob someone for booze. But why drag him to the bathroom?

I stepped inside. Shadows, cast by the dying sun peeking through boarded-over windows, stretched across the wall above the claw-footed tub. Its sides had been rubbed clean as though something had been forced inside. Chills raced up my spine. The layer of rust and grime on the bottom had been disturbed. Could be where the drunk slept it off. Chances are, they'd be back as soon as night fell.

I rubbed my arms, but the chills remained.

"Let's go. Your contributors get a look at this they'll lock their checkbooks in a vault."

"Don't be such a killjoy." Ozrick frowned at me like a mother scolding her child. "We have thirty in our company, each with special talents. We'll have this place in shape by the New Year."

"That's four days away."

Four days before Morales might find my body in a dumpster. Four days before Tolson might get that date, after all. Four days until . . . I closed my eyes and shuddered.

"No, smarty-pants. *Next* New Year."

It would take more than twelve months and thirty would-be women to shape up this place. I almost suggested he start praying; ask the eternal spirit to take pity on them.

I left him to get the rest of his photos and waited in the car. Down the street, oversized candy canes (plastic with aluminum fringe) swayed from hooks on light poles. A strip of ribbon, once bright red and now dulled and wet, slapped the asphalt as wind carried it to the gutter.

The rose and mirror filled my mind. And the lawsuit. I didn't want to get thrown in jail. I rubbed my temples. Too much to deal with just now. Later. I'd think about Parkston and his lawsuit later. I'd stashed my notes at home. It wasn't beyond Grigsby to rummage around my cubicle, and I didn't want him finding anything. He'd buckle beneath the pressure of a lawyer on his ass. He'd done it before, sold out and revealed a former reporter's source. If I'd had any respect for him, I lost it then.

Ozrick returned. Twenty minutes later, he parked in my duplex's short driveway. I started to bail out, but he clamped my arm.

"Before you go in, I need to tell you something. I've made a few changes."

"What kind of changes?" I eyed the front door as though it were the gateway to Hell. Since moving in, he'd given me one shocker after another. With the day I'd had, I wasn't sure my heart could take another jolt.

"I gave the place some . . . *Pizzazz*. I mean really, girlfriend, that garage-sale-special look you had going was nauseating. No offense," he quickly added, and toyed with his pink-tipped hair. "It's wonderful. You're going to absolutely love it. Oh just call me Oz because I am a *wizard*."

Already he'd thrown out my Budweiser and stocked the fridge with white wine. Red wine filled the counter where my ten-year-old Mr. Coffee had sat. He purchased a monster machine from Starbucks and I haven't had a simple cup of Folgers since. Then he started trashing my furniture. Not that it wasn't much more than garbage to begin with, but that wasn't the point. It was *my* garbage.

Closing my eyes I drew several deep, calming breaths and slid out of the car. I really wanted that bath, cold beer and movie. But I had a gig in less than an hour. I played a six-piece kit. I'd always told myself drums was the heart and soul of music, but when it came to setting up I wished my job was as simple as putting an amp on stage and plugging in.

A mauve flowered wreath with *Welcome* strung across its center adorned the door. He'd replaced my *Solicitors; Knock and you'll face criminal charges* sign with a frilly invitation to bug me on my days off.

God, I hoped he hadn't dumped my Bacardi. If this were a prelude to what I'd find inside I would need a stiff drink. Yep. Get a little buzz going and research the rose. Find those notes Parkston wanted and burn them.

I must have had a look of disdain. *Oz* pursed his lips.

"Don't be such a sour puss. You're going to absolutely love it. You've got to trust my vision, honey." He sashayed up the sidewalk, ducked around me and, holding the key as if he were unlocking the secrets of metaphysical interior decorating, spun around and plugged it into the deadbolt. He flung the door open and stepped aside. "Welcome to your new world."

I was to enter first? I didn't want to. Hesitantly, I stared inside. No blinding pink paint. Good so far.

I passed between the staircase and kitchen, entered the living room and my breath hitched in my chest.

"Where's my couch?"

"That thread-bare thing? Salvation Army wouldn't even take it. It's in the dump where it belongs. But look." He spread his arms wide and twirled in the center of the living room like a novice ballerina. "Isn't it *wonderful?*"

Dark walnut benches with green cushions and floral pillows flanked the bookcase against the far wall. A lavender-upholstered La-Z-Boy occupied the space where my Bentwood rocker had been. Fabric sagged from the joints where ceiling met walls and formed a peak near the light fixture, which he'd replaced. No more generic-glass plate with gold sparks painted on. Oh no. Now we had a dangling hunk of brass and crystal that I couldn't help but see as a phallic symbol: It drooped like a flaccid penis.

"Oh. Ah, it's—" I realized I wasn't breathing, and sucked in a lungful of air. "This is—*Oh God.*"

"Breathtaking, isn't it?" He swooped down on a bench and stretched out like a male version of Cleopatra. I couldn't help wonder if he'd been dropped on his head as a baby. "That light fixture? It came from a gallery in New York's SoHo. Really sets the place off, don't you think?"

"I . . . I . . ." *Oh shit.*

"It was a quaint little place a block from the off-Broadway theater where I played a lead in *La Cage au Faux—The Birdcage*. Sentimental value. It gives this room color and style—It's a brave new world."

Brave, all right. "Where's my old shipping crate? I like that crate."

"Don't worry. It's in the garage. I sanded it and stained it and got some of those cute little brass corners to nail on and oh, it's going to look absolutely wonderful."

The image of Quint when we were kids, crossing himself in the Catholic fashion, came to mind, and I realized I was raising my arm to follow suit although I'd been raised in Ruth's Mormon faith. I clenched my fist and headed for the kitchen in search of Bacardi.

A better car. Living with Oz would help me save money. I needed a car that wasn't fifteen years old and ran on a promise and a prayer, as Grandma Monakee used to say.

I found the rum beneath the sink, chucked a few ice cubes into a tall glass and filled it half way. Looking in the fridge, I remembered Oz wasn't a Coke guy. A two-liter of A&W sat on the shelf. Mentally thanking him for not being an orange soda guy, I uncapped the bottle and added it to the rum. Root beer I could take. Orange soda made me puke.

I took the drink and hurried upstairs. Glancing at the old Hewlett Packard, I measured the time it would take to boot up against how quickly I could shower. Ten minutes, if I skipped shaving my legs.

I jabbed the power button, stripped down, set my ring in the soap dish and jumped into the shower before the water warmed. A quick shampoo job and a once over with a bar of Zest, and I climbed out. From the rack, I snagged the towel, dried off and wrapped it around my hair.

I slipped into a pair of hip-hugger jeans, pulled a tank top over my head and added a blue cardigan sweater. Beneath the bed, I found my Adidas and tugged them on without untying the laces.

Then I selected Webster's Online site from my favorites list and typed in Barkarole. Not found. But alternate spellings appeared. I selected *Barcarolle* and waited.

A boating song of the Venetian gondoliers—and—*A piece of music composed in the style of such songs.*

Great. Not *Guns and Roses*, but music and roses.

In the bathroom, I ran a comb through my thick mane, glanced at the clock and wove the mass into a long braid instead of drying. I'd freeze but halfway through the first set it wouldn't bother me. Drumming had a way of generating heat.

I shut off the PC and hurried downstairs. "Oz? Think you can drive me to the club?"

"Got to hurry," he said in his singsong voice, and grabbed his purse from the bookcase at the foot of the stairs. "My guests will arrive any minute. Think you can get a lift home?"

"Sure." I'd twist Jimbo's arm, which wasn't hard. He'd swim San Francisco Bay if I asked him. Dad would drop off the truck in the morning, so I wouldn't have to inconvenience anyone again. And it would give me opportunity to hunt down the kid on the skateboard.

I had to get through the gig first. The last thing I felt like was entertaining, but it was a hundred bucks I could put toward that more-gently-used car.

During the drive I told Oz what happened that morning. After all, he lived with me. If someone was actually after me, Oz should have the option of getting away until the killer was caught.

Oz stopped for a red light, turned and stared at me as though begging me to cry uncle. When I didn't, he clung to the steering wheel and uttered an exaggerated sigh.

"I've got a weapon." Raising one hand to warn me against a rebuttal he added, "I know you don't like guns but sometimes, girlfriend, we've got to do what we've got to do. It's a stun gun, and it gives off a pretty nasty jolt."

Not lethal but it sure beat the aluminum bat I kept next to my nightstand. "Where is it?"

"Between my mattresses. If you need it just say the word and it's yours." He cupped his hand over mine. "You must be absolutely chilled with fright."

Scared and pissed off was more accurate. I didn't have patience for the killer's charade. Which it wasn't. The two prior victims gave testimony to that.

"Lock the door, even with your friends there. Don't open it for anyone. Morales has my key but the spare is beneath the railing. I'll let myself in."

"I don't care if it's that yummy UPS driver in those tight-fitting shorts. I won't even take a peek."

"Maybe you should take that ski trip, after all."

"And leave you?" He shook his head, sending the pink spikes brushing the headliner. "What kind of friend would I be if I went traipsing off when you need me most? Huh-uh, sweetie. Me and my stun gun are here for you."

He stopped in front of The Dock, a wooden structure designed after the old fish markets that once lined San Francisco's wharf—complete with pilings and round, stubby logs sitting on end and bound with rope. Out back, a pier extended over the river, reduced to a thin stream in the winter.

Cars packed the lot. Before I could get out, Oz wrapped his arms around me in a tight squeeze.

"You'll pull through and figure out who this wacko is. Let me help, okay? I can be Tonto to your Lone Ranger, Robin to your Batman, Super Girl to your—You get the idea."

"If I have a role, I'll let you know." I gathered the snare and leather bag with my drumsticks and headed for the glow pouring from the club's double doors.

The rain had stopped. Security lamps cast light on shimmering pools in the asphalt. My breath hung in plumes. Before stepping into the restaurant I scanned the lot. Couples entered cars while others exited and made their way toward the restaurant. Near the road idled a steel-gray Camaro so much like Richard's I did a double take. It eased from the lot and turned south on Elm Street.

The creepy feeling that someone was watching sent my flesh tingling. For the next five hours I'd be on stage behind four men. If the killer were there he'd have a hard time getting to me.

Unless he hid backstage.

Chapter 9

Inside, out of the damp night air full of shadows, I still couldn't shake the feeling of being watched. Fine hairs at the back of my neck prickled. I scanned the crowd, as if I could pick out the killer.

"Where are you?" I whispered. "Where are you hiding, you coward?"

I'd found the rose that morning, but Morales said the body was dumped sometime after midnight. Was that the killer's start time? That left me seventy-six hours to figure out who he was and why he wanted me dead. Petty's voice filled my mind: *Hey baby, there ain't no easy way out.*

Glancing at every face I passed as though I might recognize the killer, I wove through groups of people waiting for tables. Buttery odors of steamed lobster and charred steaks filled the air. Chatter as families discussed their days created a hum as I made my way to the dimly lit club in back.

The din of chatter faded as I stepped into the club. Against the far wall, the fifties-style jukebox played The Byrds' "*Mr. Tambourine Man.*" Maroon, leather topped stools lined the long mahogany bar. Amber light reflected off the antique mirror framed in intricately carved wood. Wine and fluted champagne glasses hung upside down from racks like crystal spider webs. I deposited my belongings on a tall, round table near the resident Baby Grand where drunken patrons clustered on St. Patrick's Day for the obligatory version of *Danny Boy*. The bartender and owner, Brian, saw me coming and set a glass of rum and Coke on the bar's surface, worn to a deep shine the color of merlot.

On stage, Steve and Robin set up their amps. Half my kit had been assembled on the carpet. Looked like I wasn't the only one late: Jimbo hadn't arrived.

A man with a patch over his left eye arranged my floor toms next to my twenty-six inch Ludwig bass. Tall and lanky, he stepped easily from the platform, picked up my cymbal stands and returned in one fluid motion. Other than the patch, he was as nondescript as white wallpaper on plasterboard. Short cropped hair, blue jeans, chambray shirt and black boots. No belt. No jewelry.

Steve lifted a monitor and positioned it along the stage's front edge.

"Who's that?" I asked.

"Dobbs." Steve scratched his scalp beneath the three-inch Afro that covered his small, round head like a golf ball sprouting mold. His complexion the shade of dark rum spoke of his African heritage, an alluring clash with his stark blue eyes. "Our roadie."

"Why is he setting up?"

"That's what a roadie does. He's also a drummer."

"No one mentioned this to me." Even if he was a drummer, he wasn't touching my baby. That was a vintage kit Richard gave me, a Seventies original. No one played those tubs but me. "When did this happen?"

"Missed the corporate meeting," Steve said with a smirk. "Got a problem?"

"Hell, yes. He's messing with my rig."

"He's not interested in your rig." Steve swept his gaze over me, and I could sense a nasty remark squirming in his mind. I folded my arms over my breasts. "You missed practice all week."

"Two nights," I corrected. "What's that got to do with it?"

"There're some changes. He sat in. If you can't keep up, he can."

"Still trying to edge me out? My brother started this band."

"Which is why you're still here."

"I'm here," I shot back, "because I play those tubs better than anyone."

"Dobbs keeps a beat."

Anger tightened my chest. I shook my head. "Not on my kit."

Dobbs apparently caught wind of our discussion, abandoned my drums and helped Juan with his keyboard. Then he retreated to the bar, ordered a beer and paced in a tight, six-foot rotation.

"Where'd he come from?" What I really wanted to know was how he lost the eye and why he paced in a manner consistent with the space of a prison cell.

"Moved from So-Cal," Steve said, using the California abbreviation for cities south of Bakersfield. "Needed a job."

"I don't have a say in this?" No way would Steve edge me out, but Dobbs' presence told me that's exactly what was happening. Well, not without a fight. "I thought this was a democracy."

"Would've had a say if you'd come to practice." Steve reached around me, snagged the power cord to his Marshall amp and stretched it taunt across the platform. "Finish setting up. You already cost us fifteen minutes."

Robin set his Les Paul bass in its stand and flashed me his boyish grin. In black leather pants, matching vest over black shirt and long ebony hair, he looked like a male version of Cat Woman. He was wound up like a two year old on Sugar Smacks; bouncing from foot to foot, jumping off stage, back on.

"Glad you made it. Steve was gonna put Dobbs up here."

"That won't happen." I'd have to get Morales to run a background on Dobbs. He wasn't taking my job. Full name, date of birth and Morales could dig up dirt on anyone. From the way Dobbs paced, I'd say he had plenty of secrets to unearth.

Robin slung his arm around my neck and planted a wet kiss on my lips. "I'm so stoked. This is gonna be freakin' awesome."

"Robin—It's a gig. We're here every weekend."

"Guess I'm . . . *maudlin*."

"Your word of the week?"

He nodded. "Hard figurin' ways to use it."

Setting aside my snare case, I glanced around, found the high-hat and slid it onto its stand. "Where's Jimbo?"

"Got another doo-ie," Robin said, his own term for *Driving Under the Influence*. "His third."

"Our lead guitarist is locked up?" This would be a fun night. Steve was a decent rhythm player but couldn't carry lead. Even on rhythm, he was no match to Richard. "That's just great."

"Chill. Steve took care of it." Robin handed over my crash cymbal. I slid it onto its post and tightened down the wing nut. "Might want to go outside. Take a breather. Your aura's all red and stuff. Gotta calm down, or you're gonna stroke."

"My aura's pissed off." Readjusting my toms, I scanned the crowd hoping to spot the guy we dragged in last time Jimbo was arrested. Hubert or Huey or Harold. Something like that.

"Slip outside and meditate," Robin suggested. "That'll help."

"I'd rather medicate." Satisfied my kit was properly adjusted, I jumped off stage, finished half the drink and waved at Brian. He nodded and set about making another.

At the bar's far end, Morales gripped his longneck and motioned me to join him. As I settled on the stool I realized he'd shaved. His clothes weren't rumpled either. Odd. Did he hope to get lucky?

"You're looking good tonight," I said.

"Been a long day. Showered. Got a problem with that?" Morales asked.

"No problem," I said, and part of me knew he'd cleaned up on my behalf. He could be a gentleman, after all. "Any new leads?" Brian set the glass before me. I pulled out the twin straws and drank.

Morales turned around and rested his elbow on the bar. The other he kept tucked to his side, touching his holster. Over the years I'd picked up on several of his peculiar motions. This translated into *always guard the gun.*

"You talked to Quint. Did it have to do with the case?" I tried again.

"That why you asked me here?"

"Know how you love to talk shop." I searched my mind for another avenue of discussion. "How long have you known he was back?"

"Week. Little longer." He took a pull from the Corona and rolled the bottle's neck between thumb and forefinger. "You?"

"Found out today. How'd you know he'd be at the Gazette?"

"Badorini. Been watching you, remember?"

Ah, yes. My babysitter with a badge. I glanced around, spotted the detective against the wall nursing a can of Mountain Dew. Two tables away, snug in a corner by himself, Tolson flipped a page in a paperback. He glanced my way, grinned and returned to his book. That flutter I'd felt in the Gazette parking lot raced through me again, and I smothered it.

"Know anything about him?" I asked Morales.

He followed my gaze. "Lover boy?" he grumbled. "Eddie Tolson. Thirty-five, single, hired two months ago. Ex-military from Stockton. No priors."

"You run a background on him?"

Morales nodded. "When they're too busy, we do it."

I drank until ice touched my lips. "The first victim. What was left with her rose?"

"Nothing."

I set the glass down, considered ordering another but I'd have to get through the next hour and a half under hot lights. Instead I asked Brian for a bottle of water. "You just won't tell me."

"Ongoing investigation."

"I hate those words." I thanked Brian for the water and spun around on the stool. "You wouldn't tell me anyway."

"Didn't find anything," Morales insisted.

"Quint bought a rose today."

"Oh? Sharing info. Sweet."

"You question him. He buys a rose. Seems odd to me."

Morales upended the bottle, drank, glanced at me and drained the Corona.

"Do you really think he's involved?" I asked.

"You?"

"Not at all." I'd exchanged maybe a dozen words with Quint and none constituted a confession. "Is there *anything* you can tell me?"

"No."

"We could work on this together," I suggested.

"It'll cost you." The slightest hint of a smile tugged his mouth.

"I'm running out of time," I said. "It's making me nervous."

"Cute when you're nervous."

I glared at him. I didn't have the patience for his games. I had less than eighty hours before he'd be digging my body from a dumpster and he wanted to play games? "You infuriate me."

He chuckled. "We'll catch him."

"Is that a promise you can keep?" He wasn't fooling me. He knew more than he was telling. So I dug a little deeper. "Did you learn anything new on today's victim?"

"Off the record?"

"Do I look like I'm working on a story?"

"Never know," he muttered. "Borden resident reported missing two days ago out of Fresno. Boyfriend called it in."

Finally, a flicker of hope. I had contacts in both their sheriff's and police departments. "Who's the boyfriend?"

"Unknown. Fresno PD is tracking him down."

"You said her clothes were theatrical. Was she in a play?"

"Opera. Stepped out for air. Didn't come back."

"Two nights ago?"

Morales nodded.

"When did she get the rose?"

"Five days ago."

A slight measure of relief edged through me. I breathed deeply. "Then maybe the four-day timeline isn't a pattern."

"Died late Thursday. Guy dumped her sometime after midnight."

"How do you know?"

"Feed store owner was working inventory. Left at midnight. Didn't see or hear anything."

Steve picked up his guitar and motioned toward the stage.

"How's Quint connected?" I slid off the stool.

Morales glanced at me through the corner of his eye and shifted his attention back on the crowd.

"*Is* he connected?" I asked.

"Just following leads."

"Which means you don't have anything on him."

"Still digging." Morales stood. "Gotta go. Esteves is working your car tonight. Autopsy's early morning. Gotta get some fuckin' sleep."

Damn-it. I couldn't let him leave until I had information to help point me to the killer. I touched Morales' arm. He glanced at my hand, at me, and raised his brow.

"Any chance you'll call if you find something?" I asked, softening my tone.

His flint-like gaze melted. Maybe there was tenderness in there, after all.

"You'll be the second to know."

"Not the first?" I asked.

"Chief first. Then you. Keep in touch." He slipped past the crowd at the doorway and left.

I had a pleasant buzz going by the time I settled on my throne. Lights overhead flashed on. I focused on my bass' rich, amber shell until my vision adjusted.

Steve and Robin strapped on their guitars and plugged in. Juan settled behind the keyboard. The first number was Guns and Roses' "*Welcome to the Jungle*," which would sound like shit without lead.

I leaned over my snare to poke Steve with my drumstick, ask him if he wanted to change up the set since Jimbo was out. Before I could reach that far, a man stepped beneath the lights and looped the strap of a familiar, blond Fender over his head.

Quint turned around and gave me that cocky grin. "Take us in, Babe."

Chapter 10

I stared out at the crowd—faces I couldn't see beyond the blue, green and yellow lights pouring down in cone shapes from above the stage. Was the killer in the club watching me? Waiting for his chance to gouge out my eyes? I shoved the thoughts from my head. Over the rim of my toms, I peered at Quint, his snug-fitting Levis, the guitar strap cutting across his back. Had to admit, he sure wore those jeans well.

Drumsticks raised, I tapped out a sharp, four-four count. Quint took over with the brief guitar solo. I stumbled into the song on my high-hat, quickly recovered and set into a fast, steady rock beat. Steve belted out Guns and Roses: *We are the people who can find whatever you may need.*

I focused on my pounding, did a cross up and struck out the rhythm on my toms.

If you got the money honey, we got your disease--

Soon Steve's voice faded and I lost myself in the music. The next number threw me, something I hadn't heard or played since before Richard died. Quint leaned toward the microphone and brought those memories flooding back with a near-perfect rendition of Tom Petty's *"Letting You Go."*

By the time we finished our first set I'd adjusted to the fact Quint was on stage. I propped my sticks against the snare's rim, pulled off my sweater and tied its arms around my waist.

Passing Robin I muttered, "Not telling me? That was rotten."

"Steve didn't tell you? Aw, man. Steve was supposed to tell you." Robin bounded off the stage beside me. "But having Quint back is freakin' awesome, right? Almost like old times?"

Awesome? No, I wouldn't call stirring up long-dead emotions, ones I worked hard to bury, awesome. But in a way, it was like old times. Minus Richard and his small-town groupie girlfriend, Claire. She was a brunette with eyes greener than mine, tall and shapely, a cheerleader who only dated football players. She'd gone out with Quint a few times, but he wasn't the quarterback. Richard was the quarterback.

Even without them, I had to admit some of the magic was back. *Miles Creek* hadn't rocked like this in years.

Quint settled at the table where I'd deposited my coat. His own latter-day groupie, Patty Newburg, leaned against his chair and toyed with his shirt collar. A platinum blond, she reminded me of the small-town tramp in *It's A Wonderful Life*, always running with no destination in mind. They'd had an on-and-off relationship through high school. I never understood why he kept taking her back.

Yep. Just like old times.

I wiggled my water bottle at Brian. He tossed me a cold one. I caught it and settled on the edge of the stage. A few moments later, Quint sat beside me and rested his arms on his jeans-clad thighs.

"Forgot how good you are," he said. "You really rock."

I uncapped the bottle and drank.

"Steve was supposed to tell you."

"So Robin says." Yep, Steve was supposed to inform me, purposely forgot, and probably loved every moment of my discomfort. If he thought bringing Quint into the band was going to drive me out, he was wrong.

"Don't mind, do you?" Quint asked.

Across the room, Patty glared at me. Ever since grade school, we'd had a mutual understanding: we hated each other. I shot her a smile, and quickly shifted my attention to Quint. "Why are you back?"

"Jimbo's in jail. Steve needed someone--"

"No. Back in Borden." God I sounded like such a bitch. But Quint's return, now, when Jeremy was out, and I was in the throes of a stalker who wanted to cut out my eyes, unnerved me. Why was it, when the world came crashing down, Karma threw in an obstacle like Quint that I didn't know how to deal with? "What are you doing here?"

He held his glass in both hands and poked the ice with his lean finger. "Sometimes going back is the only way to move forward."

"Soul searching?" I glanced around. Without the stage lights, I could see more clearly. And although I had no way of spotting the killer, hairs prickling at the back of my neck told me he was watching.

"Guess you could say that." He tilted his head, studied me intensely enough to make me squirm. "Do I make you nervous?"

"Are you trying to?" I rubbed my sweaty palm against my jeans.

He grinned. "Not at all."

"Why did Holmes drag you to the station?" I scanned the room, looking for anyone who shouldn't be there. Outside Badorini, everyone looked normal. Well, as normal as anyone in a bar could look.

"You heard him. His sergeant wanted to talk." Quint poked the ice, licked his finger and drank.

"What about?"

"Always working, aren't you?" Shifting his gaze, he fixed me with those soft hazel eyes.

Refusing to get caught in that dreamy look, I waved the remark aside. "You bought a rose this afternoon. The Barkarole. Why?"

"Day's full of interrogations." He raked his fingers through his hair. "Okay. I'll play the game. What do you want to know?"

"The rose."

"Morales mentioned it. Name's familiar, but I can't place it. Thought if I saw one I'd remember."

"Ruth's garden."

"Oh. Right." That crooked grin spread across his face. "You, me and Rich got busted smoking pot in there. Those were good times." He frowned. "Why'd you call her Ruth? She's your mom."

"Not anymore."

"Oh?"

"After Richard died things got worse," I explained. "The day of his funeral, she informed me I wasn't to call her mom or mother. Just Ruth."

"That's cold, Babe."

"She's always been cold." I rolled the water bottle between my palms, uncapped it and drank. "You talked to Richard that night, didn't you?"

"Tried to." Quint poked the ice in the glass again. "He didn't feel like talking. You and Ruth fighting—that shit ate him up inside."

"That's what he was angry about?"

"Yeah. He got really depressed when you two went at it. That night, he was more than depressed. He was sick. And I wasn't there for him."

Right. Quint had been in bed with me. "Wish I could go back and change everything."

"Me too. Then Rich might be here, playing with us." He glanced across the room. I followed his gaze, which settled on Patty. "Surprised she's still around."

"I'm not."

"Oh?"

"Every town has its resident whore."

"Shit, Monkey. Just say what you think."

"Thought I did." I brought my knee to my chest, hugged it against me, stretching the muscle at the back of my thigh. Old times. Almost. "All we need are Richard and Claire."

"I remember her," Quint muttered. "She was . . . interesting."

"She was a toned-down version of Patty."

"Jesus, you don't like anyone."

"That's not true. I like Robin." My nerves were shot, and the clock kept ticking. I only had about seventy hours before some eye-gouging bastard planned to kill me. "Besides, Claire led Richard around by his nose."

"Nah, by his dick."

"You would know," I muttered, and mentally kicked myself.

"I dated her once," he said defensively. "One time. She saw Rich and that was it."

"Broke your heart?" I hoped Claire dumping him had left him feeling empty inside. Then I'd know he'd suffered in some capacity, even if I wasn't the culprit. He deserved to suffer after all those days I'd waited to hear from him. What a fool I'd been.

He shot me a quizzical look. "It pissed me off. But nothing got broken in the process."

Patty left the table and settled across from Tolson. She picked up the straw he'd pulled from his ice tea, smiled and stroked it against her bottom lip. Had she seen the look Tolson gave me? Was that her motive behind turning on the tease? *Have at it, Patty.*

"The interview," I said, bringing us back to Morales' interrogation. "What did you talk about?"

Quint shrugged. "Mrs. De La Cruz, the first victim, she hired me to shoot her portfolio in Memorial Park. Someone left one of those roses on her towel. Four days later she died. That sergeant thinks I know something."

"Do you?"

"No. And he'll realize that. He had a cop serve a warrant at Robin's place. I'm staying there until I find an apartment. They confiscated my computer."

"What's on the computer?" Reporter mode. Ask questions; dole out apologies later—if necessary. I wanted answers. I wanted to know what Morales had on Quint. If I sounded short or bitchy, oh well.

"The shots I gave the client."

If I could see those photos I might see the rose, might see someone in the park I'd recognize. Might see what the killer left, the equivalent to the mirror in my car.

"Was there something with the rose?" I asked.

"Didn't pay attention." Again he studied me, and I shifted uncomfortably. I didn't like being scrutinized. Then the color of his eyes softened to that warm caramel shade. I knew that look. It's what made me fall for him years ago.

Setting the water aside, I stood, raised my foot behind me, gripped the toe of my shoe and stretched my quad muscle. "Right. Who would pay attention when photographing someone?"

"Why all the interest?"

Good. Morales hadn't told Quint about the rose in my car. "Job hazard?" I said, but it wasn't very convincing. "You didn't keep copies of those photos, did you?"

"Everything's backed up on a flash drive."

"May I see them?" Finally I'd gotten a break. He wasn't so dumb after all.

"Have dinner with me." He leaned closer and I caught a whiff of sandalwood mingled with sweat. Not a bad scent. Kind of alluring . . .

Damn it, don't go there. He wasn't *that* attractive.

"Well?" he prompted.

I let my foot drop and lifted the other. "I told you—"

"Yeah. I know. You don't dance with the devil." That cocky grin returned. He stroked my cheek. "Dinner. Tomorrow night. I'll pick you up at six."

"We can use the computer at the Gazette," I offered.

"I've got a laptop."

"Okay. Six."

Damn. My principles were taking a pounding.

Chapter 11

Half an hour into our third set, Oz showed up with his acting guild. Even beneath the glaring lights I could pick out his lime green shirt. It glowed in the club's dimness. At least the thespians weren't in drag. They ordered Rob Roys and chatted, clapped at the end of each song, even danced a few times. Girl's night out.

Around midnight, we took our final break. I rushed to the ladies room; last chance until two A.M.. When I returned, Quint had packed his Fender and headed for the door.

"Where are you going?" I asked.

"SAR call," he said, referring to the county's Search and Rescue team. He pulled a cigarette from the pack in his black leather jacket.

"What's the scoop?" If there was a hot story brewing, I wanted to know.

"I don't have details yet. See you tomorrow. Six o'clock." He grinned, sending a flutter through my heart like a moth beating its wings against a glass jar. Heat flared in my cheeks. I touched the cold water bottle to my face, extinguishing that flame.

"Can't believe I agreed to a date," I muttered.

I imagined him chuckling while he headed through the restaurant. As he pushed beyond the club's doors, Tolson closed his cell, and stood.

"I'm on call," he told Patty. He glanced at me, smiled and exited after Quint.

On call, huh? Search team plus EMT usually equaled breaking news. I glanced at the pager clipped to my purse—old technology Grigsby wanted me to surrender in exchange for a Blackberry and Bluetooth thing that looked like an overgrown cockroach nestled in the ear. I declined. I knew how to use the pager. And if someone were trying to contact me the screen would light up. Nice and simple. This time it hadn't, which meant it wasn't a story in my beat or Grigsby didn't think he needed me.

In the darkened corner, Badorini poured Mountain Dew over ice. I'd ask him. Maybe he had his scanner going. But if he was like most cops, he only tuned into police frequencies. Morales listened to them all, but he wasn't *most cops*.

"Where's Quint going?" Steve glared at me as though I were Quint's keeper.

"He got a call. Which means we're minus lead."

"I play decent lead," Steve said. "I got it covered."

"I could get called out if there's something to report on."

"Good. I'll put Dobbs in." Grinning, he waved to Dobbs, perched on a barstool near the stage.

Anger stabbed through me. My face grew hot. "Like hell you will. You're taking this too far, Steve. Back off."

Great. Do my job—get the story—and lose my status with *Miles Creek?* Or finish the night, and try not to sound like shit without lead? Gripping the water bottle, I stepped onto the platform. We still had three minutes before launching into our last set, but we had to decide what to play now that Quint left.

Robin joined me, tapped his fingers across my crash cymbal's brass surface. "We changin' up the set?"

"Yep." I motioned for Juan and Steve to join us. "Brainstorm, guys. What do we play?"

"I told you," Steve said. "I got it covered."

Robin glanced at me, then Steve. "Aw, come on, man. No tension, okay? Let's all take deep breaths, exhale and clear that negativity out, man. Just let it go. We gotta think of something we can play that don't need strong lead."

Steve, his blue-eyed glare locked on me, picked up his guitar and looped its strap over his Afro-capped head. "We stick with the schedule."

"I've got a better idea." I sat on the leather-padded throne, picked up my sticks and twirled them between my fingers. Steve wanted to play hardball, I'd give him hardball: Strong lead he couldn't handle. "Edgar Winter. *Frankenstein.*" Turning to Juan, I added, "What are you waiting for? Let's go."

Juan took position behind the keyboard. Robin retrieved his bass. Steve's jaw hardened, and that glare turned into daggers. He loved the attention singing brought him. Frankenstein had no lyrics. It did, however, have kick-ass drums.

I dove into the number, Juan joined, and Steve tried to keep up. Finally, he caught the rhythm, but sounded weak.

Halfway through, I launched into my quasi solo with series of hard-hitting rolls on the toms, snare, toms again then cymbals. Right on queue, Juan brought the pulsing thread in, a sound I used to imagine traveled from one speaker, through the wire, and out the other side. I ended with strong rolls once, twice, third on brass, crashing to the end. I love that number—hell of a workout.

Before Steve could choose the next song, I leaned toward the boom mike and ordered, *"Forward."*

Linkin' Park. Not exactly our classic-rock style, but I liked the song. Although it was written for a man, I had a Stevie Nicks voice and while I usually stuck to backup vocals, the words suited me. And "Forward" had solid lead. Kick me out of my band? I don't think so.

"Sometimes I need to remember just to breathe," I sang. Shoving aside the battle with Steve, my date with Quint and the killer stalking me, I threw myself heart and soul into the number, let

the music take over. *"Forget our memories—forget our possibilities—"*

By two o'clock the crowd had thinned to Oz and company, detective Badorini and a few drunks the bouncers escorted out. My head buzzed with the residue of our last set as it often did. Sometimes I wondered why I hadn't gone deaf.

With the hand towel I kept in the drumstick bag, I moped perspiration from my face and stared at the kit. I didn't have the energy to break down only to reassemble tomorrow night.

"Brian? Okay if I leave this?" I gestured toward my Ludwig.

"Won't be responsible if something's busted." Poking fingers into the mouths of three glasses, he gathered them up. "Your call."

"Thanks." The worst that had happened was a dented head—some people didn't restrain their children. I packed my snare—it was too fragile to leave—and hitched a ride with Oz. During the trip home, the calming diversion rocking out had provided me drained away leaving me with the killer to think about. Only three days left. A few hours of shut-eye would recharge the brain. But I wasn't sure I could sleep.

Biting my thumbnail, I leaned against the window heavy with condensation. I rubbed a circle in the fog, peered through the hole. Near the river's edge, Borden's resident bum, Mathers, parked his empty shopping cart, crawled into a sagging cardboard box and pulled a dingy, brown blanket in after him. Even sleeping in the rain, Mathers would get a better night's rest than I would.

Oz reached for the disc player, and pulled his hand away. Good. No more *Boy George*.

"Since you're playing our New Year's Eve Gala Monday, I thought it'd be a good idea if the group heard you." Oz turned south on Elm and then hooked a right onto Norton Drive. Lights in Save Mart were dim as the night crew restocked shelves. The tall sign perched on the roof winked out. "They love your band. I knew they wouldn't be disappointed. And where did that gorgeous blond come from? Oh my God he's yummy. He wasn't there before, was he? I couldn't have missed *that.*"

"He's filling in."

"You know him? Oh *please* tell me he's gay."

"Unfortunately, no." I gave Oz the abridged version of my relationship with Quint. "Like an idiot I agreed to have dinner tomorrow night. I'll see the photos and that'll be it. Hopefully, it'll be quick and painless."

"Oh sweetie, that was years ago."

"I omitted some details," I said in defense. Slouching, I stared out at the black, storm-laden sky. "He's playing a game. I just don't know what."

"Ever occur to you he might really be interested?"

"Why?" I immediately regretted the outburst. It wasn't impossible a man might be interested. Morales was. "I mean, why now? I waited for a phone call, checked the mail every day, hoping for something." Tears stung my eyes. I brushed them away. Damn-it, I wasn't going to cry. Wasn't going to waste time thinking about Quint. "After I see those photos, I want nothing to do with him."

"But he's working at the paper and he's playing in your band," Oz reminded me. "Seems you don't have a choice."

"I can't figure out why he came back." Poking my glasses into place, I straightened. "He could have gone anywhere when he got out of the Navy. Why here?"

"Connections? His family's here, right?"

"His mom and sister moved to Elk Grove."

"Huh. Got to admit that is odd."

"Why did you move here?" I glanced at Oz. A somber look fell over him.

In the driveway, illuminated by a sixty-watt bulb, Oz cut the engine and leaned against the padded headrest. "Clancy. His parents are here, his brothers and sisters—my God there's a whole slew of them. We thought we'd be together forever. Know what I mean? That feeling you want to be with only him and no one else. Then he found himself some man whore, and here I was. Stuck."

"That's when you started the guild?"

"And it's been the best thing in the world for me. I've had a few flings, and they didn't work out. But I never give up hope. Mr. Right is out there. I just know it."

"For you," I muttered. I'd had some long-term relationships, if one could call seven months long. That was Morales. Suddenly I realized I'd had few dates. Hell, Oz had a more adventurous love life than I did.

Dad's words echoed through my mind—*You don't want to be alone forever*. Yes, I did. If it meant compromising my time, giving up what I really wanted in a man, I'd rather be alone. Problem was, I wasn't sure what I wanted. Who could fit a bill I hadn't yet created?

As though plucking the thoughts from my mind, Oz asked, "What do you want in a man?"

"Tenderness. And he can't be needy. Or clingy. I hate clingy men."

"I know what you mean."

"Enough talk about men." My head ached, and all I wanted was to soak in the tub and crash. I'd Google the rose tomorrow. Nothing would make sense if I didn't get some sleep.

"Quint Rydell—he doesn't know about the rose in your car. Does he?" Oz asked.

"No, and I want it kept that way."

"You can count on me, girlfriend," he said, and went through his lock-the-lips motions.

I followed him to the door. In my mind, I was already soaking in that hot tub. Since my beer was gone I'd make do with a glass of wine. Red. The only white I liked was Moscato and that wasn't on Oz's list. He reached for the door and snatched his hand away.

"What's wrong?"

"Sweetie, I locked it. I'm sure of it."

The door stood two inches ajar. From somewhere inside, light flickered like a strobe. Shivers worked my spine. The key. I spun around, knelt and ran my hand beneath the porch railing.

"Oh God, it's *gone.*" My hands trembled. Thoughts scrambled for cover in my brain.

"What's gone?" Oz backed up on the sidewalk.

"The key." Dropping to my knees, I searched the shrubs for the scrap of duct tape. There it was, tangled in the boxwood. I started to stand and spied a cigarette butt beneath the shrub.

Oz didn't smoke. Neither did I.

"Any of your guild smoke?"

"No."

Unless a solicitor had crushed it and kicked it into the flowerbed, it shouldn't be there.

Using a twig, I turned the butt over. Marlboro. A popular brand, which would make it harder to determine who left it. Still round so it hadn't been stepped on. Hadn't been crushed either, the cone-shaped ash was intact.

"I need a flashlight. Have you got one in the car?"

He wrung his purse strap and glanced at the driveway. "Don't you think we should call the police?"

"Do that. And get me a light."

Oz sprinted to his car, returned with a small LCD flashlight, handed it to me and found his cell phone. As he jabbed the buttons, his fingers trembled.

"What if he's still in there? Shouldn't we wait in the street?" Oz asked, a tremor in his voice.

"He's not in there."

"How can you know that?"

"He's watching me." My voice became monotone. Numbness filled me. "Knows where I am, what I'm doing. Anticipating the moment he takes me and cuts out my eyes." I looked at Oz. "Three days left. He hasn't deviated from his pattern yet. He's showing me who's in control."

I trained the tight, bluish beam on the cigarette. The porch overhang and the shrubs kept the ground dry. A dropped cigarette would have burned out, left ash and traces of its heat. There wasn't so much as a scorched leaf. Tossing the twig, I stood and brushed my hand on the seat of my jeans.

"They're on their way," Oz said. "Come on. Let's wait in the driveway."

Fear touched my spine like icy fingers of a corpse. I peered through the narrow gap in the doorway and shuddered. The flashlight dimmed. Then died out. I gave it back to Oz.

"Who knows you keep a key there?" Oz asked.

"Me. You. Morales. And Dad." Had I told anyone else? "Maybe Quint."

"Thought you hadn't seen him in years."

I shoved my hands in my coat pockets. "Dad always kept a spare under the railing and Quint knew about it. He was like family. If he needed to get in, he knew where to find it just like me and Richard."

Quint smoked Marlboro cigarettes. He left two hours early. And he'd bought that rose. But if he wanted to kill me, why plan a date? The first victim was married; the second had a boyfriend. Quint could have dated De La Cruz, but after meeting her husband, I doubted De La Cruz would mess around behind his back. His glare was almost like a physical blow.

I didn't like the image forming in my mind. But Quint couldn't be involved. I knew him as well as I knew Richard. Quint wasn't a cold-blooded killer.

Something you know and I don't, Bro? Sure could use some help here.

I waited for that subtle feeling to tell me Richard heard, but all I got was emptiness in the pit of my stomach.

Oz had called the burglary in. Cops would be here soon. Morales would be here. Whatever evidence the burglar left I would never know because Morales couldn't compromise his *ongoing investigation.* I didn't like my life resting in anyone's hands except my own.

Oz looked at me, and his eyes widened. "Oh, honey. You're not going in there."

I peered through the darkness at the rain-slick road. Beneath the street lamp's hazy glow was a blue compact car. Badorini. I could just make out his silhouette beyond the wet glass.

"Hannah? Please tell me you're not thinking about going in there."

"I have no choice. I have to see for myself."

"You may not like what you find, sweetie."

"I know. But hiding from the truth will only make the killer's job easier. I have no intention of making anything easy for that bastard."

Across the street, the light inside Badorini's car flickered on. He'd gotten the call. He stepped out and bolted toward us.

Heart pounding, I turned toward the door, tucked my hand into my coat sleeve and pushed.

Watch over me, Bro.

Chapter 12

Inside, a broken lamp flickered and shot quick blasts through the living room like a strobe. Beyond that, the house fell to darkness.

I stepped into the entryway, looked left, right, left again, catching glimpses of the stairs and kitchen, which lay in shadows. Tears born of panic stung my eyes. Images of life I couldn't see stirred the air around me, life that lived only in shadows and please-oh-please-God don't let him be there, in the darkness, waiting for me.

Empty eye sockets, blood streaking down pale flesh, filled my mind and I choked down a scream. In that moment, I realized that I didn't fear death as much as the horror of mutilation, and that fear swelled inside me.

Next to the kitchen, I paused and studied every inch: Blackness beneath the table, the space between the wall and fridge. I listened for any hint of sound, hoping to hear him breathing before he saw me so I could bolt outside.

Splintered remains of a mirror caught the strobe and sent knives of light slashing the living room. I half expected him to creep downstairs, grab me by the throat. I wanted to run, God how I wanted to get out of there. But I had to see for myself what he'd done to my home, had to know because it might give me insight into the mind of the man who wanted me dead.

Mentally grasping Richard's hand as I'd done so often in childhood, I crept toward the living room. Blood pulsed in my ears. Another step, and I cleared the short hallway.

The room had been wrecked, pillows slashed and bleeding shredded cotton. Oz's prized light fixture dangled by a brass bolt. The crystal had exploded in a billion pieces over the carpet.

Spray-painted words in foot-high letters were scribbled on the far wall: *Come back to me.* Clamping my hand over my mouth, I smothered a scream.

Roses had been ripped apart and thrown all over the room. Broken stems, decapitated flowers, petals crushed and ground into the furniture and floor. Red streaked the wall by the cryptic message where he had smeared petals over the fresh paint.

"Hannah?"

Morales.

I turned toward the door. Jittery strobes of light flashed in sync with the throbbing in my head. The picture frame on the fireplace mantle caught my attention. The photo of Richard and me had been ripped out and thrown onto the floor. My image was intact but Richard's had been mangled, his eyes scratched out.

"*Hannah, get out of there.*"

My world tilted precariously. I felt like I'd tip over and fall off. My knees buckled. Morales rushed in, caught me with his arm around my waist and yanked me to my feet. I collapsed against him.

"My home." A blend of fear and anger churned inside me. "That bastard violated my *home.*"

My sacred space was no longer sacred. I'd never view these rooms the same. On the air, I detected something musky. The odors of him mingled with my own fear? I pushed away from Morales and turned toward the stairs. The fear and anger ebbed, leaving behind cold numbness.

"Sonofabitch." He grasped my arm. "Can't go up there. You know that."

"Evidence? Protect the integrity of the scene?" I laughed, but it came out like a choking sob.

"Only way to catch him." Morales led me toward the door. "Gotta trust me. Not going to let this fucker kill you. Told you that."

As we passed the staircase, I glanced into the darkness. Three steps up lay a pair of white cotton panties. He'd taken them from my clothesbasket; I'd stripped them off that evening to shower. A shiver rippled my spine.

Frigid air needled my face; the fog lifted from my mind leaving stains of the images I'd seen inside. The roses. The photograph. The message begging me to come back.

Back to whom?

A blend of worry and contempt flashed in Morales' eyes. But even his anger couldn't cover the facts we both knew; someone wanted me dead and I had less than three days to figure out who that someone was.

*　　*　　*

The switch in his brain clicked off.

The chaos in his mind—once a roar—wound down like water sucked into a drain. It gurgled and died leaving stark silence, the kind that made an imaginary buzzing sound in his head.

He slammed the mind-door shut. The *Do Not Touch* sign rocked on the dull, brass knob.

"Don't touch," he whispered.

Maybe Mom had been right.

"Don't touch. *Do Not Touch.*"

His heart thudded. Sweat dampened his palms, made the small object he clutched slippery. He tightened his grip until his knuckles whitened and ached. He couldn't lose it. Part of

Hannah was inside; he could feel it pulse with a life of its own like a tiny heartbeat throbbing against his fingers.

A grin cracked his face. From the safety of darkness that spread through the Save Mart parking lot, he peered out the car's rain-streaked glass at the duplex across the street. Cops stood guard outside while that dark-haired detective forced Hannah into the fag's car.

Earlier, he'd watched her go inside and waited for a scream. But he'd been trapped beyond the mind-door, the switch still on and everything from outside had been muffled. If she screamed, he'd missed it.

He stared at his fist. Getting out of his special place proved difficult this time, and that fact frightened him just a little. Something had changed. The hinges on his mind-door had rusted, groaned in protest as he fumbled with the switch and tried to leave. If he got stuck in there, someone might find his body on *this* side. Then they'd stop him before he could complete his task.

He couldn't let that happen. Not when he was so close.

Maybe he should listen to Mom. Not go in there so often. Save it for Hannah. He would need those special talents to lure her away, so he could finish his job.

The fact it had been difficult to get out this time made him wonder what would happen *next* time. Would he be there forever? Stuck in that special world without Stella? Would he miss that all-too-important date with her again?

No. He wouldn't.

Do Not Touch.

"I won't," he whispered. Closing his eyes, he leaned his head back and clenched his teeth. *"Oh my loves whose memory will remain in my heart forever."*

He couldn't have them in this world so he'd have them in his own. Soon he would gather the last piece, bring them together in the body of a warm, elegant woman he could keep for eternity.

Calmness abruptly snapped through him, yanking away fear and confusion with a magician's smoothness as he pulls cloth from beneath dishes. His nerves rattled a bit, just as those dishes did, but they quieted and an overwhelming sense of serenity washed through him.

He opened his fist and stared at the silver ring.

He'd taken a little longer in the duplex than he intended. But just standing in her private world thrilled him. Although he remembered to wear gloves and couldn't really feel much through them, he touched and imagined what things felt like.

Where she showered. Where she dressed. Where she slept. He'd clutched her bed sheet, brought it to his face and breathed in the sweet, clean scent she'd left behind.

He knew her routine and habits. The way she nibbled her thumbnail when nervous or trying to hide something. Knew how she dropped her clothes to the floor and studied herself in the mirror. Imagined how she might touch herself and moan in the darkness when no one was looking, and he wanted to reach through that imagined scene, touch his fingers to her, feel that slick warmth nestled in that furry patch between her legs.

Closing his eyes, he summoned the feeling of her cool panties against his cock as he'd first caressed then wrapped the fabric around his stiffness and the motion mingled with images in his mind—*Oh, how he wanted inside her.* His jeans tightened over his crotch, and he breathed deeply, quickly, forcing a cold, black void to fill his mind until his erection softened.

Across the street, the red Neon backed out of the driveway.

The cops went inside. He started the engine, circled back behind the store and rode the alleyway reserved for deliveries.

He knew her private world as intimately as she did. When the switch clicked on, he captured her thoughts, shared her sensations of touch. Could lick his lips and taste the wine she drank.

Fog crept over his thoughts, wrapped him in cold dampness and tugged him back toward the door.

He shook his head and dispelled the fog. Not now. Not so soon after getting out. In his mind, he peered over his shoulder. Corrosion covered the door's hinges; acidic-like foam seeped from the old-fashioned, skeleton key lock. Tentacles that looked more like blood-filled veins stretched out and slapped against the sign, immobilizing it, covering up the middle word so it now read *Do – Touch*.

Not now. Not yet. Not so soon.

That world helped him capture Olympia's youth and Antonia's music. It would help him get Giulietta's sensuality.

Giulietta—*Hannah*—really didn't know the power of her eyes. The moment he looked into them, he knew he couldn't resist giving of himself. He'd given her the ultimate gift, his reflection, heart and soul. Given them so she could keep them close to her heart. Now the connection between them was a strange, sweet terror that thrilled and excited him.

"Beneath her splendor," he whispered, gripping the ring tighter, "Hell intoxicates me."

Youth. Music. Sensuality. These elements belong to Stella. He wasn't taking anything that wasn't his already.

He might only be able to pass through the door one more time. He'd use it after he brought Hannah home, captured her eyes and with them, the last piece of Stella's soul. Then Stella would see everything he'd done for her. She'd see that he had searched six months to find her again, that he had killed to make her whole. She'd be so grateful he gave her a second chance that this time she wouldn't try to get away.

This time he wouldn't have to kill her.

Chapter 13

Dad agreed to let Oz and me crash at his place, a single-bedroom apartment on the west side. He didn't ask, and I didn't explain, just kicked off my shoes and curled up on the recliner.

I woke early to the scent of coffee brewing. Stark white walls surrounded me, and for a moment I couldn't remember where I was. Then the events of last night filled my mind like a flash flood: Living room trashed, mirrors shattered, the cryptic message *Come back to me*.

Oz snored on the couch. With a gentle nudge, I tried to wake him but he was out like a drunk.

I needed to record every detail of last night while it was still fresh in my mind. Maybe if I saw everything in writing, it would help me sort through the mess. Leaving Oz to sleep, I found my pen and notepad and slid onto one of two stools at the kitchen's bar. The metal rim around the stool's legs chilled my bare feet. I put on my glasses and scribbled the message down. Next, I added broken mirror/mirror in car, light fixture destroyed and cigarette butt/Marlboro: Dropped? Planted? Beneath that, I jotted *Barkarole*.

"What have you got there, Kiddo?

I jumped at the sound of Dad's voice. I'd been so absorbed in trying to recall the details I hadn't noticed him in the kitchen. Not good. Better watch that. Someone could walk up behind me, and I'd never know it. Like the killer. But I was in Dad's place and, even though it wasn't the home I grew up in, it was filled with the familiar comforts of his gasoline-scented jacket, the recliner, and a hint of Old Spice.

Dad set a steaming mug on the bar, pushed the sugar dish toward me and got a carton of milk from the fridge.

I doctored my coffee and drank. Folgers. I closed my eyes and savored the taste. "My place was trashed last night."

"Seems like this town's going to hell," he muttered. "Did they catch the guy?"

"Not yet."

I stared at my notes. I'd forgotten something. Closing my eyes, I mentally walked through my living room. The photo. I made the note, adding that Richard's image had been scratched up. Not with a pen. There were no telltale ink lines. Whatever had been used was sharp enough to distort without cutting all the way through. The tip of a knife? But there hadn't been any indentations. A scalpel? The first woman had been dismembered in an almost surgical manner. Maybe I was looking for a surgeon.

"You hungry?"

"Uh-huh." I turned back to my notes. How did Richard figure into this? His eyes had been green, but they'd been buried with him. At least, no one told me if they were missing.

Come on, Bro—Got a secret to share?

I waited for that twinge of warmth, his way of saying he was with me. A faint chill shot through me, like the ghost whisper I'd felt the day before.

What did that mean? Why did I feel him in a whisper both now and at the opera house? He was telling me something. Was that where Richard died? We didn't know for sure. Whoever he'd been with drove to the ER parking lot, rolled his body out and left. A nurse starting her shift at two A.M. found him.

Dad would know if Richard's eyes were missing. I watched him, standing before the stove, as he cracked an egg against a bowl's edge. I couldn't ask. Maybe Carley would know. I'd drop by the funeral home later today.

I jotted down De La Cruz, victim two and my name.

De La Cruz had brown hair and green eyes, as did the second victim and me. If I could figure out what else we had in common I might understand the killer's motive.

De La Cruz wanted to be a model, so it was safe to assume she was tall and willowy. Hispanic. She was a twenty-three year old stay-home mom from Borden's east side, so it was also safe to assume she lived in poverty.

I didn't know enough about the second woman, only that she lived in Borden and worked at the opera house in Fresno. I'd ask Carley about her, too. With any luck I'd glean a few facts for comparison.

As for me, I grew up in northwest Borden. Not the well-to-do section but middle class before the economic slowdown killed them off and turned them into the working poor. My musical background might connect to the second victim, but there was a gulf between opera and classic rock. If De La Cruz had musical talents, that information hadn't been released.

Physically—other than similar hair and eye color—there wasn't a common factor. I didn't have De La Cruz's height or the opera singer's weight. I had a feeling the singer wasn't Hispanic nor did she share my Irish heritage. Seemed to be more inconsistencies than parallels.

As I made notes, Dad fixed fried eggs, toast and sausage. He set plates on the bar and settled on the stool beside me.

"What's that you're doing?"

"A puzzle." I forked a sausage link and bit off one end. Maybe I needed to focus more on the killer and less on the victims.

"I read your story this morning about that murder." He glanced at the notepad, lifted his mug and drank. "Is that what you're working out?"

"Yeah." I closed the pad and set the pen aside. "Can I still use your truck?"

"Keys are on the shelf by the door."

"Need me to drop you at the station?"

He folded an egg beneath his fork, poked it into his mouth and chewed. "I've got the Toyota. Your mom doesn't like it. She wasn't taking it to Texas, anyway."

With the edge of my fork, I cut an egg. The yolk oozed out and soaked into the toast. I glanced at the clock embedded in the stove: Seven. They'd be starting the autopsy in an hour. Until then, Oz and I could clean up the mess at home. If I could force myself to go inside.

"How long you gonna wait to tell me?"

I looked up and met Dad's worried frown. "Tell you what?"

"Whatever's giving you them wrinkles." He ate a sausage link, washed it down with coffee and went to work on the other egg. "Whatever brought you and your friend here in the middle of the night."

"I told you. Someone broke in. The cops had to process the scene."

Dad drained his mug, wiped his lips on a sheet of Bounty and headed for the coffee maker. "The cops take your car and your place is broken into. Seems to me there's more to this than you're saying."

"You'd make a good investigator," I said, a weak attempt at humor. But the worry in Dad's eyes told me loud and clear he didn't find anything humorous about my situation. I told him about the message and the rose, toyed with my food and finally set the fork aside.

"How's that connected to you?"

"Maybe he knows I'm on to him."

"You're playing a dangerous game, kiddo."

"Job hazard." I wasn't about to tell Dad all the facts. Stress over the divorce had taken its toll, evident in the dark half moons hugging his eyes. He didn't need to know someone wanted me dead.

"Job's more hazardous than I'm comfortable with."

"Covering crime has its drawbacks," I admitted.

"Just so long as you don't get hurt, is all." He carried his plate to the sink. "Don't wanna pick up the paper and read about someone finding *you* in a dumpster."

Unable to look at him, I gulped coffee. He had an uncanny way of reading me, and I didn't want him knowing just how close to the truth he'd come.

"What've you got so far?"

"The first victim received a rose four days before she died. Another was found with the body. Yesterday's victim had a rose, too, so it's a safe assumption she got one before she died."

"A special rose?"

I nodded.

"Like them your mom grows?"

"The Barkarole."

"They might have come from her garden." Dad poured himself another cup, lifted the pot in an offer. I shook my head. "Someone got into her greenhouse. Tore it up. She was heartbroken. You know how she loves them flowers."

"When?" I flipped open the notepad and gripped my pen.

"A week or so ago. Before Christmas. She was going to put a bouquet in the house, them dark red ones. She always cuts a bunch for the holiday."

I scribbled the note, finished my coffee and slid off the stool. "Looks like I'll be visiting Ruth after all."

"Get them boxes while you're there. She's threatening to throw stuff out." He cleared my plate, looked at the uneaten food and gave me a frown. Apparently deciding it wasn't worth an argument, he scraped them into the disposal. "Maybe you shouldn't go anywhere alone."

"I'll bring Oz."

"Your mom will have a fit."

All the more reason, in my opinion. Although poking Ruth had only gotten me bitten in the past.

"Wait until after work. I'll go with you."

"Okay," I said, remembered my quasi-date, and added, "I can't."

"You're not playing until nine. We'll go at six."

"I've . . . got a date."

Turning to face me, Dad grinned broadly.

"Don't get too excited. It's Quint. And it's only so I can see his photos."

Dad continued rinsing the plates, but his grin didn't fade.

"He took photos of the first victim the day she got the rose. If he caught something in those frames I might get an edge in this case."

"Over that cop friend of yours?"

"Morales won't tell me anything." I crammed the notepad and pen into my bag and grabbed my coat. "I'm on my own."

"If you find something are you gonna tell him?"

"Maybe." I needed to get out of there. That skin-prickling sensation that Dad was on the verge of catching on worked my spine. I nudged the couch with my foot in an attempt to wake Oz. He snorted, rolled over and snored.

"Hannah." The only time Dad used my given name was when he edged toward anger. "Looks like you need that cop, with someone breaking into your place. And he's got a job to do. Anything you find could help him do it."

I wanted to protest. After all, I wasn't entitled to information in Morales' *ongoing investigation.* But Dad was right. Together we might compile enough to form a theory, and that was a step toward solving the case.

"Don't make it personal, Kiddo."

"Fine. I'll tell him what I learn. Oz," I said, and kicked the couch harder. I forced my shoes on and slipped into my coat. "We've got to go."

Oz peered up and smiled as though still caught between wake and dreamland. With a smile like that, the dream must have been awful good.

He followed me home. In the driveway, Esteves packed his tools of the IT trade into the cargo space of his ten-year-old Volvo. He placed a paper sack sealed with red evidence tape on the passenger seat, precious cargo he wouldn't trust to the car's tail section.

Morales bunched the yellow tape under his arm, tossed it into his Bronco and slammed the door.

"Finished?" I asked.

"All yours." He set his tackle box on the passenger seat. "Fuckin' tired. May have overlooked something. If we did, call. Careful upstairs. Dumb fuck shattered your mirror."

"What did you find?" Mentally crossing my fingers, I shifted my attention between Morales and the duplex.

"Might've got lucky. Stains. Could be semen. Might wanna bleach your bed."

"I'll bleach the whole room," I said. "Let me know if the test shows anything? And don't give me that ongoing investigation crap. I'm a victim, and I have rights."

"Tell you what I can." He climbed into the Bronco.

By ten we had most of the debris bagged up and stacked in the garage. After a canister of Ajax, Oz finally admitted the spray paint wasn't coming off. He still had half a can of the antique white he'd used on the wall so we covered over the message. The words bled through the first two coats, but the third worked. Which left me decidedly uncomfortable knowing the killer's words were still there, trapped beneath a layer of eggshell-finish latex.

Upstairs, I scanned my room. The heap of laundry overflowing the wicker basket had been rummaged through. The bed had been stripped of its sheets, the green spread lay rumpled in a heap. I couldn't shake the sick feeling of knowing he'd been there, in my private world, touching things. Bleach. Lysol. But I still wasn't sure I'd ever lie there and sleep.

I went into the bathroom to scrub the paint from my fingers. A billion tiny reflections of myself stared back from mirror fragments in the sink. Above the sink, a naked, steel door covered the medicine cabinet. Not only did the freak want to terrorize me, he had to inconvenience me. That had been the only mirror in my room.

Carefully, I picked up the pieces and tossed them into the wastebasket. One sliver dug into my finger. Blood splashed the sink's white enamel. I tossed the shard, turned on the tap and rinsed the cut until the water ran clear. I reached for the soap in the ceramic dish and stopped. My ring was gone. I'd left it there last night as I did every time I played.

Panic cramped my chest. I pulled the plastic wastebasket from the corner by the vanity and searched the floor. Then I rummaged through the wads of tissue, mirror fragments and Q-Tips inside the trash. That ring was all I had left of Richard.

"You sick freak," I shouted. He took it. He took my only link to Richard.

I stepped out of the bathroom and peered around, trying to find something else out of place. The closet doors were closed and I usually left them open, a habit stemming from childhood and nightmares of the Boogeyman.

Most kids had a boogeyman with red eyes. My boogeyman had black eyes. Dead eyes. Almost like empty sockets.

Although Esteves hadn't found prints, I grabbed a washcloth from the dirty clothes pile, wrapped it around my hand and pulled the closet door open. The row of boxes I'd stacked on the shelf had been pulled down. The contents were spilled over more boxes and shoes that I never wore.

Inside one box, half buried beneath a nappy sweater I couldn't bring myself to toss, lay my freshman yearbook. Several pages had been ripped out and shredded into long, even strips. I pushed the sweater aside and picked up a scrap of paper. Even with only a portion of his face and that thick, unruly hair showing I knew the image was Richard in his football gear. Beside him, Claire snuggled against his shoulder.

Chapter 14

Fury rose inside me, and formed a knot in my throat. I swallowed hard. My room would never be the cozy environment it had always been.

"That twisted bastard won't rule my life." I tried to gain strength from the words. I had to remain strong, no matter what happened. I needed to view my situation with the same detachment I gave a story in order to keep a clear head.

I had Oz shoot photos of the closet then set about collecting the scraps. Since no prints had been found downstairs, I wasn't worried about destroying evidence. The photos would go to Morales.

This particular yearbook had been in the bottom of a box, three other editions stacked on top. Those were still intact. If I doubted Richard's connection before, I didn't now. Whoever wanted to kill me knew my brother. He'd probably gone to school with him—how else would he know which yearbook to destroy?

I needed to know what was on those pages. On my desk I found the depleted pad of Post-It sheets and went through the tattered book page by page. I made a list of those that had been destroyed. Seven, including the M-section of the senior class. The library kept copies of all the high school yearbooks but, because of the holiday, they wouldn't open until Wednesday. Quint might have his copy. If not, Steve would. They were both in Richard's senior class.

What about that cop who'd shown up at the Gazette crime scene? Morales said he'd gotten there quick. Did he live in Borden? I'd only gotten a glimpse of him, but enough to peg him as close to Richard's age.

I shrugged into my jeans jacket and scooped the keys off my desk. Downstairs, I snagged the phone off the answering machine and thumbed in Detective Brad Ismay's cell number. In addition to being my *Crime Stoppers* contact, he was a friend and had been with the Fresno police force long enough to know most of the cops. If anyone had sent an officer to the Gazette, Brad would know.

I hung up after he promised to check dispatch records.

The autopsy was underway. I needed to know what the coroner had discovered. It might help peg the killer, or at least give me information I'd need to fight back—Were there defensive wounds that showed she tried to fight him off? Had he used the drug to incapacitate her?

Leaving the vacuuming to Oz, I climbed into Dad's Ford and headed across town. The rain had stopped, but the sky remained thick with steel-gray clouds that drooped over the city. I drove down Norton, hung a right on Sycamore and followed the Fresno River to Ashberry Drive. Metal guardrails framing the bridge were crumpled and scarred, evidence of a recent crash. Embedded in eroded banks, leafless trees shuddered in the wind. As with every winter, the river was depleted to a weak stream perhaps three feet across at its widest point.

The old section of the cemetery spread out before me, granite monuments and crypts scarred with black streaks from years of wind and rain. Briefly, I considered stopping to visit Richard but I needed to get in and out of the funeral home before Morales spotted me. I pulled into the mortuary's lot and parked.

Morales' Bronco sat next to a white Crown Victoria. Carley Summers' car was tucked into the carport reserved for loading caskets into the hearse. A Jetta stood beneath the protection of a century-old Elm. Toward the back of the lot sat another Crown Victoria, black, the *Exempt* plate tagging it as law enforcement.

Badorini's pale blue compact eased to the curb in front of Borden Funeral Home. Waving an acknowledgement of his presence, I dropped from the truck's oversized cab and hurried toward the yellow-with-white-trim, two-story Victorian. Pushing past the glass-framed doors, I slipped into the funeral home's cool dimness.

Gladiolas and carnations filled vases to either side of the door. Candles sent spicy aromas into the air to mask the stench of decomposition—with a friend in the business I learned details I could have lived without. These scents were cinnamon and nutmeg.

Morales was probably in the autopsy room. He usually turned off his cell while viewing the procedure, so Badorini couldn't alert Morales. Maybe I could slip in and out before he caught me.

Two dark haired, brown-eyed men, younger versions of the woman with whom they sat, nestled in the entryway at the base of the curved, wooden staircase. Scant light reflected warm hues off the rich, walnut paneling.

The mother, her round, age-creased face streaked with tears, clutched a rosary to her chest. She dabbed her eyes with a lace-trimmed handkerchief. One of the sons, who appeared to be in his early twenties, glanced up as he consoled his grieving mother. Their clothes spoke of wealth. I didn't know brand names that weren't on Wal-Mart's clearance rack, but these clearly came from an equivalent of Macy's or Sak's. They wore wool suits, cashmere sweaters and leather shoes.

Gripping my pen to the point I feared I'd crack its plastic housing, I paused in the hallway. This was the hardest part of my job. I never liked questioning a victim's family and wouldn't now if my life weren't at stake. Usually, once I introduced myself as a reporter, their eyes glazed over. And the emotions, if they agreed to speak, overwhelmed me. I'd never been good at dealing with others' pain. But if I wanted the story, I had to adopt the attitude of a hard-nosed cop. There'd be plenty of time for sobbing when I got home. I steeled myself and approached the trio.

"Are you the Pardini family?" I asked when the son glanced up.

"Who are you?" His gaze wandered from my face to the notepad clutched in my hand. He narrowed his eyes.

"Hannah Monakee." I sighed. "A reporter with the Borden Gazette."

"My sister's dead," he said with the hint of an Italian accent. "Momma's upset and *you want to interview me?*"

"Not an interview. A few questions, that's all. I have personal interest."

"Go away," Mrs. Pardini said. "My Christina is dead—*My baby is dead.*"

She buried her face in a pink embroidered handkerchief and wept.

"I'm sorry for your loss." Weak, but it was all the sympathy I could muster under the circumstances.

"You—a story, that's all she is to you."

"No," I responded, trying to sound convincing. "She's much more."

"You knew Christina?" the younger son asked.

"No." I lifted my hand to bite my thumbnail and tucked it into my fist instead.

He patted his mother's back and stood. Gripping my elbow he led me across the Persian rug and deeper into the long, dimly lit hallway. "Why are you here?"

"I need to know all I can about your sister."

He studied my face and frowned. "Why?"

Tightening my grip on the notepad, I bit my lower lip. I'd have to trust him if I wanted information, but for all I knew he could be the killer. Anyone could.

"Whoever killed your sister is after me," I finally managed. This time, I studied *his* face. Creases furrowed his brows.

"You think it's the same man?" he asked with a note of hope. Yet the caution—and suspicion—still darkened his eyes.

"I don't know. They found a rose with her body. The same variety was left in my car." I peered back at Mrs. Pardini, now leaning heavily against her older son. "I think he killed another woman a couple weeks ago."

"This rose. A red one?"

"Almost black."

"Christina had a rose someone gave her. She brought it home from work on Monday."

"Four days before she died." I glanced up the hallway, at the double steel doors marking the autopsy room. "Did she have anything else? A gift of some kind?"

"I don't know."

"Giovanni," the woman said, but instead of looking at him she glared at me. "These, you take to that lady?" She held a cardboard hatbox trimmed in pink silk. Probably the clothes her daughter would be buried in. "Come. You get these."

"One moment, Momma." He turned to me. "You're not lying, are you?"

"No."

As he considered this, the frown deepened. Finally, he said, "Courthouse Café at noon."

Relief flooded over me. "Thanks."

"I'm going to trust you. Don't do anything to make me sorry I did." He turned to join his family, paused and peered over his shoulder. "Find who killed my sister."

He returned to the couch, took the box from his mother, set it aside then resumed his position of comfort.

Since I was there, and Morales was occupied, this would be a good time to see if my friend had more information. I turned to the office, the door of which stood ajar. Inside, Carley Summers sat at her mahogany desk filling out paperwork. Behind her, heavy blue drapes had been tied back to allow a view of the manicured lawn. Storm-hampered light filtered through, casting the room in a bluish wash. I knocked lightly. She looked up and waved me in.

A petite woman with black curls tumbling over her narrow shoulders, she exhibited elegance and style. I'd known Carley since third grade, when we banded together to keep the boys off the monkey bars. We later discovered they came around to look up her dress. I wore jeans. Later, it struck me as odd that she'd choose to run a funeral home. The business had been her father's, and her grandfather's before him. I expected her brother to step into their shoes, not Carley.

I ducked inside, firmly closed the door and sank on the plush wingback chair. "They're still on the autopsy?"

"They're almost finished."

"Why aren't you in there?" I asked.

"About halfway through, Morales ordered me out." Carley toyed with her diamond stud earring and gave me a sideways glance. "Did he ask about me?"

"You mean, does he know we talked?" I shook my head.

"When he told me to leave, I didn't press the matter," she said, "but I think he suspects I'm leaking information."

Somewhere in the hall, a door opened. Closed. I glanced around, hoping to find a closet I could duck into.

"You're taking a risk coming here," Carley said. "For both of us."

"I'll get out without him knowing I'm here," I said, hoping it was the truth. No closet, but there was a window. I could dive onto the lawn if necessary. I planted my elbows on the chair's padded arms. "How much do you know about this murder?"

She wove her fingers together on the gold-trimmed desk blotter and leaned toward me. She always looked like she had a secret, and usually she did. I only hoped she'd release this one, considering Morales' suspicion, and that it would give me insight. For several moments, she remained silent, and I wanted to urge her to hurry before Morales caught me and made good on his threat to arrest me.

"I know both women were killed by the same person," she finally said.

"The eyes?" Chills crept over me.

"Enucleated. Same as the first."

The image of the photo on my mantle, Richard's eyes scratched up, came to mind. "Your father ran this place when Richard died, right?"

Carley quit toying with her earring, reached across the table and patted my hand. Sadness filled her gaze; she knew Richard's death had crushed me. "Yes. Why?"

A familiar voice drifted through the crack beneath the door. Morales? No, Father Fink, the priest at the local Catholic parish. Unfortunate name, and someone I'd bumped heads with a few times. But a good priest.

"What's wrong?" Carley prompted.

Elementary school. Chasing off boys—someone who shared that kind of history wouldn't think me crazy. *Right?*

I swallowed hard. "Would you ask him if Richard's eyes were intact?"

She straightened and spread her mauve-lacquered fingertips over the blotter. "You think Richard's death might be connected?"

"I know it sounds crazy." I stood, paced, slid back onto the brocade cushion. "It's a long shot. Just ask, okay?"

"Sure, honey. I'll ask."

Breathing deeply, I turned the topic back to the victim. I tilted my head toward the door. "Has anyone asked about her?"

"A man called," Carley said in her *wanna know a secret* manner. "But he wouldn't leave a name."

"Who's viewing?"

"You know Morales is in there—I can tell. You're jumpy. With him are Esteves, the medical examiner and Commander Leo from Fresno police."

Fresno would be working the missing person's end of the case. But why attend the autopsy? I almost asked but realized Carley wouldn't know. Anyone with a badge could view the procedure.

"They'll run a toxicology analysis," Carley continued, "but I can already tell you she was drugged just like the first one."

"Oh?"

"No sign of a struggle, no skin beneath the nails, no defensive wounds. The body's clean except the permanent bruising around her neck."

"What'd they find next?"

"That's when Morales made me leave. Which is what you should do," she added. "He catches us together, I could lose my contract with the County."

"I'll leave soon," I promised. "Do you know any personal details about the victim?"

Carley lifted one narrow shoulder in a noncommittal shrug. This wasn't privileged information. "Christina Pardini, forty-six years old, an opera singer who hails from the northwest side. Old money. The family moved here about thirty years ago and opened up a chain of restaurants throughout the Valley. She divorced six months ago and returned from LA. She sang in the opera there, too."

"Everyone seems to be moving back." I caught Carley's smile. "You knew about Quint?"

"Ran into him Christmas Eve. He was shopping for someone, and it wasn't his mother."

"Oh?"

"Unless his mother's into pink silk trimmed in lace. And even if she is, that's not the kind of gift a man gives his mother."

So, he and Patty had hooked up after all. I wasn't sure how I felt about that. And why should I feel anything? He meant nothing to me. I shoved the issue from my mind.

"Was Pardini sexually assaulted?"

"No sign of anything. This body was clothed. The first had been stripped to bra and panties, but they found no lacerations or fluids to indicate she'd been raped."

Footsteps in the hallway, only this time it wasn't one set. I added the information to my list and headed for the door. With any luck, I could slip outside unnoticed. I rested my fingers on the knob. It twisted beneath them.

"Crap," I muttered.

"Hide," Carley insisted.

"Where?"

"Under the desk." She slid back, stood and straightened brochures advertising caskets, jewelry for cremated ashes and LifeGems.

I dove beneath the desk just as the door to Carley's office opened. In the space between the privacy panel and floor, I spied Morales' brown hiking boots. I held my breath.

"Finished," he said.

"Good. I can get started making her presentable for the family then?"

"She's all yours." He paused. Didn't move. Didn't leave and damn-it I wanted him to *leave*.

Sweat dampened my palms. I resisted the urge to dry them against my jeans. If I did, he'd hear me. If he heard me, he'd arrest us both.

"You seen Hannah?"

"Earlier. She came by to ask about her brother."

"Oh?" Morales said, and I imagined that eyebrow shooting upward.

"I bet it's because Quint returned," she said and I wanted to hug her. "He must be stirring up a lot of memories."

"Could be," Morales said, but I could tell by the hard edge to his tone he wasn't convinced.

"She still can't accept the fact Richard killed himself. She refuses to believe he would ever use drugs."

"Yeah. Told me that." Another pause. "Truck in the lot. Looks like her father's."

"I wouldn't know. I didn't see her arrive."

Dull pain edged into my back. I fought the need to shift, knowing he'd hear me. But if I didn't move soon that pain would migrate up my spine, create a knot in my neck that only a chiropractor could fix. I'd be getting through the gig tonight on rum and Aleve.

When Morales finally left, I tumbled from beneath the desk and sprawled on the floor.

"Close call," I said, and slowly stood.

"You can't leave through the parlor," she whispered, and glanced at the door. "The window."

"I thought about that." I peered through the glass. The lawn was ten feet below. Drop and roll? Risk the back and save the ankles so Dobbs couldn't get my job? "Call if you learn anything else?"

"Of course. Oh, and Hannah?"

Rubbing the knot at the back of my neck, I turned and faced her.

"I was wrong about the eyes."

"They hadn't been gouged out?"

"Removed. On both women. Clean and neat. And they're missing."

Chapter 15

I had three hours until my meeting with Giovanni, which left plenty of time to go by the skate park and track down the kid who'd paid for the flowers. Then check out Ruth's greenhouse. While there, I could collect whatever of mine she intended to trash.

On the corner of Ponderosa and H streets, Sycamore trees towered over the expanse of lawn in Rotary Park. Where the soccer fields used to be stood a dog park encased in eight-foot cyclone fence. The police sponsored the effort—they were tired of arresting adults who busted each other's heads when their children fouled up. A bad call on a play too often landed someone in jail, and someone else in the hospital.

Beyond the playground, where rain dripped from monkey bars and sling-type swings, three boys stood around the edge of the city's newly constructed skate park. Concrete walls dipped and swooped up like a soft-lined, inverted sandcastle. Two of the boys had shaggy black hair, loosely fitting the description the clerk at the florist had given.

A blond, his hair spiked in a three-inch Mohawk and with a crude tattoo on his shoulder announcing him as a punk rock fan, turned toward me as I approached. He fingered the twenty-five-caliber bullet dangling from a chain around his neck and met me at the gate.

"Whatsup?" He folded his arms over his banged-up skateboard.

"I'd like to talk to those two." I gestured at the boys.

"What? You a cop or somethin'?"

"No. A reporter."

"Cool. So's my mom. You work for the Bee?" he asked, referring to the daily that serviced Fresno County twenty miles south of Borden.

"The Gazette." I glanced at the boys, almost identical except one wore glasses and the other had a mouthful of colored rubber bands hooked on clear braces. "Are you their keeper?"

"They're buddies of mine," Mohawk said. "If you wanna talk to them, you talk to me."

I bit my lower lip. Although the kid seemed harmless, his attitude unnerved me. He wasn't a Sureno or Norteno. They were Hispanic gangs. But he could slip easily into one of the white supremacists groups. Peckerwood? Neo-Nazi?

"I ain't no fuckin' banger," he said as though reading my thoughts. "Jus 'cuz someone looks different don't mean they're a banger. I'm punk. I respect the art. Sid Vicious, Johnny Rotten. Fuckin' *geniuses*."

"I know their work. They had tight sounds." I propped my elbow on the fence. "I'm looking for a boy who ordered some roses. About a week ago."

"Whatcha wanna know for?"

"I need to know about the man who paid him."

"Dunno. Not like he gave a name."

I flicked my gaze at the other guys, no longer standing at the edge of the inverted sandcastle but now watching me. "Either of you buy roses for a man about a week ago?"

Mohawk straightened and motioned to his friends, both dark-haired and with lightly tanned skin as though they shared a blended heritage. "Eric. Will. This lady seems cool. You guys know anything about some flowers?"

"Yeah." Eric stepped toward the gate, lifted his eyes and gave me a wide grin exposing the multi-colored bands. "What's it worth to ya?"

Damned little shark. I rummaged in my purse, found a ten and waved it before him.

"Aw, that's the shits. I got twenty bucks just to make the order."

"Ten's all I've got."

He tore the bill from my fingers. I made a mental note to take it easy on the bar tab tonight. "What did he look like?"

Eric shrugged. "Old."

"Gray hair?" I offered. Old to a kid meant anywhere between twenty-five and eighty.

"Nah. No gray."

"Brown? Blond?"

"I don't remember. He wore a beanie."

Great. No hair color. "Eyes? Do you remember what color they were?"

"Kinda brown. I only noticed cuz he stared at me like real hard. I was afraid if I didn't do it he'd shoot me or somethin'." He stomped one end of the skateboard—black with a white-lined skull sporting a Mohawk much like the blond kid's. Eric caught the board as it flipped up. "But hey, twenty bucks is twenty bucks."

"Was he tall? Short? Thin? Heavy?" I asked.

"Tall. Not skinny but not fat." He crammed the ten into his jeans pocket. "Hey, that's all I know. Like, I didn't check the guy out, ya know? I ain't a fruit fly."

"Anything else?" I asked, and mentally crossed my fingers. "Anything you can remember that might help me find this man?"

"Nope. 'cept, I got this feelin' he was like a cop or in the Army or something, like he had a gun and would use it. He didn't threaten me or nuthin' like that but had this attitude, ya know? A tough guy."

Tough guy. Brown eyes, wore a hat, not fat but not skinny—Hell, that fit half Borden's population.

"Oh, and he wore boots. Doc Martins, or they looked like 'em. Black."

"Do you remember what else he wore?"

Eric shook his head and studied the ground. "I dunno, man. Jeans, I think. And a jacket. He was a white boy. Hell, they all look alike."

I scribbled my home phone number on the back of a Gazette card and gave it to him, knowing he'd drop it in the garbage once I left. But I held a fragment of hope that he'd keep it, and if he remembered anything else he'd give me a call.

Back in the truck with R.E.M. singing "*Losing My Religion*," I wished I could reach inside the kid's head, pluck out the information I needed as easily as he plucked the ten-spot from my fingers. I needed a solid description of the man who had purchased the roses. Black boots—hell. That could be anyone. Army? A cop? Yeah, if he was SWAT. Street cops wore boots, though, with their uniforms. Gang members had taken to wearing Doc Martins. Could the killer also be a gang member? Was this some sort of initiation? I'd known them to target specific people to gain rank, but usually those people were cops or lawyers with the county's prosecutor's team.

With plenty of time before I needed to meet Giovanni, I drove across town and parked facing the wrong direction on the Mulberry tree-lined street before Ruth's house. Maybe I could get her to talk about the significance of the rose and get my hands on Richard's yearbook.

I opened the truck's door and knocked over a couple green plastic bags. One had split its seam. The other hadn't been tied properly and its contents spilled over the sidewalk.

Groaning in an effort to keep from cursing, I started shoving things back inside then realized most of this was my stuff: Old report cards, class photos, a newborn-sized pink dress with matching bonnet. Great. My childhood lay in the gutter. She was cleaning house all right, putting the past behind her for a fresh start in Texas, and Dad and I were part of that past.

I pulled the plastic together, tied and propped the bag against a box she'd also left for collection. Books from my old room. The entire collection of Dr. Seuss from childhood, Christopher Pike from junior high, Stephen King, John Sandford and Dean Koontz shoved in with Poe and T.S. Eliot. Wedged between *Eyes of the Dragon* and *Invisible Prey* lay a stack of letters bound by a rubber band. On top were five programs from productions in San Francisco. *Cosi fan Tutte, Phantom of the Opera, Tales of Hoffmann*, a couple others that had faded beyond deciphering.

"Bitch," I muttered, and crammed the programs beside the letters. I lifted the box onto my bent knee and propped it against the truck. After depositing the books onto the bench seat, I tossed in my old ballet slippers and slammed the door.

How could anyone who had given birth—*who had a daughter*—be so cold? That was the question I'd asked myself most of my life, a question that, for years, made me wonder what I had done to make Ruth so distant. And for years, I'd sought her approval, tried anything to make her proud of me. After Richard died, the gulf between Ruth and me widened, and I realized there was nothing I could do. I didn't mourn the loss of my mother— she was never there to begin with. I mourned the empty place in my heart where the thought of her—of the close relationship we could have had—resided. I mourned the death of a little girl's desire to become the daughter her mother could love.

And this, memories of a childhood most mothers would cherish now scattered in the gutter, was yet another reminder that while I grew up with two parents, I really had only one.

Skirting the remainder of the junk on the curb—I didn't want to know what else she'd tossed—I strode up the flagstone walkway trimmed with Irish moss.

Mini-blinds covered the windows on the two-story brick-and-mortar house, painted subtle shades of tan and brown. Modest, just like Ruth. Not the gaudy shades of pink and turquoise some of the newer neighbors had chosen, and I could hear Ruth comment in that hard-edged tone how inappropriate such colors were.

Ruth answered before I knocked and regarded me with a blank stare. I'd always thought of her as exotic and beautiful, but inside she was as warm as a winter night in Siberia. She stood with her perfect posture, hands clasped before her, an unspoken command of respect. She had the same green eyes as mine, same dark, shimmering hair only she wore hers pulled back in a tight bun. But the resemblance stopped on the surface. Beneath, she was as caustic as a blend of bleach and ammonia. Even her slim-fitting skirt, which hit just below her knees, and cream-colored blouse with the slightest hint of lace, seemed rigid and cold.

"I trust your father told you I am leaving?"

"He mentioned it." I peeked beyond her to the stacks of cardboard and furniture protected beneath thick blankets. "When do you fly out?"

"Wednesday morning." She didn't move. I almost left, but I needed to see the yearbook and greenhouse.

"Dad said there's some things I should get."

She looked past me toward the mound on the curb.

"I see." I hooked my thumbs in my jeans pockets and again peered past her. "What about Richard's stuff?"

"I will take his belongings with me."

"May I come in?" I finally asked.

She stepped aside, and I squeezed past her. Several boxes were stacked near the foot of the stairs, all with my brother's name and clearly marked with the contents: Photos, clothing, trophies, books. On top rested the Fender guitar case under a layer of bubble wrap.

A spiral-bound notebook lay open on the case. In it, she'd made a list of each box and an inventory of what they contained. Below, she'd itemized those that would go into storage and those she'd keep with her. At the end of the page she'd noted ones she never intended to open. Three. All marked *private*.

"Is his senior yearbook in here?" I tapped the box beneath the Fender.

"It is."

"May I see it?" I had the list of missing pages in my purse.

"It is already packed."

Fifteen, twenty minutes at the most was all I needed. "I'll repack them," I offered. "I'll tape it up. Everything will be as they are now."

"I made myself clear." She stood there. Stoic. The Ice Queen.

I balled my hands into fists, gritted my teeth, blocked the argumentative words I wanted to shout so badly it hurt my chest. Lashing out would only strengthen her resolve, would be like trying to turn hardpan into fertile soil.

"You're leaving Wednesday?" Maybe I could sneak in before the movers came.

"Yes. Everything will be moved on Tuesday," she added, as though reading my mind. And somewhere in that void she'd created inside me, I believed she could.

She turned toward the back of the house where Carmen stood in the kitchen wrapping Ruth's china and packing the pieces in a heavy crate. "Carmen? Make us some tea."

Ruth never asked, always ordered and Carmen obeyed. Although she couldn't like Ruth any more than I did, Carmen stayed and served and never said a word. Literally. I wasn't even sure she *could* speak.

I almost declined the offer—I wasn't fond of hot tea—but it would give me the opportunity to broach the subject of the roses. Glancing wistfully at Richard's belongings, I followed Ruth through the formal dining area and into the pale blue kitchen. She slid onto the colonial-style chair and gestured me to sit across from her. Like Carmen, I obeyed.

Carmen, her floral dress pinched beneath the sterile, white apron, set the blue-onion patterned tea pot on the table then brought the tray of cups, saucers, honey and lemon.

Ruth filled my cup, then her own and set the pot aside. "Why are you here? I do not believe you came to see me."

I spooned a lemon slice into my tea, tried to set the spoon in the saucer as soundlessly as possible but it hit with a subtle clink. "Dad said your garden was vandalized."

She lifted her cup, drank, set it down. Then she fixed her gaze on me, and I could swear her eyes fossilized.

"Look. I'd just like a peek at the garden."

"Do you know who did it?" Had I not known Ruth, I might have been offended.

"No."

"Then why look?"

"Curious." I clenched my teeth, drew a deep breath and exhaled slowly. Maybe I should have waited, as Dad suggested. My fingers trembled as I reached for the tea. "Several of these roses have shown up at crime scenes. I think the . . . *culprit*," I exchanged for *killer*, "may have gotten them here."

"Another of your stories?"

"Ties in, yes." I bit my thumbnail, caught her scornful look and quit.

"The murder? I saw the headline in the newspaper." But didn't read the story, I'd be willing to bet.

"Two murders," I said. "And I'd like to figure out who this guy is before he kills again."

"You are not a police detective," Ruth said. "Remember? You are only a newsperson. It is not your place to investigate crimes, although you have never seemed to understand that."

"Hobby." I sipped the tea, bitter and hot. "I'm helping the cops."

That didn't score points, not that I ever could. And it wouldn't help me get closer to the garden. She peered through the lace curtain. I followed her gaze to the backyard and, beyond the gate, the plastic-enclosed greenhouse that covered the rear lot adjacent to Pine Street.

"Did you report the vandalism?" I asked.

"No."

"Why not?"

"I do not want people here. I cherish my privacy. You know that."

"A crime was committed," I said, attempting to reason with her.

"They are not going to find the person, so I saw no need to call."

"May I look?" I drank, set the cup down and slid the saucer away.

"There is not much to see." She sipped, peered outside, sipped again.

"Were all the roses destroyed?"

"No. Only one variety."

I tapped my fingers against the table, drumming out a Beatles tune: *That Boy.* She glared at me, and I quit. I stood, wove through the maze of boxes and headed out the back door. I'd gotten halfway across the yard when she stepped onto the porch.

"Hannah." She didn't raise her voice, but inflicted a hard edge that made me flinch. "You do not have my permission. If you go in there I will call the police and have you charged with trespassing."

Anger churned in the pit of my stomach. She had no reason to stop me, but Ruth never needed a reason. Bitch came naturally like a talent for writing or painting. Some people were gifted.

I stepped past her, marched through the house and left. Shoving the box onto the passenger seat I realized I was muttering *no place like home* over and again, as though it was a mantra that might change my world.

I climbed in, started the truck and drove around the corner. On Pine, I cruised past the chain-link fence. At the corner, I parked in shade beneath a pine's wide boughs. The greenhouse filled the quarter-acre lot adjacent to Ruth's backyard. Beyond the plastic walls, rose bushes were reduced to spindly forms. Even from this distance I could hear the humming sound as the automatic sprinkler system kicked on.

Cold wind raked across me as I slid out and eased the truck door closed. I jogged across the street, up the sidewalk and approached the eight-foot fence. I hadn't climbed it since high school, wasn't sure I could anymore. But I needed to see the garden and wasn't leaving until I did.

"No guts, no glory," I muttered, hooking my fingers in the cold, steel fence. Icy needles seeped into my hands. I poked the toes of my shoes in the diamond-shaped links and climbed.

Chapter 16

Fifteen years ago I could have scrambled over the cyclone fence with the agility of a cat. Even with the constant exercise from drumming, my arms ached by the time I reached the jagged cuts of steel on top left exposed to deter intruders.

Those sharp, steel peaks snagged my jacket sleeve and scraped my flesh.

"Damn-it," I spat.

Burning pain, like fire following a trail of gasoline, spread to my elbow. I tried to lift my arm high enough to release the material but it wasn't letting go. I scanned the street: No sign of Badorini. Wiggling out of the jacket, I gripped the pole that ran the length of the fence. Then I pulled myself higher, brought my legs over the top and dropped on the far side. My jacket flapped in the wind, as if angry I'd left it behind.

Frigid, late December wind pierced my cotton blouse, chilling me. Hugging myself, I rubbed my arms and studied the greenhouse. Plastic walls were nailed to the frame. A strip of metal protected the seams. No way could I pry it off. I should have checked the truck. Dad always carried tools. The only way in was to tear the plastic.

A willow tree draped over the south side of the fence. I grasped a handful of the bare, whip-like branches, pulled them low, gripped the base of one and broke it off. With the sharp end,

I created a quarter-sized hole. I tossed the branch, worked my fingers through the plastic, stretched and ripped it apart.

Inside, misters hummed while a fine veil of water drifted over the roses. Goosebumps prickled my arms. I again rubbed them in a futile attempt to get warm. Scents of damp earth and fertilizer—the same scents from the dairies that lay on the outskirts of town and swept through Borden when the wind shifted—filled the air.

Other than the watering system it was still and quiet. Which meant Ruth hadn't caught on to my plan. I ducked through the tear, straightened and looked around. Thorns slashed my blouse as though her plants didn't like the intrusion any more than she would. Thin lines of blood soaked my sleeves.

In the distance, a car door closed. A dog let loose a series of sharp barks that grated my nerves. A lizard—gray and scaly—scurried across the red cobblestone and darted into the wood mulch.

Air thick with the scent of roses pressed in on me. Poking my glasses in place, I waited until my vision adjusted to the dimness then stepped between bushes and onto the walkway.

Most of the roses had bloomed and died, Ruth's neglect leaving dead clumps on thorny stems. I edged along the path until I reached the center where the Barkarole grew.

The shrubs had been hacked. Most of the roses were now dead or gone. The stems were pinched, cut with dull scissors just like the one in my car.

A trail of petals led away from the bushes. I glanced around and licked the icy mist from my lips. Then I followed the trail the killer left like Hansel's breadcrumbs through the wicked forest. The thought that I stepped where *he* stepped, touched what *he'd* touched, terrified me. The trail ended near the north wall. He'd left a spray-painted message identical to the one in my living room: *Come Back to Me.*

"Who are you, you bastard? Who am I supposed to come back to? Huh?" I clamped my hand over my mouth, closed my eyes, breathed through my fingers until the anger subsided. The coward. Hiding behind cryptic messages. "Come out and face me, you creep."

Footfalls slapped the sidewalk outside. Voices, muffled by the plastic, drifted toward me. Ruth. I recognized her precise speech pattern. The other I couldn't peg.

I crouched behind the row of plants. The door, about five yards away, opened. Cold wind sliced through as they stepped inside. I spied the patrol cop's dark blue pants.

I glanced at the tear I'd made in the plastic. Keeping to the relative safety of the shrubs, I inched toward my only chance of escape. The distinct sound of a bullet being chambered cracked the silence. Turning, I faced the black barrel of the cop's gun.

"Don't move."

I froze.

"Come out, hands up where I can see them."

I laced my fingers behind my head, crawled on my knees to the cobblestone and stood. Raising my gaze, I met Holmes, his gun wavering unsteadily in his outstretched arms. A small measure of relief washed over me, but only a small one. This was probably the first time he had pulled his weapon in the line of duty, and I was lucky he hadn't shot me.

"Don't shoot," I cried.

"Ms. Monakee." Even in the gloom, I could see Holmes' face redden, turning the freckles purple. "Mrs. Monakee wants me to arrest you."

What was that bird that laid its eggs in other birds' nests and abandoned them? They should rename it Ruth. A colder, more heartless creature didn't exist.

"I'm not surprised." I turned toward Ruth. "You'll call the cops on me but not when someone trashes your garden?" To Holmes, I added, "Call Morales. Tell him I found the source for the roses."

"He heard the call and radioed dispatch. He says if someone's here to hold them. That'd be you."

"I know it's me," I snapped. "Can you get that gun out of my face?" Pain pressed against my temples. I looked at Ruth. "How long ago did this happen? Before Christmas I know, but when?"

"It might help if you tell us." Holmes lowered his weapon, but gripped it firmly in both hands. Adrenaline. I hoped the guy didn't have an itchy finger. He'd shoot himself in the foot.

"I discovered the destruction five days before the holiday." She lifted her chin and focused on Holmes. "I came to cut flowers for a bouquet."

"Didn't you see the message on the wall?" I asked.

She continued to address Holmes. "I chose not to call the police. There is not a thing you can do. Am I right?"

"If it was just vandalism, probably not," I answered for him. "But this goes beyond vandalism."

"Please take her into custody."

Holmes eyed me and shuffled nervously. He re-holstered his weapon. "I'm going to have to wait for the Sarge, Ma'am."

Ruth glared so true to her Ice Queen persona I wanted to strike a match and thaw her out. But there was no thawing my mother.

"Arrest her," she repeated.

"Uh—This is a civil matter, Ma'am. We're not supposed to get involved. All I can do is hold her until the Sarge gets here."

"Do so. Make sure your sergeant knows I intend to press charges."

"Yes, Ma'am."

Ruth left. I wanted to shout after her, tell her to go ahead and have me locked up but was afraid Holmes would change his mind about waiting for Morales.

"Lovely lady, isn't she?" I unbuttoned my cuffs and rolled up my sleeves. Scratches riddled my forearms. But they were thin and, once cleaned up, shouldn't be too noticeable. I'd wear my black suit to dinner.

"What's the time?" I asked.

He studied his wristwatch, a gold-tone Seiko with stretchable band. "Quarter past eleven."

Forty-five minutes until my meeting with Giovanni. I was about to ask Holmes to get on the radio and hurry Morales up when the detective ducked into the greenhouse, looked around and zeroed in on me. His dark gaze hardened like obsidian.

"Ought to arrest you right now," he grumbled.

"Civil," I said. "Thought you didn't get involved in civil cases."

"Willing to make an exception—You're pushing it." He looked past me at what remained of the Barkarole. "That them?"

"Seven plants. All destroyed. And he left a message." I gestured toward the wall.

Morales stalked up the walkway and paused before the foot-high letters. "Sonofabitch."

"He did this the day the first victim got a rose."

"Holmes, get your kit." Morales pressed his palms together and lightly tapped his index fingers against his lips. "You knew about this?"

"Dad told me this morning."

"Should have called."

"So you could shut me out again? Huh-uh. I'm not playing that game."

He grabbed my arm and swung me around to face him. "Murder's no game, Hannah."

"Keeping information from a potential victim isn't either." I shrugged him off and turned back to the foot-high letters. "It's the same as on my wall. Do you think he knows I lived here?"

"Knew you as a kid?" Morales tapped his lips, his brows creased into a frown. "Could be."

"Me and Richard used to hang out here. Quint, too," I said, and immediately regretted the admission. Morales was already suspicious of Quint. I didn't need to fuel that fire.

"Can't figure out where Rydell's been."

"He has nothing to do with this," I said.

"Not so sure. Don't like it when things won't add up."

"You're off track. That's why they don't add up."

"Steer clear of him."

"Can't. I promised to have dinner with him." I caught the flicker of anger in Morales' eyes and added, "We're old friends."

"Are you listening?" Morales gripped my wrist painfully tight. "This guy wants to *kill* you. Got that? I *can't* let that happen."

"Did Esteves test the fluid you found at my place?" I asked, referring to the semen sample. "Or are you going to withhold that information, too?"

"Type O. Non-secretor." Morales let me go.

"Fine. Bring me a blood-soaked glove, then I'll listen." I headed for the door.

"What about this?" He swept his arm through the garden's damp air. "Just said Rydell knows of this place."

"A lot of people know. Ruth's had this for years. Before Richard died, she showed her roses at that big event in Southern California."

"She seen anyone hanging around?"

"You talk to her. She won't tell me. I've got to be someplace. I guess asking you to call if you find anything is too much?"

"Go home. Leave this to me."

"My faith in your performance is a little thin. You missed something in my bedroom."

His brow darted beneath that shaggy hair.

"Huh-uh. This is give and take, and all you're doing is taking. When you give, I'll give."

"Arrest you for withholding evidence," he ground out.

"I don't think so."

Before I could reach the door, Morales caught me around my waist and tugged me close. He held me in a half-hearted embrace, glanced around and said, "What the fuck are you looking at?"

"Nothing, Sarge," Holmes said.

"That's right. Go . . . look for prints or something."

Morales touched his lips to my ear. "Monakee, you make me crazy. Don't wanna find you in a dumpster, got that?"

Dad's words. Ones I hoped wouldn't come true. Yep, I got it all right. I leaned away and studied his eyes. Not that hard, flint-like gaze of anger but softer with a hint of concern.

"Badorini's watching. I'll be okay."

"Watch you myself if I could," Morales grumbled. "Don't trust Badorini or anyone, not with you."

"I'm touched."

"Quit bein' a smart ass." He pulled me closer, again touched his lips to my ear. His breath was warm and moist. "You wanted to go, fine. I let you go. But I'll never stop caring what happens to you. Get used to it."

Touching my fingers to his cheek, I nodded. I'd always suspected somewhere beneath that Dirty Harry image was a real, flesh-and-blood man. I only wished I'd discovered him sooner.

I pulled away and stepped toward the door.

"If anything happens, I'll call." I followed the sidewalk around the block to Pine Street.

Climbing into the truck, I sighed. Morales was right, I am a smart ass. I'd gotten out of there without cuffs on my wrists this time, but that wouldn't happen again. Morales was itching for an excuse to confine me, and his post-relationship revelation would make him even more vigilant.

I had thirty minutes before I had to meet Giovanni. I needed to focus on him, forget Morales and Ruth. I was about to find out what connection the killer had with Christina Pardini.

I started the engine, twisted on the radio and found 105.1 FM out of Fresno. Classic rock. While the Beatles sang of a *Hard Day's Night*, I steered south until I hit Yosemite Drive, and hooked a left.

I turned on Elm and parked next to *Courthouse Café*, an old trolley car from San Francisco someone had carted to the Valley and hitched to a building. It was named for the business it drew from the hundred-year-old Courthouse across the intersection.

Inside, air warm with scents of grilled beef chased the chill from my limbs. The EMTs, Kurkis and Tolson, sat at the counter eating hamburgers and fries. The only available table against the row of windows was wedged between Quint, drinking coffee and working on a salad, and an undercover cop who poked at a patty melt. I'd never met him but he kept his elbow tucked against the bulge at his side, guarding his gun.

I slid onto the booth unnoticed, ordered coffee and set the menu aside. Giovanni entered with a gust of wind. He sat in the opposite seat and looked me over.

"Did you have an accident?" he asked.

"A minor incident. Thanks for meeting me, Mr. Pardini."

"You wouldn't lie to me, would you? You're not writing a story?"

"Honest. No story. Personal reasons, like I said."

"Okay. What can I tell you?"

"Did Christina have a boyfriend?"

"There was someone, but she rarely spoke of him."

Hope surged through me. I resisted the urge to pull out my notepad. "Did she give his name?"

The waitress, pencil tucked into her tight, platinum curls, set my coffee on the paper placemat and turned to him. He waved her away.

"No name," he said.

"Did you ever see him?" I dumped two packets of sugar into the cup and tore the seal from a small tub of cream. "It's important you remember."

"That cop who called me. He asked me. I told him she had letters, but never brought the boyfriend to meet us."

I'd be willing to bet that cop was Morales. "Did you give him the letters?"

"Not yet. He'll meet me at the police station at two."

"You have them with you?" My mouth went dry. I'd crossed the line into an *ongoing investigation*, and Morales would have a fit. "May I see them?"

"I don't know." Giovanni glanced around uneasily.

"I'll read them and give them right back." I reached out, my fingers twitched with anticipation.

He pulled three envelopes from his blue blazer's pocket and set them on the table. "That's all I could find."

I pulled a letter free and scanned the loose script. Scrawled across the bottom was the name *Clio*. I picked up the envelope and searched for a return address. There wasn't one. The postmark was from Fresno.

The letters were written to a vibrant woman full of promise and talent, one who grasped life and lived it to the fullest and who, now, lay dead in Carley's funeral home. With my finger, I traced her name, so carefully written by a man who longed for her affection. Who was he? How did he feel now that she was gone? Did he have answers as to who killed her? Answers that might save my life?

Last night, you were so wonderful—Your voice resonated within me and touched the very core of my soul like the whisper of an angel. You are heaven, and I am but a soul striving to reach the heights where you dwell—

Sappy, but nothing that would peg the author as a killer. The others were similar.

"There might be something else." Giovanni's hands quivered. He stared at the place mat.

"Oh?" I stirred more cream into my coffee and drank.

"The day Christina got that rose, she got a necklace. A winged serpent?" He shook his head. "I didn't see it, and Momma, she doesn't speak good English."

"Where is it?"

"Momma would know."

"Do you think she'll let me see it?" I returned the letters to the envelopes and set them aside.

"She'll give it to me. I can meet you later? Tonight at six?"

"Good." Damn. I had a date at six. "That won't work. I'm playing at The Dock. Can you bring it by?"

The waitress paused by the table with a steaming pot, topped off my cup and left.

"What time?"

"We start at nine, break at ten thirty."

"Okay. I'll bring the necklace."

"Did your mother say who gave it to Christina?" I mentally crossed my fingers. If she had a name, I'd have a suspect.

He shook his head. "Christina, she was very quiet about this boyfriend. I think maybe he had a wife."

Afraid of getting caught cheating, he killed her? Possible. But where would the first victim fit in? And me?

"She said he wore a uniform," Giovanni added. "Maybe he was in the service."

"Did your mother say anything else about the necklace?"

"She said only that it's a winged serpent. Wings and serpents. Like maybe more than one."

I studied the postmark again. Four days before the first victim, De La Cruz, died. The day Ruth's garden had been vandalized.

"The boyfriend lives in Fresno?"

"That's what Momma said."

"And he reported her missing?"

"The cops, they spoke to him. But when I ask, they won't say who he is."

Which meant they were trying to protect the boyfriend. Maybe he'd been threatened. Maybe he had incriminating information as to the killer's identity.

Or maybe, he was one of their own.

Chapter 17

I left the café feeling hopeful. At least I knew the killer left something with Christina. Winged serpent. Mythology? Demonology? I'd research both.

I climbed into the truck and headed for the Gazette. While I could have gone home, I wasn't ready to face that fresh paint with the killer's plea trapped beneath. And, the Gazette computers were better than mine: High Speed versus dial-up.

Seven minutes later, I parked next to Vi's PT Cruiser, a purple bubble with feathered-boa trim in the back window and vanity plates *I-(Heart)-Trirs*. It took several attempts to decipher the abbreviation until I remembered our community reporter's quasi-children consisted of three Rat Terriers: Poppy, Lula and Izzy.

The only other car in the lot, a beaten-up Jeep, belonged to the sports editor. Probably recapping last night's Borden Crows game for the Sunday edition. He usually kept to himself, so I could research the necklace in peace.

I dropped from the truck into a rain puddle, shook off my feet, although the water had soaked to the socks, and keyed my way inside. The police scanner in my cubicle crackled with static. A cop reported he was *ten-ninety-seven*—at the scene. I hadn't heard sirens, which meant he was on the far side of town or the situation wasn't critical.

Depositing my purse on the desk calendar stained with coffee rings and assignments, I glanced at the Post-It-notes to make sure I hadn't forgotten anything. I hadn't.

I booted up the computer, selected Google from the toolbar and typed in *Valley unsolved deaths*. After more than ten thousand options surfaced, I added Central CA and tried again. Links to news articles and crime victims' websites filled the screen. Bakersfield, Sacramento, Stockton, Fresno, Merced, the list went on and on. I started at the top and worked my way down. After two hours and three sludge-like coffees from the break room vending machine, I found a two-year-old article from the Stockton Record involving a hit-and-run. Claire Rougue of Borden, California.

She'd been struck down in a parking garage while leaving work late one night. No witnesses. No evidence except silver transfer marks on the garage wall.

I scrolled down until I found her photo. Older, her hair not so shiny, the smile more subdued. But it was definitely Richard's high school sweetheart.

"Poor Claire," I muttered.

According to the article her mother resided in a Borden nursing home at the time of Claire's death. I pulled the phone book from beneath the stack of papers, rifled through and found two retirement facilities. One was pricey, had two dining rooms, a spa, and an in-home theater. It offered golf, shuffleboard and day trips. If I remembered correctly, Claire's family wasn't well to do. The other offered long-term nursing care.

I scribbled the addresses and phone numbers to scope out Monday. Right now I wanted to research the rose and Christina's winged serpents. Then get ready for that date.

I sent Google on a search. Crystallinks: Origins in mythology, history, legends and fantasy. The link took me to a page where Ouroboros, the snake eating itself, filled the screen.

"Winged gods who came to earth to create the human race," I muttered, scrolled down, and delved into dragon symbolism.

"Alchemy, Chinese—eternal change. Spiritual perfection, powerful amulet of luck." I scoffed. Christina's amulet hadn't brought her luck.

"What are you doing here?"

I jumped, looked up at the cubicle wall where Tom Withers, his Crows cap backward on his crop of graying hair, peered down at me.

"Research." I jabbed the screen's button. The image faded to black. "How was the game?"

"We won. Barely. Twenty-one to twenty, Dos Palos missed the extra point. Pretty exciting in the first half, but the second sort of fizzled." He popped sunflower seeds into his mouth, cracked one and spit the shell into a Styrofoam cup. "Grigsby was in earlier. It seems that new guy—Jeremy's temp—got a hell of a story. It's going to be tomorrow's lead."

"Quint? What story?"

"Some guy got lost up by Mammoth Pools. Quint tracked 'em down and got some photos, too."

"That's my beat." Heat burned my face. I slapped my notepad on the desk. "Not only is he working with me, playing in my band but now he's moving into my territory?"

Work and the band I could handle. But don't mess with my job. Dinner was going to be interesting, after all.

"Careful there," Tom motioned toward my computer. "The server's been going down all day. I just booted it up twenty minutes ago."

"Noted," I said, and gave him my *is that all?* smile. He took the hint, slid out of view and moments later the clacking of his keyboard drifted through the air.

Snatching up the phone, I called Robin. He answered immediately.

"Peace," he said.

"You're going to be home tonight, right?"

"Yeah, man. Gonna get a brain-drain with the tube. X-Files marathon. Got a major crush on Scully. Why?"

"Just checking. I'll be there with Quint, and really don't want to be alone."

"Whatever, man. I gotcha covered."

"Thanks." I hung up. Never hurt to be cautious.

Re-activating the screen returned it to the Google page. Wikipedia focused on Dungeons and Dragons. No rose. Next I tried Ancient Objects and Sacred Realms. Rituals. None using serpents or roses.

Another search took me to garden serpents, sky dragons and Egyptian jewelry representing Isis. I tried Serpent, Mirror, and Rose. *Serpent and the Rose*, a movie about voodoo, and a novel titled *Mirror Lake*. Beneath those were Harry Potter, and *The Serpent's Shadow*.

When I tried to backtrack, nothing happened. I shook the mouse. Still nothing. "Damn-it."

"Server's down again," Tom announced as he passed my cubicle. "It'll be thirty minutes before it's back up."

I didn't have thirty minutes. Quint would pick me up in two hours, and I still needed to shower and figure out what to wear. I shut down and left.

Driving home, I considered what I knew so far which amounted to little. Nothing I could fit together at any rate. Nothing tangible. Nothing that made sense.

Oz had made considerable progress. The duplex almost looked normal without the fabric and giant dick hanging from the ceiling.

I piled my belongings on the bookcase and joined him in the kitchen.

Donned in a hot pink apron that matched the spikes in his hair, Oz turned eggplant in the skillet, fried it to a golden brown and transferred the slices onto paper towels. From a pot simmering on the stove, scents of garlic, tomatoes and basil drifted on steam. Fettuccini rested in a colander beside the sink.

"Smells great," I said.

He lifted the lid on the sauce, scooped a bit onto a wooden spoon and brought it to me. "Absolutely yummy. Taste."

I blew on the sauce, let him feed me and closed my eyes. God, it was more than yummy. It was fantastic. Since breakfast at Dad's, I'd only had coffee and hadn't realized how hungry I was until now.

"Thought you might want a bite before your big date." He returned the lid and set the spoon in the sink of sudsy water.

"He's buying."

"Oh, sweetie. Didn't anyone teach you dating rules? You never go on a date hungry," Oz said. "Last thing you want is Quint thinking you're a pig."

"So I eat first?" Didn't make sense to me. A free meal was a free meal, and on my budget I learned to take advantage whenever possible.

"Going out for dinner isn't about the food. It's about the company. *His* company."

"It's a sacrifice to see his pictures," I said. "All I want are those shots."

"But you can't let him know that. After all you've told me, you want to go in there prim and proper and every bit the lady he wishes he had."

"Make him suffer?" I uttered a sharp laugh. "That's not going to work."

"Oh yes it will. Sit. It's ready, and you're going to eat. Then we'll get *you* ready."

We? What the hell was this *we* business? I pretty much had my night planned out. Eat, get to his place, study the photos and dump him once we got to The Dock.

I sat at the Formica-topped table and picked at a gold fleck embedded in the Fifties-era relic, one of the few items of mine Oz hadn't trashed. He dropped pasta into a plate, poured on sauce, added slices of eggplant and sprinkled it with freshly grated Parmesan.

"Oh, and don't worry about your room. I took the liberty of purchasing a new mattress. You'll love it. It's one of those pillow-top designs. Real comfy." He met my gaze. "What? I couldn't buy it without giving it a test drive." He wiped his hands on the lace-trimmed apron. "You don't mind, do you? I'd never want to sleep on a mattress that some freak jerked off on. I mean really, honey, that's just creepy."

"How much?" Mentally calculating my checking account balance brought me close to the red.

"Don't worry about it. Peace of mind has no price. I couldn't sleep in this house knowing that bed was in there."

"Knock it off your share of bills." I wanted to kiss him—I wouldn't have slept there. Ever.

"If you insist." He fixed himself a plate and sat at the table's far end. "But really, I did it for myself as much as you."

"I'm glad you moved in," I said.

"Me too, sweetie." He brought a small piece of eggplant to his mouth. "Me too."

At a quarter till five I scooped up the last bit of basil and tomatoes, devoured it and jogged upstairs. If I hurried I'd have time to shower, dress *and* dry my hair, which took thirty minutes. Maybe I'd just braid it.

A half hour later, clad in a pair of cotton panties and white undershirt, I stood before the closet and rifled through my wardrobe for the third time. It had never occurred to me what a limited selection I had: Jeans and more jeans, modest sweaters, a couple suits I saved for important meetings and blouses that looked more like men's shirts than anything a woman might wear. I opted for a suit, laid it on the bed and searched for my low heels.

"Hey girlfriend." Oz knocked softly on my bedroom door. Not waiting for permission he stepped inside with two boxes, one large and one small. He eyed the suit. "Oh, *please* tell me you're not wearing that."

"I wished I'd never agreed to this." I found a pair of knee-highs and slipped them on.

"Every picture tells a story," he said in his singsong voice. "And this isn't the story you want to tell. He's a gorgeous hunk of man. If only I could walk in your heels." He glanced at the Mary Jane flats, and his hand fluttered near this throat. "I took the liberty of picking up a little something for you."

"You *what?*"

"Clothes, sweetie. *Women's* clothes. That *Annie Hall* look of yours just won't do."

Redecorating my home wasn't enough; he had to redecorate me? "Oz . . ."

"Button those lips, baby. Tonight's your time to shine." He pushed the suit aside and set the boxes on the bed. "He's going to faint and drool and regret the day he walked out of your life."

"Payback?"

"You got it, girlfriend, and it's going to be a real bitch." He opened the shoebox and pulled out a pair of black pumps. Stiletto heels.

"I can't."

"Yes you can. Heels say sexy and that's the order of the evening. Got that?"

I stared at the larger box, imagining some slinky outfit more fitting a transvestite. "I don't know about this."

He flipped the lid and pulled out an elegant, short black dress. Spaghetti straps, delicate V-neckline, cut to fit the waist and hips. Might look like I had some shape. Setting it aside, he removed a matching bolero jacket, lace insets on the back and sleeves, trimmed in small back beads. I glimpsed the New York label: Chauncey Street.

"Must have cost a fortune," I said.

"Clearance rack. You've got to learn to shop. You look like a three. Hope it fits." Lifting the dress, he started to hold it against me. His features twisted in distaste. "Oh sweetie. That just won't do."

I glanced at my knee-highs, white cotton panties and tank top.

"Find black panties—Lace if possible. I've got a little something that might work in place of those granny socks."

I rummaged in my drawer, found a pair of lace-trimmed underwear and quickly changed. But a black bra—one without straps—had never found a home in my dresser. Looked like I'd go without. The material was heavy enough to hide the fact I didn't own a slip either.

Oz returned with a long mirror and pair of silk, thigh-high stockings. I didn't ask where he got them, just pulled off the granny socks, worked the hose over my toes and smoothed the lace trim against my thighs.

"From my role in *Victor-Victoria*." He stood back and looked me over. "Gorgeous."

Poking my glasses into place, I glanced at my reflection. Lifting onto my toes I studied my legs. Not bad.

"Hair next, then makeup, and didn't you get those contacts?"

"Forgot."

"You don't have a pair at all?"

"One for emergencies," I said. "In case the glasses break."

"This, girlfriend, is an emergency. Get them."

I'd already given up control and wasn't going to argue over my last pair of contacts. I took them from the medicine cabinet and touched the lens to my eyes. I hadn't worn contacts in weeks and immediately tears formed. I added drops and blotted my cheeks with a scrap of toilet paper.

A dime-sized amount of liquid silk and thirty minutes with the hairdryer smoothed my unruly mane to a straight, shinny cascade I never believed possible. He kept the makeup to a minimum; touch of mascara, blush and the lightest hint of wine color to my lips.

In the bedroom I turned my back, stripped off the undershirt, picked up the dress and stepped into it. He pulled up the zipper, straightened the straps, slid the bolero accent over my arms and urged me to face the mirror again.

"It's still you and oh, sweetie, you are absolutely radiant. The heels," he said, and set the pair before me.

I stepped into the spiked shoes, wobbled and grasped his shoulder.

"You'll get the hang of it. Walk around. He'll be here any minute."

Too late to back out now. "Really. Does this work?" I glanced at my suit, rumpled on the spread.

"Don't even think about it." He pushed my hair over my shoulders. "You're beautiful. And he's going to hate himself the moment you come downstairs." He drew his brows in concern. "Sweetie, you really don't know how lovely you are, do you?"

"You think so?" I glanced at my reflection in the mirror leaning against the wall. What I saw wasn't me, as though the glass captured a fragment embedded in my soul I didn't know existed. "Dating rules—Give me the rundown?"

"You've dated," he said, the concern deepening into sadness. "What did your mother do to you? How could you have lived all these years without knowing what it is to be a woman?"

"I dated Morales," I reminded Oz. Oh, there'd been a few others, but they had wanted someone to take care of them. I didn't want a man I had to take care of, or a man who wanted to take care of me. My independence threatened their masculinity.

"Okay," he said, and rummaged through my closet. He withdrew my black wool coat. "Quick summary? No matter how good the date is, no kiss. And never, ever on a first date do you come home and try out that new mattress. Got it?"

"No problem with that one." Climbing into bed with Quint was the last thing I'd do. This was about the photos. I turned and let Oz slide the coat over my arms.

"There," he said, lifting my hair from beneath the coat's collar. "This'll give him just a glimpse of ankle. A teaser. At the restaurant, you take off that coat and he'll lose that cocky attitude."

Oz scampered downstairs. I buttoned up the coat. It hit six inches above the heels. I crammed my wallet, pen, notepad and lipstick in a black clutch purse and paced, getting used to the shoes. Oz's efforts would be lost if I fell on my ass.

In my jewelry box, coated with a layer of dust, I found the modest set of pearl earrings and necklace Dad gave me for college graduation and put them on. Underneath lay the silver ID bracelet with Quint's name etched on the plate. He'd given it to me, and I gave him mine, all those years ago. I ran my finger over the engraving and closed the box.

The doorbell rang. My heart jittered unsteadily. The door opened, closed and Quint's muffled voice drifted upstairs.

Chapter 18

Quint alternated his attention between the road and me to the point it made me uncomfortable. But I'd made a deal with the devil, and I'd get what I wanted—the photos. I could suffer an evening of scrutiny.

His black suit, starched white shirt and narrow tie suited him even though the look died out in the Eighties, when he wore navy slacks and sweaters with the Catholic school's emblem.

I peered at the storm-heavy sky, brooding clouds that blocked the stars and moon. Ahead, square boxes of light broke through the darkness like a beacon guiding us to the outskirts of town. He drove beneath the awning before Little Italy and shifted into park.

Finally he said, "You look so different."

"Disappointed?" Suppressing a smile, I released the seatbelt and reached for the door's lever.

"No." He shook his head vigorously, cleared his throat. "Wait."

"For?"

"I'm attempting to be a gentleman," he said and gave me that crooked grin.

I toyed with the beads on the small black purse while he handed his keys to the valet attendant and opened my door. He offered his hand. I took it to steady myself on the spiked heels and allowed him to lead me into the restaurant.

Golden light spilled over red carpet. The walls were rich with art depicting Italy's mountains, vineyards, and crowded streets lined with centuries-old buildings.

"Rydell," he said to the dark-haired host in a red blazer at the podium.

"Ah. The special order. Right this way."

Hand against the small of my back, Quint guided me through the narrow dining area, beyond another set of doors and into a courtyard. Tall, propane-fed heaters chased the chill away. Miniature Christmas lights glimmered in trees growing from redwood planters. In the center, a cloth-covered table held thick-pillared candles and a white rose surrounded by daisies.

"Special order?" I worked the coat's buttons. "I'm impressed."

He helped me with the coat and draped it over a nearby chair. Then he straightened and his grin faltered. "Damn. *I'm* impressed."

He held my chair. I couldn't help but think what a far cry this was from years ago. I tried to hold back the laughter, but couldn't. He gave me a quizzical look as he sat opposite me.

"Seems like such a short time ago you tried to drown me in the pool."

"Dunked you." His grin returned. "It's not like I held you under. You were such an easy target."

I touched the daisies, stroked their soft petals.

"They're still your favorite, right?"

"I'm surprised you remember." I drew my hand away. "Have the cops returned your computer?"

Resting his elbows on the table, he laced his fingers and studied me through flickering candlelight. "What are you looking for, anyway?"

"Something he left with the rose."

"He?"

"The killer." I glanced around. Beyond the light's warm glow, the courtyard fell to shadows. Chills crept over me. The sensation that someone was watching sank in with that chill, bringing a mild sensation of panic. I breathed deeply and scanned the patio, searching for movement.

"Do you ever stop working, Monkey?"

"Excuse me?"

"You're preoccupied. Thinking about work, right?"

I shook out the panic along with the cloth napkin, and draped it across my lap. "Speaking of work. What's with the story? Breaking news is my beat."

"I was there, had the camera." He shrugged. "Grigsby asked me to write it up. So, what's with this rose?"

The waiter pushed through the doors with a bottle of red wine, poured and left.

"You're either obsessive or there's a connection I'm not seeing," Quint added.

"Both. That's how I get the big stories."

"Is that why you're here? To get the story?" He sat back, picked up his glass and drank.

"This is my price for seeing the photos, isn't it?" A smile tugged my lips and I struggled to suppress it. "My dance with the devil."

"Why do you keep saying that?" His grin faltered slightly, nothing anyone else would notice. But it was nice to know Mister all-confident-Quint Rydell had a touch of insecurity, after all.

"Well?" he prompted.

"Why did you come back to Borden?"

"I already told you."

"Ah, yes." I picked up my glass. "Soul searching."

He drank, watching me over the goblet's rim. "Yeah, I'm looking for something."

"So am I." I sipped the wine, a smooth Cabernet. Nice. "Something in those photos."

"They were right."

"Who was?"

"Tom, Vi, Grigsby. They said you're the job. They were right."

"Eight years as a crime reporter takes its toll."

"At least you figured out what you wanted before someone figured it out for you."

"The Navy wasn't your first choice?"

"Wasn't mine at all." He toyed with the butter knife, slowly rolling it over. "After Rich died, Mom freaked. I guess she thought I'd follow him—we did everything together. She called my grandfather and next thing I knew I was in Florida for three months of hell."

"Why did you stay?"

"Somewhere through all that I realized I'd found direction in life. But I didn't want to scrub decks or work artillery. So I signed on for SEAL training."

"You stayed in Florida?"

"Nah, training in Coronado then on to Georgia. What about you? Ever leave Borden?"

"College in Fresno. That's as far as I've strayed."

He reached across the table and grazed my hand. I wanted to pull away, but his touch was gentle, and I realized I liked that touch.

"I thought you and Patty were back together." Not what I wanted to say, but it worked to shift his attention.

Leaning back, he retrieved the glass and drank. "You know how she is. I was her fall-back guy."

"Are you satisfied with that? Picking up other men's leftovers?" Ouch. I hadn't meant to say that, either. The old wound really hadn't healed.

"*Was*," he reiterated, raked his fingers through his hair and gave me that cocky grin. "That was a long time ago. How about you? Anyone special?"

"When did you get out of the Navy?"

"Subject not to broach." He toyed with the knife. The blade caught the tree lights and glimmered. "Last summer."

"Where have you been?"

He warmed to the topic, rested his arms on the table and ran his fingertip over the glass' stem. "All over. Skiing in France, climbing in Arizona. Tried K2 in Pakistan, but a storm hit, and we had to abandon the climb."

"Navy must have been good to you." It cost money to travel and engage in high-dollar sports.

"I made some investments. I've done all right. How about you? What do you do when not working?"

"The band." I sipped more wine and licked my lips. "That's it."

"You still hike?"

"Haven't in years."

"We should go sometime."

Fishing for another date? I'd have to wait and see about that. Not that I wanted to date him, of course. What was that saying? Been there, done that? Yep. And got a nasty burn in the process.

"How did the De La Cruz woman find you? Did you run an ad in the paper?"

He chuckled, shrugged as though resigning himself to the game. "I've got a show at the gallery. She saw my work."

"What do you remember about that day? Who was in the park?"

"If you wanted to play cop, you should've brought your cuffs."

I wasn't sure if he was attempting to end the conversation, or making a proposition. Then he grinned.

"You're really into this crime stuff."

"It's my job."

"Nope." He shook his head. "It's more than that. You're a junkie."

"Crime fascinates me, all the evidence, the forensics. It's a puzzle with most of the pieces there. You just have to find what's missing."

The waiter set salads on the table. Odd how he didn't take our orders. Well, maybe not. The lights, heaters and candles were a well-thought-out plan. I really was impressed.

"Is that why you're here tonight? Looking for pieces?"

"That was the bargain."

"After dinner." He jabbed his fork into the salad. "I'd like to get reacquainted first."

"Time heals all wounds? Is that it?"

"I'm willing to believe that." He ate, chewed slowly, watching me.

Maybe I wasn't willing. He hadn't been left with wounds. *I* had.

He frowned and set the fork on the plate. "Wanna talk about it?"

"There's nothing to talk about." I speared a tomato, ate and sipped more wine. No, I wasn't going to discuss how he left and never looked back, never considered I might want to hear from him. *Hell* no.

"You're angry." He pushed chunks of lettuce around on the plate. "Are you going to tell me why?"

I let my fork clatter against the china. "If you think hard enough then maybe, *just maybe*, you'll figure it out."

"Is everything in your life a puzzle?"

"Seems that way." He couldn't be brainless, not if he made it through SEAL training. Time to change subjects. "You studied piano."

He sighed. "Yeah. Lessons twice a week for seven years. Until Dad died."

"Barcarolle. It's a type of music. Are you familiar with it?"

"Back to the rose?"

"Spelled differently."

"Venice." He wiped the napkin across his mouth, and lifted his wine. "It's got this certain melodic structure that's supposed to imitate the fast and slow motions of the gondoliers. One of the last things my teacher taught me."

"Can you play it?"

"I was sixteen, not sure I remember. Beautiful music, though. Which puzzle piece is this?"

"Something I found on the Internet." Probably didn't fit anyway. "What's the music from?"

"An opera, I think. I'd have to look it up." He pushed his salad aside. "Tell you what. When we get to Robin's, I'll Google it."

Over the next hour I drank, nibbled on tortellini smothered beneath Parmesan sauce, and limited the conversation to our childhoods. We'd edge toward that night, but took turns diverting and I realized he didn't want to revisit that encounter any more than I did. Yet every smile, every tender touch of his fingers on my hand took me back to that night—the first time I'd loved a man heart, body and soul. Then he disappeared for almost thirteen years. Yep, I really had a way with men.

I played emotional tag with those memories, but by the time we reached Robin's house shortly before eight I'd managed to bottle them up. Night had fallen and with it the thick, Valley fog seeped from the ground. Red, blue and green Christmas lights trimming houses were reduced to faint orbs as they struggled to shine through the mist. They looked lost now that the holiday had passed.

Quint helped me out of my coat, draped it over a hanger in the closet, headed down the hallway and stopped.

"Computer's in the bedroom. Unless you're uncomfortable with that," he quickly added. "I can set up at the table."

"That'll work. The table."

Disappointment flickered in his eyes. He continued down the hall.

On the couch, Robin huddled beneath a blanket and snored lightly. X-Files credits flashed on the television, then the news reported on the fur queen's fight to justify a wrongful death suit. The prosecution's witness, a juvenile at the time, had lied and was directly responsible for her husband's death, Emma Langtry told newscasters from the steps of the Sacramento courthouse. Now, he's an adult and can pay for those lies.

I hadn't realized Quint returned until I glanced up and saw him watching the newscast. Laptop tucked under his arm, he bounced the flash drive in his free palm.

"Ready?" He found the remote tucked in Robin's blankets and thumbed off the set.

I crossed the kitchen, normally cluttered with dirty dishes and frozen food packages. It was spotless. I recognized the pecan-wood dining set from Quint's house when we were children. The china cabinet held bare shelves, but they were dust free.

He pulled the end chair to the side of the table and motioned for me to sit. Pain darted through my feet, and I resisted the urge to kick off the heels. I sat while he plugged in the flash drive and booted up the Apple computer.

"Are you going to tell me about this rose?"

"It ties the two murders," I said.

"What else?" He opened a folder on the flash drive, selected five images and jabbed Control-O. While the images opened, he uncorked a bottle of Merlot and filled two long-stemmed glasses half way. "If you know the rose is there, why look?"

"He left something else."

"Oh?" He handed me a glass and returned to his chair.

"Christina—the second victim—whoever gave her the rose gave her a necklace."

"Doesn't mean it's a pattern."

"I think De La Cruz was given something symbolic. He chooses his victims. The items are given to them before they die."

"You're talking present tense. He's already chosen the next victim, hasn't he?"

"You'd make a good cop." I drank, even though the wine with dinner had left me light-headed. "There's only three days to nail this guy."

"Another pattern?"

"It's the only evidence I have. The roses, necklace and mirror."

"Mirror?"

I gripped the glass' stem. "The one he left in my car."

Until now, I hadn't realized how little evidence existed. Every lead I'd tracked down, except breaking into Ruth's garden, had been a dead end. With less than three days left, that made me decidedly uncomfortable.

Maybe I was wrong to trust Quint, but I wanted to. Residue of the past, perhaps. Or, despite the fact Morales suspected Quint, he hadn't shown any reason not to trust him.

I set the glass on the placemat and stared at the computer screen. The images had opened. The one in front showed De La Cruz in a fur-trimmed parka. Young. Beautiful. And now dead.

Chapter 19

I told Quint about the break in, Richard's ring, and the yearbook. I told him how the women died. Then I told him about the eyes.

I closed mine. A tear squeezed free. He caught it against his knuckle, slid his arm around me and drew me into a tight hug.

"I have to know what he left De La Cruz," I said, feeling safe in his arms just as I had all those years ago. "If I can link the three items, and the rose, I know I can figure out what game he's playing. Then I might figure out who he is—" *Before he kills me.*

"We'll find this guy," Quint said, his voice muffled against my hair. "If it takes all night, we'll examine every photo, get on the Internet, whatever it takes."

"Morales thinks you're involved."

"Morales is a dick."

"He's doing his job."

"Defending him?" Quint leaned back and studied my face. "Shit. You and that cop?"

"That ended months ago." I reached for the wine. My fingers trembled. Quint retrieved the glass for me, and I cupped it in both hands. This time I didn't sip but drank, draining half the contents. Warmth snuggled lazily inside me, smothering Morales' warnings about Quint. I'd known him all my life. He couldn't be a killer. I leaned back and met his gaze. That caramel color softened the look in his eyes, and I was hooked. Yet, Morales' words nibbled at my brain, and I wasn't sure which frightened me more: being hooked, or the possibility Quint really was the killer. I pulled from his embrace and drained my wine.

He snagged the bottle off the counter and refilled my glass. "The yearbook photos. Rich and Claire?"

"Some."

"The others?"

"Richard alone, you and Richard."

"Maybe we should track down Claire."

"Can't. The Gazette ran her obit a couple years back. She was struck by a hit-and-run driver in Stockton." I swallowed a mouthful of wine, set the glass down. "You don't have your yearbooks, do you?"

"Mom's got all that." As though closing the subject, he turned back to the computer and shut one image at a time. They were close-up shots with bare oak branches behind De La Cruz, the granite World War II marker peeking through. No one else. Nothing else.

He opened five more.

They were the same.

Another five.

Nothing.

Fear cinched my chest. I watched as he worked in earnest, trying to find photos that showed the park. Halfway through the images, feeling a little drunk and depressed, I was almost convinced this was another dead end. Then the park opened up behind De La Cruz. I gave Quint a peck on the cheek.

"Now. Where was the rose?"

Glancing at him, it dawned on me that I'd kissed the devil. Again his gaze softened to that warm, caramel shade.

"Where?" I repeated.

"It's, ah--" He breathed deeply. "With her stuff." He closed the image and scanned the next. "There."

"Right--" I reached out, touched the screen in unison with him, and the words tangled in my throat. His hand hovered over mine. The thin buffer of air between us tingled my flesh, as though currents passed from his hand to mine.

I knew I should pull away. My slightly intoxicated mind told me to. But I lifted my hand instead, lightly grazed his. My breath hitched as he slid his fingers over mine in a gentle touch.

Common sense overrode the alcohol haze and I pulled away. He laced his fingers over mine and kissed my palm. Then he brushed his lips against mine in a feather-soft caress. Parting his mouth, he ran his tongue over my lower lip and murmured, as though savoring the taste. He leaned back, studied me, gauging my reaction. Then he moved in for more, but I turned my head.

"We can't do this."

"Yeah we can." He fingered my hair away from my face and touched his lips to my neck, sending a shudder of heat through me. "I know I can."

"No." Planting my hand against his chest, I gently pushed him back. "We can't pick up where we left off."

"That's not what I'm doing."

"Sure looks like it." I tapped the computer screen, where a non-descript pile sat next to a bench. "Let's see how big you can get it."

Quint burst out laughing.

Heat stung my cheeks.

"The image," I said, but couldn't help smiling. "Get your mind out of the gutter, Rydell. You haven't changed at all."

"You have."

"Wine tends to make me . . ."

"Horny? I'll remember that."

"I'm sure you will," I said, trying to sound scolding. "The photos. We're running out of time."

He worked while I gave orders: closer, sharpen that, it's too blurry. Finally, he closed the image and moved to the next.

I studied the background. The blue Honda parked at the curb behind a black van, a man walking his Golden Retriever, someone in a navy blue jacket leaning against a tree and reading a paperback, a silver Camaro across the street.

"I've seen that before." I touched the Camaro on the screen.

"Looks like Rich's old car."

"No, I've seen it recently." I bit my thumbnail, and searched my mind. "Last night, when Oz dropped me off at the club."

"That doesn't mean much. The lot was packed."

"Focus in on it. See if you can get a plate."

"Plate?"

"License number. If you get enough, Morales can run it."

"Long shot, don't you think?"

"It's a start."

Quint zoomed in and sharpened the image. "No plate."

The chrome frame attached to the bumper was empty. "Did you see who drove it?"

"I was doing a job," he said. "Not watching who climbed out of which car."

"Let's look at that bundle by the park bench." I eyed him closely, wondering if my demands irritated him. But he just toyed with the mouse, drew a dotted line around the bench and zeroed in on a purse. Blurry.

Before I asked, he sharpened it and adjusted the color levels to cut back on the sun's glare.

Next to the bag, a dark splotch nestled against a towel. The rose?

"That's it," he said, as though plucking the thought from my mind. "That's where she found the rose."

"Can you get closer?"

He worked on enlarging the lower left corner, hit some keys, brought up a box and made adjustments on what looked like a sound wave. Then he closed the box, leaned back and retrieved his wine. "Good as it gets, Babe."

I leaned over the computer, as though I could make the object clearer. Next to the rose laid a silver-tone box, oddly shaped, not smooth but bulky. "What's that?"

"Makeup kit?"

What a guy thing to say. Makeup wasn't one of my daily rituals, but even I knew cases were either zippered cloth bags or plastic. And certainly not silver-toned plastic.

"It doesn't have a handle," I said.

"It's got something." With his fingertip, he outlined an odd shape to one side. "Maybe it tipped over."

"Did you see the kit?"

"Nope. A bag, the towel."

"What kind of bag?"

"Like those women take to the beach."

"Like this?" I touched the screen where a blue striped case sat next to the towel.

"That's the makeup, isn't it?" he asked sheepishly.

"Most likely." I swirled the Cabernet. The wine's thick legs draped down inside the glass. "Did you notice the silver box when you got there?"

"Wasn't paying attention."

"*Think.*"

"I am. And, I don't remember."

I slumped in the chair and bit my nail. The silver box might as well be a flying saucer. It was as clear as those on UFO documentaries.

"Hey." He stroked his finger against my cheek. "We'll figure this out."

"Within the next two days? Because that's all I've got."

"He's not going to get you."

"Oh?"

"I won't let him."

"Oh God, don't turn macho on me now." He sounded like Morales. I stood too quickly, and my head swam. "He's watching me. He's probably out there right now, knows everything we're doing and he's laughing his ass off. I have *nothing*."

"The pieces are there, isn't that what you said? All we have to do is fit them together, and that'll show us what's missing." Quint pushed up from the chair and ran his hands over my shoulders. "We'll find them."

"We?" Joining the game at this point could get him killed. Although I'd been furious with him, I wasn't any longer and I sure didn't want him *dead*.

"Let me help you." He slid his hand over my back, stepped closer and cupped my cheek. "I've had a lot of . . . *specialized training*," he said, and I got the distinct impression he referred to killing with his bare hands. "It'll give me an excuse to stick around."

"You need an excuse?" I closed the gap between us.

"A reason."

He touched his wine-moistened lips to mine, caressed them in slow, sensuous motions that robbed the air from my lungs. Combing my fingers in his hair, I parted my mouth, scraped my teeth over his lower lip. He groaned, pulled me closer, pressed his firm, warm body against mine. His kiss deepened, his tongue teasing, but he didn't rush, didn't let the passion overwhelm him. He kissed me with the tenderness I'd wanted so long, tenderness that told me I was special.

A cabinet opened and closed. Then ticking sounds, like pebbles spilling into a bowl. Crunching noises drifted from the kitchen.

I pulled away and peered at Robin, sitting on the counter, a bowl of Captain Crunch cradled in his palm. Milk dribbled down his chin. A boyish grin spread across his face. He waved the spoon, spilling cereal onto the tiled floor.

"When did this happen?" he asked.

I stepped away from Quint. He shoved his hands in his pockets.

"Isn't this a *maudlin* moment."

"What time is it?" I asked.

"Eight forty five."

"Damn. I wanted to change before the gig." I headed for the door.

"No time, Babe." Quint caught up with me, pulled my coat from the hanger and held it while I slid my arms through the satin-lined sleeves.

"I can't play in this."

He gave me that crooked grin. "You can play in anything."

"I'll look real graceful straddling my snare in this dress."

"Nah. Sexy."

*   *   *

I had kicked off the heels to accommodate the pedals, tucked my dress between the snare and my crotch, and managed to get through the night. Giovanni never showed, which dampened my spirits. I wanted to see that necklace.

Because we wouldn't be playing Sunday, I packed my snare in its padded case and set about breaking down my kit.

Behind the bar, now brightly lit, Brian dried glasses and stacked them on a glass shelf. I slid onto a stool.

"Did anyone drop by looking for me?"

"Nope."

"No one?"

"Sorry." Brian dunked a beer mug into the sink of sudsy water.

Quint carried my bass to the van, returned and started to take out the floor toms. A deputy, in department issued khaki and Smokey Bear hat, approached the stage.

"Quint Rydell?"

He set the toms down and straightened. "Yeah?"

The deputy handed Quint an envelope, and left. I caught a peek at the return address: Sacramento.

"Everything okay with your mom?" Katherine Rydell and Quint's kid sister, Breezy, lived in a suburb just south of the state's capitol.

"Yeah."

"What's with the letter?"

He folded and tucked it into his back pocket, then retrieved the drums. "Better get these loaded before Steve takes off."

"In other words, mind my own business?"

"Yeah." He softened the word with a grin. "Get the snare, and I'll drive you home." He carried the drums out back.

I donned my coat, tucked the snare case beneath my arm and stepped into the cold, damp night. He slid the van's door shut, and then led me around the building to the side parking lot.

Once I settled in, he folded his long legs in the driver's compartment and started the engine. Air blasted through the Mustang's vents, quickly warmed and chased the chill from my feet.

"Back to my place?" He let the car idle at the roadway. "We could do some Google searches."

"Home." I really needed sleep, and these shoes were killing me. Felt like my little toes had permanently merged with their cellmates.

With a slight nod, he turned south on Elm, brought the car up Norton and parked at the curb outside my duplex. Digging the keys from my purse, I waited until he came around, opened the door and helped me across the rain-filled gutter to the sidewalk.

He trailed his hand down my arm, laced his fingers with mine and walked me to the door. Then he kissed me in a series of soft, warm strokes. I wanted to invite him in, but knew we'd end up in bed. I wasn't ready for that. I didn't think I'd ever trust him again, much less stand on my porch in his arms, lip-locked in a sensuous moment that prompted me to throw away my conservative upbringing and drag him upstairs.

I couldn't. I wouldn't.

Caressing my back, he drew me closer. He brushed his lips against my ear, kissed the sensitive spot just below my earlobe and I thought I'd melt. I gripped his shoulders and leaned my head back, inviting him to explore. He accepted, and trailed the tip of his tongue over my neck. He moaned, and returned his attention to my lips.

I wouldn't. *Couldn't.*

A small cry escaped me. My flesh tingled. Tiny jolts of pleasure coursed through my body. I arched my back, and pressed against him. Finally, I found my voice, but the words weren't those I intended to speak.

"We could do that Google search here," I whispered.

"Yeah?" he asked, his voice hoarse, his breathing slightly labored.

"Computer's in the bedroom," I said. "Unless you're uncomfortable with that."

He plucked the key from my hand and unlocked the door.

Chapter 20

Quint lay beside me, his breathing reduced to the soft rhythm of sleep. I couldn't sleep. My head was filled with photos of the deep red rose nestled on De La Cruz's towel. The killer was in one of those frames. I could feel it. But without a physical description, studying the photos was useless. I had to figure out what that silver-tone box was. The more I thought about it, the less I believed it was a container housing hairbrushes and spray.

Getting that answer would mean a visit to De La Cruz's husband. If he knew what that container was, I might link it to the mirror. I needed to track down Giovanni, too, and get a look at that necklace. Now, I needed sleep. But thoughts churned in my brain, keeping me on the edge of slumber.

I rolled over. Moonlight seeped through the bedroom curtains and bathed Quint in its bluish glow. He lay with his back to me, the sheet draped loosely over his hips. Across his bicep, a scar lightened his skin. A quarter-inch wide, three inches long, the disfigurement ran at an angle as though someone had struck him with a hot fireplace poker. I propped on my elbow, touched the scar, and leaned closer to kiss his shoulder.

Swiftly, he rolled over, shoved me down, grabbed my wrists and pinned them over my head. Pain shot through my arms. My heart slammed in fear.

"Don't fucking touch me." Fury burned in his eyes.

"Quint?" I squirmed against his iron grip. "Quint, you're scaring me."

Recognition flickered in his gaze. He let go. Rubbing his chest, he sank back to the bed.

"What the hell was that?" I yelled. I yanked the sheet to my chin, and resisted the urge to bolt to the bathroom and lock myself inside. "What the hell's wrong with you?"

"Sorry." Anguish furrowed his brow. A hint of sadness touched his eyes. "Ah, shit, Monkey. I'm *so sorry*."

"Lesson one." I breathed deeply and tried to calm my pounding heart. "Don't touch while you're sleeping. Did you forget where you were?"

"Yeah." He raked his fingers through his hair. "Must've been dreaming."

"Dream, hell. More like a nightmare." I shoved the pillow against the wall, sat up and tried to relax, but my whole body trembled.

"Did I hurt you?"

"You scared me." Even in the semi-darkness, I could see splotches forming on my wrists. "What were you dreaming about?"

"Nothing."

"Liar."

He gave me a half-hearted grin. Shifting to his side, he faced me and stroked hair away from my temple. He slid his fingers along my arm and gingerly touched my wrist.

"You've got quite a grip." I wanted to pull away, but part of me was afraid he'd grab me again. "Who did you think I was?"

"No one. Just a dream. That's all, Babe." He rolled onto his back. Tucking his arm beneath his head, he stared at the ceiling. The pale light from outside glinted in his eyes, and this time I detected a hint of vulnerability I didn't know existed. Before long, his eyelids closed. His breathing evened out.

I dozed the last hour before daybreak Sunday, until his cell phone gave me a jolt. He eased from beneath the blankets, and slid on his boxers. Then he pulled the cell from his suit coat pocket, and retreated to the bathroom.

I slid my hand across the sheet, warm where his body had been. Although he spoke in hushed tones, I caught snippets of his conversation through the partially opened door.

Tucking the sheet around me, I tilted my head and listened.

"Good," he said, "saw her last weekend . . . Ah, not so good. That's why I called." Silence, then, "Heat's coming down, and it's going to blow apart. Everyone's going to find out, and that can't happen." Pause. "I need your help." Longer pause, and he added, "Give me two hours."

He returned to the bedroom, tossed the phone on the green, overstuffed chair by the window, crawled across the mattress and stretched out over me.

"That's amazing." He tucked his finger beneath the sheet over my chest, took a quick peek and sank to the bed beside me. "I can actually see in your eyes those mental gears processing what you overheard."

"Job hazard." I stroked his cheek, the beard stubble scratchy against my hand. His demeanor was so natural, as if he didn't remember grabbing me. "So? What was that call about?"

He rolled off the bed, pulled on his socks, and slipped into his pants and shoes. Then he snagged his shirt from the chair and shrugged it on.

"You're not going to tell me?"

"Nope." Without buttoning the shirt, he shuffled into his coat and dropped the cell into his pocket.

A sinking feeling settled through me. I didn't like him hiding something from me, especially after wrestling me to the bed last night. I sat up and studied him. Could I trust him? I'd been sure twelve hours ago. Now, I didn't know. "Just going to run out?"

He knelt on the bed and kissed me again. "Love to stay," he murmured, his lips tickling mine, "but I've got to take care of something."

"And you won't say what?"

"You've got enough to deal with, Babe." Raking his gaze over me, he groaned and backed away. "I've got an appointment."

"In two hours."

"I should be back before noon. I'd like to take you to lunch, maybe get around to that Google search?"

"Sure."

He left. I started to snuggle beneath the covers and realized he could be in some kind of trouble. If I hurried, I'd catch him at Robin's, maybe do a little covert ops. Follow him? Why not? There were still too many unanswered questions surrounding SEAL-man Rydell. If I stayed far enough behind his car, maybe he'd never know I was there. For the case, I told myself, and pulled on jeans and a sweatshirt.

I landed on the bottom stair just as the answering machine clicked on. Grigsby's voice boomed through the miniature speaker.

"Monakee?"

Answer? Or catch up with Quint?

"*Monakee.*" Angry, as if Grigsby knew I stood there. "*You've got five seconds to answer, or I'm calling Tina.*"

Like hell he'd hand my beat over to a rookie. Cradling the phone against my shoulder, I crossed the kitchen and grabbed a bottle of Mocha Starbucks from the fridge. "I'm here."

"Have you got the scanner on?"

I glanced at the hand-held unit on the bar.

"Obviously not," he snorted. "Get to Redwood Villa. I don't have the apartment number, but the place is crawling with cops. Homicide. Mother found the body about twenty minutes ago."

My throat went dry. I gripped the phone. "A woman?"

"Man. Go. I want the story by noon. And where the hell's Rydell?"

"I don't know."

"Find him," Grigsby barked.

I stared at the receiver. The dial tone filled my head like soggy straw. Three murders inside two weeks. Maybe Dad was right. Borden *was* going to hell.

I opened the coffee, realized Oz had popped the safety seal and changed his mind. I tossed the lid onto the counter. He did that occasionally. Drove me nuts, but as with everything else I looked the other way.

I grabbed my coat and hurried outside. From Norton, I turned onto the freeway and tried to drink without dripping coffee down my chin. I took the Yosemite Drive off ramp. Three blocks past the railroad tracks and the Gazette, a police cruiser sat angled in the roadway, cutting off traffic. I tossed the empty bottle onto the truck's floorboard, parked behind the Channel 30 News van—its satellite dish extended into the air—and walked.

Yellow caution tape drooped before a ground-level apartment. The door stood open. Just inside, I recognized Morales' lanky frame. He spotted me, perched his fingers on his hips, glanced back into the apartment then sauntered up the sidewalk and ducked beneath the tape. Gripping my elbow, he led me across the street, opened his Bronco's door and forced me onto the bucket seat.

"When did Rydell leave?"

Badorini. I'd forgotten my gun-toting babysitter.

"Know where he is?" Morales asked.

"No."

"We're bringing him in."

"On what grounds?" If this was Morales' way of trying to get me back, it was down and dirty and a lot lower than I thought he'd stoop.

"Evidence links him. Cigarette butts at the Gazette scene, and your place."

An icy sensation of panic crept over me. I shivered. "That's it? He was at the Gazette interviewing for a job. He probably dropped it."

But Quint never dropped butts. He was one of those *leave no trace* people, respected the land, all that granola-head stuff. Besides, the cigarette in the Gazette lot was found hours before his interview.

"It's a popular brand," I said, but once Morales' mind was set there wasn't any changing it.

"Esteves found saliva. Tested it. Blood type's Quint's."

"Are you running DNA?"

"No white cells found." Morales leaned against the SUV, glanced at the apartment and back at me. "Only enough saliva for typing."

"It was raining," I reminded him. "Pouring. The butt from the Gazette would have been soaked. There's no way you got a type."

"Got it from the evidence at your place."

"Someone could have planted that cigarette butt." The one I'd found by the porch certainly could have been planted.

"Got trace on him too," Morales continued. "Water-soaked fiber found by the dumpster. Matches the carpet where he's staying."

I shook my head. I didn't want to believe it. But evidence didn't lie. I knew Morales pegged Quint as a suspect before last night. If I really had danced with the devil, I had no one but myself to blame.

"Odd how he showed up after all these years." Morales leaned against the Bronco and pulled a Three Musketeers from his jacket pocket.

I'd thought the same myself. But whatever the reason for Quint's return, it wasn't murder.

"Change the locks?" Morales tore open the candy bar and methodically peeled chocolate from its end.

"Oz changed them yesterday."

"Give Rydell a key?"

Anger knotted in my chest. I gripped my hand into a fist. "No."

"Just checking." Morales stripped more coating off the bar, ate it, and licked his fingers. "What time?"

"Ask Badorini." I crossed my arms and stiffened my posture, resorting to my stand-by defense. Stubbornness.

"Sonofabitch fell asleep," Morales grumbled. "When did Rydell leave?"

"You're the detective." I slid out of the car and pushed past Morales. "You figure it out."

He grabbed my arm and jerked me in a tight, half circle. "We can do this here, or in my office. Up to you."

"This morning, okay?" I twisted from his hold. "Quint left this morning."

Morales leveled his gaze in the intimidating manner he used while questioning a suspect. When he licked his lips, I knew he wanted to ask if I was lying. Instead, he bit into the Three Musketeers and headed back toward the apartment.

"Wait." I jogged across the street after him. "What's going on? Who's the victim?"

"Doing a story?"

"Grigsby sent me." I dug out my pen and notepad.

"Male. Mid-twenties. Killed sometime last night. DOJ guys are recording body and room temps. It'll help in determining approximate time of death."

They called the state Department of Justice, which meant it wasn't a gang-related killing. "Got a cause?"

"Know more after an autopsy, but it's strangulation. Ligature marks. Distinct pattern. Someone's carrying around a bloody chain. That's not for publication," he quickly added, and scowled, angry for letting the information slip. "*Possible* strangulation. *Got that?*"

"Got it. Are you releasing a name?"

"Family knows." He glanced toward a Jetta, where a young man comforted an older woman. "Giovanni Pardini. Second vic's brother. Sonofabitch got his eyes, just like the others."

I felt like someone had rammed a fist into my stomach. My legs weakened. My knees buckled and I started to crash.

Morales caught me with an arm around my waist. "What the fuck?"

"The chain," I said, struggling to catch my breath. "Was it a necklace?"

"Something you want to tell me?"

"His sister got a necklace with the rose. Giovanni was going to bring it to me last night."

"The club?"

I nodded, closed my eyes and buried my face in my palms.

"When did you talk to him?"

"Noon yesterday, at Courthouse Café."

"Remember who else was there?"

Oh I remembered, all right. But wasn't about to tell him. I didn't want to implicate Quint more than he was already.

Morales gripped my wrists, forcing my hands down. I peered up at him. Tears sliced cold trails down my cheeks.

"Sonofabitch."

Chapter 21

Sitting in his car three blocks away, he had a hard time spotting Hannah in the crowd. But that was okay. He didn't need to see her. He could *feel* her, and that was good enough. The fragment inside her—Stella's soul—reached out to him, touched him like warm threads of silk. That hadn't happened with the others. Hannah was special, and *oh how he wanted her.*

He stared at the necklace in his hand. Blood and bits of flesh clogged the thick golden links. He stripped off the gloves, caught the necklace inside and tucked them into the console compartment for later disposal.

This time, he hadn't gone through that mental doorway, hadn't flipped the switch so the music played while he strangled Giovanni. The music wasn't for him. It was only for her. Only for *them.*

The last trip beyond the door left him shaky. The corrosion locking the hinges made him wonder if, should he go in there, he'd ever come back.

At first, he'd been afraid he couldn't carry out the act without the talents the music world granted him. He'd never killed in this world before. But something cold fell over him, turning his blood to ice. Totally new feelings, like a stone man, like the Tin Man, like *Sandmann.*

Although he'd been cold, he didn't shiver and that seemed odd. His fingers didn't tremble, even when he removed the eyes. He didn't need them. They weren't even green. But he couldn't leave them, either. Couldn't stand the black, accusing stare as the dead man looked up at him. *That* made him shiver.

What he found most disturbing was, he lacked the control he had when the switch was on. He hadn't been as skillful at removing the eyes. One popped and oozed just a bit, the way an overripe nectarine sometimes dribbled juice down his chin.

When the man died, a thin trail of frosty breath curled from his lips. He'd never seen that before. Maybe the heightened awareness and abilities he had when he flipped the switch seeped through the mind-door and into *this* world. He idly wondered if he could bring the music into this world, too.

He wasn't sure he wanted to, though. He liked those special times when he flipped the switch and no one knew where to find him.

Some day, after he brought Stella back, he wanted to live in there forever. Just as he didn't want to touch the essence of her soul as it escaped its host and soaked into him, he didn't want to taint that world by blending it with this one. He was afraid that might be happening.

He peered out the windshield. The cop had thrust Hannah into his car. He hadn't realized how they would group around her, make it harder to reach her, but that was okay. She couldn't escape destiny any more than he could.

Chapter 22

Morales handed me another napkin from the cubbyhole in the Bronco's door. I blew my nose, crumpled the tissue and tossed it into a paper sack holding a half-eaten hamburger. It lay on the floorboard among Styrofoam coffee cups and candy bar wrappers.

I told him about the yearbook, Richard and Claire's photos, and Quint's phone call. I absently rubbed the faint bruise on my wrist. I wouldn't tell Morales about last night, not until I understood what happened with Quint.

Finally I told Morales what little I knew about the necklace. "That's what Giovanni said. Winged serpent."

Morales dug around in the glove box, found another crumpled napkin and handed it to me. I dried my eyes and folded my hands in my lap. I felt defeated, as though someone had beaten me half to death.

"Caduceus," Morales said.

"The medical symbol? How do you know?"

Morales gestured toward the Jetta. "The older son saw it yesterday, when Mrs. Pardini gave it to Giovanni."

"So he could show me." More tears blurred my vision. I poked the paper towel beneath my glasses. "What now?"

"Help us get Rydell." I opened my mouth to protest, but Morales held up his hand. "Knows we're on to him, he'll run. Gotta get him before he does."

"You're going to use me as bait?" The idea of getting close to Quint, after everything I knew, scared me as much as his violent outburst had.

"Nothing like that. Spoke to Keitz," Morales said, referring to the district attorney. "We've got plenty for an arrest. Good chance the charges will stick."

"You're not finished with your investigation?"

"We'll get more on him."

"You really believe Quint wants to kill me?" My throat constricted with the onset of more tears. I thought I'd cried myself out.

"Looks that way." Propping his hand against the SUV's roof, Morales leaned toward me and lowered his voice. "During the interview, he said you're the reason Richard killed himself. Something about fights between you and your mom—*Ruth*," he quickly added. "Said those fights drove Richard nuts."

"He didn't kill himself," I insisted. "I don't know what happened, but Richard would never take a needle to himself. *Never*."

"Not what Quint says." Morales straightened, peered over the Bronco's roof. "The other victims had the same hair and eye color. Could be, in his mind, he was taking revenge against you. Maybe he killed the others to get closer to you. Or divert attention. Couldn't go straight for you, that would've been too obvious. Gotta be something I'm missing, though. He's got no link to the victims, other than takin' photos of De La Cruz."

"I can't believe this." Quint's touch was tender, not the touch of a madman. Until he pinned me down.

That was where I needed to focus. Not so much on the victims, but the killer. If I couldn't clear Quint's name, maybe I could convince myself of his guilt. Right now, I didn't know what to believe.

I left Morales to his crime scene, and drove to the Gazette. The phone light blinked, announcing a voice mail message. Since the newsroom was empty, and I wouldn't disturb anyone, I hit the speaker button and punched in my password—Richard's birthday.

"Thought I'd give you one more chance to settle this outside court."

Lance Parkston. Dread seeped through me like a dead weight. I stared at the speaker holes as his voice drained out.

"The preliminary hearing has been set for next week. It's not to late to cancel. I want the documents, my ledger and your notes. I want to know who your source is. I also want a retraction, front page, same place the story ran." He sighed, *"You don't want to fight this. Call me."*

I save the message. Who knows? I might need it. If nothing else, I'd play it for the company attorney. I needed to burn those notes. And a retraction? Not on his life.

Thirty minutes later, I'd composed the murder story. It was dry, but I didn't have the energy for creativity. After I'd copied it into the system, I drove to Dad's. I needed a quiet place to think, where no one would find me. A dose of Dad's advice wouldn't hurt, either.

He wasn't home. Under the railing, I found the key and let myself in. I sat on the couch, propped my feet against the coffee table and flipped through my notebook until I found the list I'd written Saturday morning.

What did I really know? Not enough.

I added the caduceus.

Mirror and caduceus. *Barkarole* and *Barcarolle*. Roses and music—it all seemed so familiar. My brain was exhausted. Hell, I was exhausted. But with two days left, I couldn't afford to rest. I needed to know what the killer left the first victim. I scribbled *Go to De La Cruz's house.*

The cigarette butts. If the killer had planted Quint's cigarettes at the scenes, where did he get them? Ashtrays? Not from the car, Quint would have crushed them. Maybe he used the charcoal-filled stands outside The Dock? I tried to remember if he'd gone out to smoke, but I'd been so shaken to see him I hadn't paid attention.

The murders were well thought out, the victims chosen and targeted for specific reasons. The killings were personal. One victim carefully placed in a duffle bag, the other he strangled with his hands. He kept the eyes as trophies. *That* was personal.

He drugged the women, which is a type of restraint. The only evidence at the crime scenes suggested Quint was the killer, which meant one of two things: Either he was, or the real killer controlled the scene and framed Quint. But why frame him? Where was the connection between Quint and the killer?

Richard. And Claire.

"Could really use your help with this one," I muttered, hoping somehow Richard would hear me. "You've helped before, I know that's what those feelings are. Did Quint do this?"

A surge of heat bore through me—Yes or no? *Come on, Bro. Help me out.* The heat subsided, leaving me chilled and empty. Closing my eyes, I focused on what I knew.

Richard died of a drug overdose more than twelve years ago, the same night I'd shifted from Quint's girlfriend to lover. The night before he walked out of my life. If he'd wanted to kill me, why hadn't he? I'd given him plenty of chances.

I regarded my notes. Claire died two years ago in a hit-and-run. What had she been doing in Stockton? Had they found the driver?

By the time I'd filled six pages with notes, my head ached, my fingers had cramped up and I wasn't any closer to figuring out the mess.

Beneath the coffee table, I found Dad's phone book and scoured my brain for Claire's last name. Rougue. Eight thirty-seven south Wilhite, behind the high school.

I shoved the book back on the shelf and locked up. Badorini's compact pulled onto the road behind me. Fifteen minutes later, I parked in front of a single-story house, poorly maintained yet immaculate compared to the rest of the neighborhood. An old, wooden swing with cracked blue paint and rusted chains hung stagnant from the awning on the enclosed porch. Weeds had over taken the lawn, most of which were dead.

I pushed past the screen door. The porch creaked beneath my feet. From somewhere inside came the hard-hitting sound of *Led Zeppelin—Been a long lonely-lonely-lonely-lonely-lonely time.*

Before I could knock, the curtain over the window in the door parted, closed, and a man in stained wife beater and threadbare jeans greeted me. He scratched month-old beard stubble that made his face look as dirty as his shirt.

"Mr. Rougue?"

"Who wants to know?" He peered at me through glassy, bloodshot eyes. The sickly-sweet stench of marijuana escaped the house and filled the air around me.

"Hannah Monakee. I knew your sister."

"So?" He leaned against the doorframe.

"May I talk to you?"

"Ain't stoppin' you." He scanned the street, pulled a joint from his jeans pocket and lit up. "Come in. Fuckin' cops are everywhere."

I followed him into the front room. A bare bulb dangled from what used to be the ceiling light. A dented pot on the threadbare carpet caught water as it seeped through the ceiling. The stench of spoiled food, stale cigarettes and mold overpowered me. I drew short, shallow breaths. He shoved a cat from a rocker and motioned me to sit. I sat on the chair's edge and clutched my purse to my chest.

"Monakee," he murmured. "Know that name from someplace."

"Claire dated my brother in high school."

"Oh yeah. That football prick. Never liked the dude. Want some?" He offered the home-rolled reefer.

I shook my head. "Did the police ever find the person who struck your sister?"

"Struck her?" He uttered a sharp laugh. "Fuckin' smashed her to a concrete wall. Nah, man. Never found him. Hell they never *looked*. Fuckin' faggots."

The cat, a scrawny yellow tabby with matted fur, sat by my feet and looked up at me through large, golden eyes. It crouched on its haunches, shifted, ready to spring onto my lap. With the toe of my shoe, I nudged it away.

"When did she move to Stockton?"

"I dunno. Year or two before she died. Met some guy on *MySpace*, some fuckin' whacko job." He took a hit on the joint, sucked air and held it. "Told her it wasn't gonna work," he said, his voice high-pitched as he fought to keep the smoke in his lungs. He exhaled a thin cloud.

"Why is that?" I prompted.

"Control freak, ya know? Like, he tried to tell her what to do and shit just like her first old man. That dude was a bastard. Hit her. All that shit." He drew on the joint. "This guy was the same. Wouldn't let her call, wouldn't let her visit. I heard from her about a week before she died."

"What did she say?" I scooted closer to the chair's edge and eyed the Pepsi can on the table beside me. Something ticked inside, and I didn't think it was fresh carbonation.

"Whadda ya' want to know for?"

"I'm investigating some local crimes." I glanced at the can. "I think her death might tie in."

"What're you, a fuckin' Cop?" He tucked the reefer behind his back, as if I might not notice he was stoned out of his mind.

"A reporter."

"Oh. Huh." He hit the joint again. "So she's got this big wedding planned, right? Got all this cash from Mom—I mean look at this place, it's a shit-hole. She took it, man, took all this money for her wedding and bails."

"Bails?"

"Yeah. Couple weeks before the gig, she changed her mind."

The ticking sound in the can grew more impatient. I shifted my weight and tried to focus on the information, not what might be crawling around in week-old Pepsi.

"She backed out of the wedding?"

"Yeah. That's when she calls me. She was freakin', said she made a mistake. Like *duh*, the brainless bitch."

"Did she give a reason?"

"Said the guy was a whacko. Hell, I could of told her that."

"Who was the boyfriend?" I asked.

"Never met him, but he came from here. Moved to Stockton a few years after high school, from what she said."

"Did she give a name?"

"Nah. Called him *Stardust*, like he was magic and was gonna change her life." He fixed his bloodshot gaze on me. "That prick brother of yours dyin' really fucked her up."

"I know." Richard's death *fucked up* all of us. "Was she afraid of someone else? Someone she worked with, perhaps?"

"Worked for the County, said she loved the job. Got lucky, if you ask me. Never was too bright."

Inside the soda can, the ticking grew louder. A spindly black leg poked through the opening. I scrambled from the rocker.

"No problems at work?"

"Nah. Got along with them okay. Like I said, man. We didn't talk much."

I found an ink-spotted Gazette card, handed it to him and stepped toward the door. "If you remember anything that might be important, would you call?"

He took the card and stared blankly at it, then looked at me. "Yeah. Guess so. But there ain't nuthin' else."

Outside, I gulped cold air to rid myself of the house's stench and climbed into the truck. The De La Cruz home was a block away. I glanced at the clock in the truck's dashboard. Quarter of ten. Plenty of time to pay Mister De La Cruz a visit.

I wished I'd told Morales where I was going. But Badorini was out there, somewhere, and this time I wanted his company. If De La Cruz's bite was worse that his bark, I wouldn't have to worry about the killer.

Chapter 23

The mailbox on the age-rotted fence looked like a miniature barn, a futile attempt to add hospitality to a house that should have been condemned. I climbed from the truck and pushed the door closed.

Fear tingled my spine. What if Badorini was asleep again? If I had a cell phone, I could call Morales and let him know what I was up to. But I didn't, and he was busy with Giovanni's autopsy. Besides, he wouldn't see the logic in visiting De La Cruz, anyway.

"Badorini, I hope you're out there." I hadn't spotted his car since leaving Dad's apartment. If De La Cruz came after me, I'd scream. That should bring the detective out of hiding.

The lawn, mostly puddles of mud, had abandoned its struggle to grow. The porch, host to car parts and a busted washing machine, sagged on one side. In the yard, sun faded, resin chairs sat beneath a leafless Willow. A tricycle with one wheel missing stood askew beside a food-splattered garbage can.

Next to the steps, the De La Cruz's two-year-old boy played with a rusted dump truck. He filled the bed with twigs and leaves, deposited them near a brittle rose bush and made puttering sounds as he worked in earnest to fill the bed again. He abandoned the truck for a chrome-colored plastic robot, scratched on one side. He played as though oblivious to the fact his mother had been murdered. He must realize she's gone, but was he aware of her death? Maybe not now, but he'd have questions when he grew up. I hoped he'd have more to learn from than old news articles. If nothing else, I wanted to give him that final article on the conviction of her killer. He deserved that much.

A glimpse of De La Cruz's world might help me do just that. I needed a peek at her house, her room, wherever she kept personal articles. Where, hopefully, she'd stashed that item left on her blanket that would connect to the mirror in my car.

I pushed past the wooden gate and walked up the uneven sidewalk. The boy stopped and peered at me through large, brown eyes. He shoved his bangs from his face, leaving a streak of mud across his forehead.

"Is your daddy home?" I asked.

He lifted the robot, showing off his new toy.

"That's nice," I said. "Your daddy. Is he inside?"

Hitching his finger over his bottom lip, he clutched the toy to his chest and backed toward the porch.

A moment later the door swung open and a burly man stepped outside. His wild gaze unnerved me; he looked like Charles Manson on steroids. His hair corkscrewed out, his low forehead and tight brow ridge shadowed dark eyes burning with anger.

Heart pounding, I stepped back and forced a smile. "Mr. De La Cruz?"

"I tell you already, we don't want you here," he said. "Leave. You get away from me and my family."

"I only want to talk."

"I call the police," he warned, and turned toward the house.

"The rose," I said, hoping that would get his attention. "Your wife found one that day she was in the park. Did she say where it came from?"

"I know of no rose." Fury reddened his face. "You think my wife cheat on me?"

"Not at all." I needed to choose my words carefully, or the only thing I'd see is the backside of De La Cruz's hand. "That rose connects to another crime, and a potential third." The boy toddled toward me, gripped my jeans leg in one muddy fist, and looked at me as if asking me to hold him. "She had several bags with her that day. There might be something in them that would help us discover who killed her."

"You're not a cop," he spat. "You write about my wife like she was not alive, just some trash. Jesus—get away from her." He yanked Jesus' fragile arm, and pulled him onto the porch. The child cried out in pain. De La Cruz slapped the boy's head, uttered "Shush," and tore the robot away.

"We don't need your charity." He slammed the toy to the sidewalk, brought his boot down and crushed the robot.

The child whimpered and scurried into the house.

"I said to you. You leave us alone or I call the police." He stormed inside and slammed the door.

That went as well as expected. I spun around, intent on getting out of there as quickly as possible. I glanced at the crushed toy. Across the breastplate, broken from shoulder to hip, letters had been scratched into the surface: OLYN. The rest of the word had been obliterated.

I clambered into the truck, gripped the wheel in sweaty palms and breathed deeply. My heart had gotten a workout and, for a brief moment, I feared it would sputter and die, like the toy robot broken on the cracked sidewalk.

I headed home. It was almost noon. I wasn't sure what I'd tell Quint when he came by, but I wasn't going anywhere with him. By the time I reached my duplex, I had a queasy feeling in the pit of my stomach. All I wanted was to crawl back in bed and shut out the world.

I dropped my coat and bag onto the rumpled spread, sat at the computer desk and pulled my foot onto the chair. The old PC whined and clicked to life. Once Explorer launched, I selected Google and typed in *Barcarolle*.

The Wikipedia site appeared and, below it, Offenbach's Barcarolle: *From French composer Jacques Offenbach's opera, the Tales of Hoffmann.*

I dug through the box I'd retrieved from Ruth's curb, found the brochures and leafed through them. *Tales of Hoffmann*, the winter I turned eleven. The other time I'd fallen asleep. What I hadn't told Dad was, Ruth pinched my arm until tears sprung in my eyes and my lower lip quivered. But I didn't cry. That would have brought on a whole different form of punishment. From that point on, I'd stared at the stage below, too afraid to absorb much of the performance.

I did recall thinking how odd it was that the same woman played all the female roles. The Prima Donna that preformed Mozart's *Don Giovanni*, the pale woman with round, red spots on her cheeks and long blond ringlets. What was her role? Then there were two others, and I remember Ruth telling me that the order of the acts didn't follow the original version.

Hoffmann. I typed the name in the search engine and waited. While the page loaded I ran downstairs and poured a glass of wine. Ruth always said it was uncouth to drink before noon, but as the song said, it was noon someplace. By the time I returned, the page had appeared. *E.T.A Hoffmann, 1776-1822.*

"One the darkest of the German romantics, notorious for the myth of manic passion. Combined his sense for the grotesque with Gothic novels and fairy tales."

I read on. Hoffmann's father married his cousin. Hoffmann spent his youth surrounded by the screams of his madwoman-mother, cries that echoed through his grandmother's apartment.

A woman on the top floor, mother of the visionary writer Zacharias Werner, became a great influence in Hoffmann's life. She gave him the outlet to retain his sanity: writing.

Disturbing. I sipped the wine. It flowed through me, settling my nerves. Then I scanned the Internet site for anything related to the mirror, caduceus, and eyes. There, staring back at me were the words *der Sandmann*.

In the version Dad told me, on those nights as a child when I couldn't sleep or when I was sure a creature hid my closet, Sand Man sprinkled magic dust over me to protect me from those creatures. But this wasn't the nighttime tale Dad told me, not a princess fairy that helped me sleep. Oh, no. *Sandmann* was an evil spirit who came at night and, if children weren't asleep, threw sand in their eyes that made them bleed and fall out. Then he gathered the eyes and fed them to his children, who lived in the curve of the crescent moon.

"He took their eyes," I whispered, and the connection didn't snap in my brain, didn't strike me with that bolt of revelation I'd experienced in the past. No, this connection—the obscenity and gruesome reality of Hoffmann's story—crept over me like a billion icy needles, leaving me numb and cold.

"Oh my God." The Boogeyman in my closet had nothing over the Sandmann. The Boogeyman was tame compared to this guy. At least the Boogeyman stayed in the shadows.

The doorbell rang. I spun around and stared at the clock. Noon. Quint stopping by for a lunch of eyes? I giggled, realized I sounded borderline hysterical and abruptly stopped.

My eyes. *Green* eyes. Like Christina's and De La Cruz's and Richard's.

Chapter 24

I asked Oz to get rid of Quint, crawled back onto the desk chair and raised my trembling fingers over the keyboard. Then I typed in *Tales of Hoffmann* and sent Google on another search.

Oz returned and settled on the foot of the bed. "I told him you're getting your period and had awful PMS. No man wants to be around a woman with PMS."

Great. Now I was a suffering bitch. "Thanks."

"I don't see why you won't talk to him. I mean, come on girlfriend. I saw him slip out this morning, and that grin on his face—Oh, if only I could see that on a man after a night of--"

"I get the point," I blurted out. "It's complicated."

"After one night? How complicated can it be?"

"Morales plans to arrest him."

"Oh—Do tell. Every disgusting little detail." Oz scooted closer and rubbed his hands together as though anticipating a juicy scene in one of his plays. "What did he do?"

"Morales thinks Quint killed those women. Until I know who did, I'm not taking any chances." I gripped the wine glass, and drank. This time, it didn't calm me. I doubted anything would.

Oz fluttered his hand near this throat. "Oh he couldn't have, he just *couldn't*. He doesn't *look* like a killer."

"Neither did Constanzo."

"Who?"

"Adelfo de Jesus Constanzo, the cult leader in Matamoros just south of the Texas border. Very charismatic. Good looking. And he killed twenty four men and woman, in addition to sixteen children."

"Grisly," Oz said, "but Quint's not like that."

"How would you know?" I turned to face Oz. "How many killers have you met?"

"None. But that doesn't mean I'm not a good judge of character. Oh sure, I was way off base with Clancy. But never before and never since." He crossed his legs, testing the seams of his tight jeans. His crop top—a neatly hemmed tee with *Girls Just Wanna Have Fun* in lavender glitter—left the knot of his belly button exposed. Was I so far gone, I'd take advice from that?

"Morales is convinced enough that he took it to the D.A."

"But sweetie, what do *you* think? You know Quint. Do you believe he's a killer?"

"I don't want to believe it." I scrubbed my hands over my face. What I wanted to do was scrub the last three days from my life. Wanted to scrub away the last thirteen years. "The evidence suggests—"

"Oh, poo-poo on the evidence." Oz clasped my hands, leaned closer and met my gaze. "What do your *instincts* tell you?"

"That there are way too many gaps to fill in." The computer was still stuck on Google. I shook the mouse. Frozen.

"Then let's fill in those gaps." Oz took the legal pad from my desk, scrounged around until he found a pen, sat, crossed his legs and propped the pad against his thigh. "What do you know?"

Maybe a fresh perspective might help. Wouldn't kill me to give it a shot. Might kill me if I didn't. I retrieved my notepad and joined him on the bed. Thirty minutes later, I'd given him the information I'd collected.

"What the killer's doing isn't random," I added. "These women were chosen. I was chosen. But we don't have anything in common, except hair and eye color."

"Claire fits the bill."

"I know. But she'd been dead two years." I sprawled on the bed and read through my notes. "From a hit-and-run driver. Hand me the phone."

Oz grabbed the receiver off its charger, stretched out beside me and handed it over. "What are you thinking?"

"There had to be evidence in that case. Morales can track it down."

"Oh speaking of cops, that buddy of yours from Fresno called." Oz grimaced. "Sorry girlfriend. Totally slipped my mind."

Instead of Morales' number, I punched in Brad's cell. He answered on the fifth ring.

"It's about time," he said.

"What did you find?" I wiggled my fingers. Oz gave me the pen, and I found a clean sheet in the notepad.

"Pardini's boyfriend," Brad said, and cleared his throat. "This is off the record, right?"

"Of course."

"Good. Because my ass is on the line." A heavy sigh, and I could hear him open and close a door. Probably holing up in the bathroom. "Clio? He's a cop."

I'd suspected as much. I scribbled it down.

"Not just any cop. He's a commander."

My hand trembled. I tightened my grip on the Paper Mate. "What does he look like?"

"Hannah, this guy's married with kids."

"He was having an affair with Pardini?"

"Yeah. It'd been going on about a year."

"Give me his physical." I poised my pen over the blue-lined page.

"Six three, two thirty, forty-seven years of age, brown and brown."

Fit the description of the man I'd seen in Courthouse Café, in the booth behind Giovanni.

"Detective? He's not in uniform right?" I asked.

"Works homicide."

"What's his last?"

"Leo. Commander Leo. Shit," Brad muttered. "You didn't get this from me."

"I owe you."

"Damned right." Brad hung up.

I dialed Morales' cell. He answered after a ring and a half. "Where are you?"

"Home." I lay on the bed and stared at the pimply ceiling.

"Rydell show up?"

"He's not here, if that's what you're asking."

"Slipped our tail," Morales grumbled.

"He's a tracker. I'd assume he knows how to evade being tracked. But, that's not why I called." I rolled onto my stomach, and peered through the gap in my sage curtains at the gloomy afternoon. "I've got a possible lead."

"Oh?"

"This Fresno cop who's been hanging around? He and Pardini were having an affair."

"Where'd you get this?"

He knew better than to ask. I tapped the pen against my cheek. In my mind, I saw his gaze go from hard to downright stony and allowed myself a half-hearted smile. "He was in Courthouse Café yesterday. Sat right behind Giovanni."

"Really think Rydell's innocent?"

"I think there are options worth exploring." The jury was still out on Quint, but I couldn't believe he was the Sandmann.

Didn't *want* to believe it. "Did you determine time of Giovanni's death?"

"Estimate. Between four and seven last night."

"Doesn't clear him."

"No."

"Where was Leo?" I asked.

"Unknown."

"Where were you?"

"What the fuck?"

"Just a question," I said. "Were you working the case?"

"With Esteves. Going over your car."

"Find anything?" I grabbed the pillow, bunched it under my arms and lay the notepad on the mattress. "Well?"

"Boot print. Driver's side. Anyone drive your car?"

"No one." Dad wore boots, but he hadn't been in the car since the last time it conked out. That had been a month ago. Leo wore boots. So did Quint. And Dobbs.

Maybe it was time to get better acquainted with our roadie.

"What're you thinking?" Morales knew me well. Perhaps too well.

"That guy setting up my drums? He showed up out of nowhere."

"Got a name?"

"Dobbs. That's it."

"That a last or first?"

"I assume last, but I don't know." I glanced at Oz as he stretched out beside me and peered over my shoulder. "Steve hired him."

"How long has he been around?" Paper shuffling, and the click of a pen drifted through the phone.

"I met him Friday night."

"Steve say when he hired Dobbs?"

"Sometime during the week, when I missed practice." I searched my memory, then added, "Tuesday or Wednesday. Oh, and another thing. I think he's done time."

Oz shot me a quizzical look.

To Morales I explained, "He paces in tight, six-foot rotations. Add the size of a bunk—"

"And you've got a prison cell," Morales finished.

Chapter 25

I waited on hold. Morales returned after three minutes. "Badorini's bringing Dobbs in."

"When?"

"Now."

I rolled over and sat on the bed's edge. "I want to hear this."

"You know I can't do that."

"Yes, you can." I tugged on my shoes, grabbed my coat off the green chair, punched the phone off and tossed it onto the bed. "I'll be back in a hour."

I needed to listen, whether Morales approved or not. With Sandmann's deadline closing in on me, I wanted to be there to gather every grain of information I could.

The phone rang, the caller ID showed Borden Police. "Don't answer."

"Oh honey. What are you doing?"

"I'm running out of time, and I'll be damned if I'm going to sit here while Morales moves forward with his *ongoing investigation*. I'm sick of him not sharing information."

"So you're going to crash his interrogation?" Oz shook his head, sending the pink spikes swaying. "Not smart, girlfriend."

"Keep working on that," I said, stabbing my finger toward the legal pad.

*   *   *

Eleven minutes later, in the detective's division, I sat behind Badorini in a cramped computer room. The monitor showed the interrogation room, not much larger than a pantry. The camera, hidden in the mock thermostat just inside the door, showed Dobbs, in his signature blue chambray and jeans, sitting stoic at the table.

"Sarge catches you in here," Badorini said. "And—"

"I'll toss her ass out," Morales finished. He leaned in the doorway behind me. "Badorini—*What the fuck?*"

"I don't see the harm in her listening. I mean, come on—It's *Hannah*. She's listened in before."

"Under my supervision," Morales said. "Not when she's a potential victim."

"What's it going to hurt?" I asked. "It's not like I'm writing a story."

He glanced at the pad, and then the pen clutched in my fist.

"Notes," I explained. "For myself."

A tall, slender woman, natural curls brushing the shoulders of her dispatcher's uniform, stepped up behind Morales. Darcy Sotello gave me a smile, which faded when she handed Morales a manila folder.

He flipped it open. A single sheet lay inside. Although he held it open only a moment, I glimpsed a mug shot beneath *Wanted* in bold, capital letters.

"Dobbs?" I asked.

"Thanks, Darcy," Morales grumbled, his way of dismissing her. He sank into the detective's offices and slid onto his black padded chair. The clutter on his desk had grown. A brown streak snaked down the side of a coffee mug, fashioned into a pig wearing a blue police uniform.

I slipped out of the computer room and sank onto the chair beside him. He glared at me, but I didn't care. If he wanted me out of there, he'd have to arrest me. I wasn't going anywhere.

"Sonofabitch," he grumbled. "Get back in there."

"Not a chance." I offered him a smile, knowing it'd piss him off. Hell, I was pissed off. He was shutting me out of a case that involved my life.

He cradled a phone on his shoulder, and studied the wanted poster. "Sergeant Morales, Borden P.D." He paused, and then added, "Get Officer Noblett."

"Dobbs' probation officer?" I asked.

Morales ignored me, and continued reading the poster. I peeked at the sheaf of paper that listed various Penal Codes, the charges Dobbs had faced, above the words *Consider Armed and Dangerous—Do Not Approach*, then, *Contact Officer J. Noblett, San Diego Probations*, followed by the number.

Among the Penal Code charges was *One-Eight-Seven*.

Murder. So, Dobbs *was* a killer.

Morales jotted notes. Although he attempted to shield the paper with his shoulder, I struggled to decipher his scribbles. Before he jabbed the air, a silent order for me to get away from his desk, I decoded one word: *Ophthalmologist*.

Cold bled through me. I backed away from Morales, and rejoined Badorini. On the monitor, Dobbs remained stoic, as though he hadn't moved at all. I stared at the black patch covering his eye. Inside, I seethed. Outside, perspiration chilled my skin. My brain churned up questions I wanted answered— When had Dobbs been released? How long had he been missing from San Diego? Who had he murdered, and why? Top of the list: *How had he lost his eye?*

Morales returned to the doorway. "Gonna question him, but the timeline doesn't match our cases."

"What do you mean?" I asked.

"Left San Diego a week ago. Wasn't around for the De La Cruz murder."

"So that's it? You're going to let him go?"

"We'll hold him on a probation violation," Morales said. "But unless the San Diego guys are covering their asses and don't know when Dobbs left, I can't connect him to the murders."

"Are you sure?" I rubbed my hands against my jeans, ridding myself of the sticky sweat. "How did he get here? There's got to be record of a plane trip, bus or *something*."

I wanted Dobbs to be the killer. If he was, I could relax. It would be over. I'd be safe and Sandmann wouldn't come for me.

"You're going to hold him?" I asked.

Morales nodded. "They'll send someone for him in the morning."

"So, we're back to square one?"

"Afraid so."

*   *   *

After asking Morales to investigate Claire's death, I returned to find Oz still on my bed, stretched out on his stomach, ankles crossed, feet swaying as he did a little brainstorming on the legal pad. I peered over his shoulder at circles with names connected by lines.

"I see Morales didn't kill or arrest you."

"He let me off with a warning." I stretched out beside Oz. "What've we got?"

"I've been busy as a bee," he said. "Look at this, sweetie. Only three people don't have direct links to the killer. That commander, Claire and Quint."

"Leo's connected to Pardini and Giovanni, both of whom are linked to the killer." I glanced at the top of the page, where he'd listed Ruth, Richard, and me. Above them, lines connected us to Claire. "Quint is linked to all of us," I added, running my finger in a circle over my family's names, "and Claire. So, Leo and Quint have indirect links."

The tattered yearbook still lay on the floor near the closet. I snatched it up and flipped through to the junior class. Sure enough, the page that once held Claire Rougue's photo had been ripped out.

"Oz, if I knew it wouldn't repulse you, I'd kiss you."

"Thanks for the sentiment. And for not doing it because you're right. It would repulse me. I just don't swing that way." He propped up on his elbows. "But I didn't really find anything that wasn't already there."

"Claire is the key. She has to be. De La Cruz, Pardini and I had—and have," I quickly added, I wasn't dead yet, "something Claire had."

"What's that?"

"Green eyes."

"The windows to the soul," Oz said. "Rather poetic, in a grisly sort of way. What about your mother? Isn't it too much of a coincidence that she grows the roses the killer chose?"

"Maybe not." The message on the greenhouse wall. Why would he leave Ruth a message?

He wouldn't. Not unless she was a target.

I rolled off the bed, snagged the phone and jabbed in Ruth's number. Two rings. Three.

"Come on, Ruth. Pick up."

Five. Six. I cut off the connection, and dropped the receiver on my desk. "Let's go."

"Where?"

"Ruth's house."

Oz drove while I used his cell to call Morales. He agreed to meet us. When Oz parked, the first thing I noticed was Dad's Toyota in the driveway. The second was the way the blinds were drawn. Crooked. Ruth never allowed anything crooked.

The third was the partially opened door. I could see the gap through the screen.

Quiet. Too quiet. *Dead* quiet. The door was ajar, the screen hung from its top hinge. The bottom had been ripped from the wooden frame, stood askew, couldn't close because something was caught in the jamb.

An arm. *Dad's* arm. Blood dripped from the fingertips and pooled on the porch.

"*No*," I screamed. A cold dagger of fear pierced my heart. I dropped my purse and bolted up the walkway. Oz grabbed my arm, stopping me.

Badorini tumbled from his car and sprinted across the street. "What's going on?"

"*Let go.*" I twisted, tried to free myself from Oz's grasp.

"Call just came through dispatch. We're going to wait right here for backup. They're on their way."

"*That's my Dad lying there.*" Again, I tried to twist free. "Let go—*I have to make sure he's alive.*"

Badorini bolted down the walkway, jumped onto the porch, ducked to one side of the doorway and carefully reached for Dad's arm. He pressed his fingers against Dad's wrist. Finally, he nodded. Alive.

My body sagged as though all the bones had been ripped out. Oz eased me to the ground, and cradled my head against his chest. He stroked my hair, murmured soothing words, but they didn't soothe. A mixture of anger and fear churned inside me, leaving me sick and scared.

I wanted Dad away from that door, from that house, from whoever might still be inside.

"That's enough," I screamed, hoping Sandmann could hear me. "Enough already. This ends *now*."

Badorini gripped Dad's arm. With his elbow, he shoved the screen wide enough to drag Dad onto the porch. He kept low, beneath window level, and pulled Dad to the end of the porch.

Morales parked and tumbled out of his Bronco. A cruiser stopped at the street, and two cops bailed out. Familiar sounds of dispatch calling all units to respond cut through the pain in my head. I leaned away from Oz and pushed to my feet.

Badorini stood, hefted Dad onto his shoulder and climbed over the railing. Then he carried Dad along the far side of the lawn, and stretched him out on the slice of grass between the sidewalk and road.

I ran toward them, and sank to my knees. Only the slight rise and fall of Dad's blood-soaked uniform told me he wasn't dead. Holes riddled his shirt. Badorini ran across the street, reached through his car's window, pulled out his radio and requested an ambulance.

Morales sent the second car to secure the back. Gun drawn, he crept up the porch steps, pressed against the wall beside the front door, and motioned for Holmes to get behind him. Then Morales opened the screen with the toe of his shoe, crouched down and peeked inside. I knew Sandmann wasn't in there. He wouldn't get caught this easily.

"You're going to be okay." I cradled Dad's head in my lap, smoothed hair from his temples. Anguish constricted my throat. My chest ached. Tears streamed down my face. I glanced at the house as Morales stepped out and shook his head.

Ruth? *Dead?* I leaned over, clutched Dad's shoulders, and pressed my cheek against his.

The ambulance arrived. Tolson slid from the passenger seat, and his eyes widened. He flung open the back doors, grabbed his kit and helped Kurkis tug out the gurney.

"One here," Morales said.

"Inside?" Kurkis asked.

"Negative."

Tolson dropped to his knees beside me, ripped Dad's sleeve to expose his arm and searched for a vein to insert the intravenous line. As if through a fog, I heard him call in Dad's blood pressure and pulse rate. He informed the hospital that Dad had been stabbed and lost a considerable amount of blood. Then Morales' words sank in—No one was in the house.

"Ruth?" I asked as he approached.

"She's not here. Signs of a struggle, though." He studied Dad, gripped my arm and urged me to my feet. He led me a few yards away. "Didn't you say your mom filed for divorce?"

"Last week. Ruth's supposed to fly to Texas Wednesday."

"Don't think they got into a scuffle, do you?"

"And she attacked him? *No.*" I glanced back at Dad. Tolson had ripped his shirt. Numerous cuts split his flesh.

"Might be on her way to Fresno."

"He took her." The words rang hollow in my ears. "Sandmann took her."

"Don't know that," Morales said, but the slight twitch at the corner of his eye told me he'd considered the same thing. "Where's Rydell?"

"Stop asking me," I shot back, but my voice was weak, all my strength had been sapped. "I don't know where he is."

"When'd you see him last?"

"Couple of hours ago? Noon," I added, recalling our broken lunch date. "Why?"

"CHP pulled him over 'bout thirty minutes ago," Morales said, referring to the California Highway Patrol. "Vehicle search uncovered a knife in the trunk."

My limbs went cold. A foreboding sense of calm filled me. "What type of knife?"

"Military."

"Sharp?"

"Like a razor. Might want to sit down." Morales gripped my shoulders and eased me into the Neon's driver's seat. He must have known I was about to collapse. Just as I hit the cushion, my knees gave out.

In a rapid-fire pace, I told him about the connections between the victims, Richard, the others and myself. "This isn't a domestic dispute. He wouldn't have left the message on the greenhouse wall if he didn't intend to take her."

A car engine grew louder. Died. I turned as Quint climbed out of the Mustang. He looped the strap of his Nikon over his head and eased the car door closed. Then he saw me, and darted across the street.

"They didn't arrest him?" I shouted.

"Cite and release," Morales muttered and added, "sonofabitch."

I bolted for Quint, and slammed my fists against his chest. "Did you do this?"

"What?" His features went slack.

"Did you?" I screamed and struck him again. *"Did you hurt my father?"*

"Christ—*why would I hurt him?*" Quint caught my hands, stopping my attack. "Is he okay?"

"No, you bastard, he's *not* okay."

I cried, although I didn't think I had the energy for tears. My eyes felt puffy and bruised. He slid his arms around me. I shoved him and backed away.

"If I find out you did this, I'll take care of you myself."

"*Hannah.*"

"Shut up and get the hell out of here."

He paled as though my words ripped the life right out of him.

Chapter 26

Kurkis and Tolson took Dad to Borden Memorial Hospital. They wouldn't let me into the ambulance, so Oz and I followed. Morales showed up shortly after they took Dad into surgery.

I sat on a hard plastic chair surrounded by drab brown walls. Tan and green tile formed a checkerboard leading to the OR's double door with the glaring red and white sign: *Authorized Personnel Only.*

Antiseptic odors clogged my nose, reminding me of the times Ruth took me to the pediatrician for booster shots and prompting memories of rubbing alcohol, and the agonizing anticipation of when that needle would pierce my flesh.

"Gonna be okay," Morales said, his awkward attempt to console me. Which was more of an attempt than I'd seen from him the entire time we dated. "Nothing you could have done," he added. "Whoever did this was long gone by the time you got there."

Tolson sat beside me, set his medical kit on the floor and gently pressed his fingers to my wrist. Checking to make sure I'm alive? I almost laughed, would have if the situation hadn't been so dire.

"I've got to find him," I said.

"Find who?" Tolson asked.

"Whoever stabbed my father. Whoever took my mother. Whoever wants me dead."

He glanced up at Morales. "I can give her something to help her relax."

"I don't want anything." No, I wanted to be as sharp-minded as possible. I couldn't track down Sandmann if all I did was sleep.

Kurkis returned the gurney to the ambulance and closed the doors, making the caduceus whole again. I stared at the symbol of the medical profession, one doctors usually had displayed in their car windows.

No, not usually. *Always.* So they'd be identified as doctors.

"Tales of Hoffmann," I whispered. "Act four—or three, in Offenbach's original version."

"How's that, sweetie?" Oz settled on the hard, plastic seat beside me and crossed his knees.

"The woman was a singer, but the physician told her if she sang she'd die. Evil, one of three, made her sing anyway."

Oz looked up at Morales. "I think the stress has gotten to her. Maybe she needs valium or thorazine or something."

Morales crouched before me, and gently gripped my knees, which trembled, as did my whole body. Instead of his usual dark glare, he looked at me with obvious concern. Then his eyes widened, and I knew he'd snagged onto my line of reasoning. "The caduceus and opera?"

I tried to speak, but my throat felt swollen. I nodded instead.

"What else?" Morales urged.

Tolson, fingers still against my wrist, consulted his watch.

"Increased heart rate." I pulled my arm away. "I already know that. I'm not suffering stress-induced paranoia, nor am I having a panic attack." I returned my attention to Morales. "He's Hoffmann. The killer is *Hoffmann.*"

"Then what happens?" Morales asked.

"I don't remember."

"Why did he kill these women?"

"That's just it." I shook my head. None of this made sense, but then it all made sense. In a sick, twisted sort of way. "He *didn't*."

"He *wanted* them dead?"

"No. He loved them." Just as Quint once loved me? Hollowness filled me, the same numbing sensation I'd felt when Morales told me Quint was a suspect. I cradled my head, rubbed my temples against deep, throbbing pain. "He loved each of them, but they were *rebound* relationships," I said, for lack of better words. "The woman he really loved was Stella."

"She rejected him?" Morales offered, and I knew he was trying to pull the information out of me. "Dumped him for some other guy?"

"I don't know."

"Sure you don't want something to help you relax?" Tolson gingerly lifted my hair over my shoulder, and stroked my arm. "Your father will be in surgery for a while. You should rest."

"I don't want to be medicated." I turned my attention to Morales. "Three women, they were like—parts of the same woman, the one he loved. He was supposed to meet her, but something happened,"

"If you change your mind," Tolson said, "day or night, you've got my number. Sorry about your dad." He touched his finger to my cheek and gave me a warm smile. Then he clutched the handle on his plastic first-aid kit and stood. Double glass doors parted as he approached, then closed behind him. The ambulance pulled from beneath the ER's carport and faded into the night.

"What about Ruth? What are you doing to find her?"

"Got every man on the force canvassing the neighborhood," Morales said. "Seems the sonofabitch took her out through the greenhouse."

"Through the hole I made," I said, for the first time feeling guilty for my actions. I'd given the killer an escape route. "No one saw anything?"

"Guy on Pine Street saw a gray Camaro."

Like the one outside The Dock, the one that looked so much like Richard's old car I had to convince myself it wasn't.

"Search party?" Two blocks from Ruth's house were fields. I'd be easy to dump a body there. No one would find it for weeks.

"Got that going," Morales said.

"I'd like to join them."

"Put yourself out in the open?" Morales shook his head. "Not gonna happen."

I returned my attention to the operating room doors, and mentally willed them to open. I needed to know Dad was okay. I wished they would find Ruth. If they found anything, they'd radio Morales. I'd know as quickly as he did.

Dad was in surgery more than five hours. The nurses got sick of my questions, but I didn't care. At one o'clock Monday morning, the doctor finally emerged through those *Authorized Personnel Only* doors.

"There was extensive damage, but he's stable."

A non-committal term for not getting worse, but not getting better.

Doctor Naz—the name embroidered on his scrubs—pulled the blue cap off his dark, curly hair. "You may see him, if you'd like."

"Thank you—Yes, I want to see him," I said.

"He's unconscious. He won't know you're there."

"He'll know." I followed Naz beyond the doors, and into I.C.U. Before I reached the doorway, I spied Dad through the wall of glass. He looked small, somehow. Frail. And I didn't like seeing him this weak. Tears stung my eyes. I slipped around the doorway, and settled on the edge of the bed.

Monitors beeped, creating an eerie undertone in the otherwise silent room. The solution in the I.V. tube dripped with an almost audible sound. Dim light washed Dad in a yellowish haze making him look jaundiced. He was pale. The gown loosely covered his chest, exposing bandages marred with thin red lines. I wanted to crawl onto the bed, snuggle up beside him as I had so often in childhood, but what if I hurt him? What if I frightened him?

My nose ran. I sniffled, glanced around for a box of Kleenex and spotted someone standing in the shadows just beyond the doorway. Tolson stepped inside, took the box of tissues from a table near the door and brought it to me.

I tore several sheets loose and blew my nose.

"Hope I didn't startle you."

"What are you doing here?" I took another sheet, and dabbed my teary eyes.

"Worried about you." He shrugged. "You need to rest."

"Playing doctor with me?"

He grinned, and I got the impression he'd like to do just that.

"I'm okay, considering my father may or may not make it and my mother is missing. Guess I'm just peachy keen."

"They still haven't found her?" Tolson set the box on the foot of the bed.

"No." I had a sick feeling they wouldn't, either. If I could, I'd search every inch of Borden. Damned if my mother would wind up in a dumpster with her eyes cut out.

He gestured toward Dad. "How bad is he?"

"They don't know. They're hoping infection doesn't set in."

"Was it a robbery?"

I studied Tolson. Why was he so interested? Because he wanted to date me, he'd made that clear. This was his way of expressing concern, and letting me know he still wanted that *dinner-that-wasn't-a-BLT.*

"No, whoever did this didn't want Ruth's jewelry or silver."

"I don't get it," he said, and sat on the corner of the mattress. "You must see a lot of this in your work."

"Yep, a whole lot. But it's never touched my family before. Strange being on the victim side of a case." I smoothed Dad's hair from his damp, clammy forehead.

"I'll leave you alone." Tolson stood and turned toward the door. "I know you've got a lot going on. But if you need a friend—"

"I'll call."

I stood there long after Tolson left, watching Dad, hoping for some flutter of eyelids, a quick intake of breath that told me he was waking up. Nothing. Because he was in ICU, they refused to let me stay. I found Oz dozing in the waiting room, woke him and he drove me home.

I crawled into bed around two thirty. I didn't think I'd sleep, but fell off moments after my head hit the pillow. When I woke, I'd lost half the morning, which I wasn't happy about. I wanted to check on Dad, maybe join the team searching for Ruth.

And I had a gig, the Carnegie Player's New Year's Eve Gala. God I didn't feel up to playing. I wasn't sure I could with Quint on stage. I'd never felt such anger and betrayal. I'd never wanted to hurt someone, but I wanted to hurt him. Still, something told me I wasn't seeing the whole picture.

My eyes felt gritty as I crawled from beneath the covers, hit the bathroom, and dressed in jeans and sweatshirt. Pulling on a pair of socks, I glanced at the computer. Still frozen. I'd forgotten to shut it down.

I jabbed the power button on my way out, and joined Oz in the kitchen. At the table, Morales bent over a plate of Eggs Benedict. I poured myself a cup of coffee, Golden Pecan from the smell of it, and hopped onto the counter.

"Checked out Commander Leo," Morales mumbled around a mouthful of eggs and hollandaise sauce. "Good cop. Decorated war vet."

"A state trooper raped women in Massachusetts." I spooned sugar into my mug, and poured cream from the carton left beside the sink. "A gun and badge doesn't make him a saint."

Morales washed down the eggs with coffee. "Affair with the Pardini woman started 'bout a year back. Not uncommon among cops. Marriage mortality rate sucks."

Oz sat in the folding chair at the other end of the table. "Why didn't he just leave the wife?"

"Dunno. Kids, I guess."

"Where was he when Pardini was killed?" I asked.

Morales ate, glanced at me and forked in another mouthful. "Home."

"His wife's his alibi." I blew over the top of my coffee, sipped carefully. Too hot, I set it aside.

"Yeah. Guy's not involved."

"Are you sure?" Oz tied his paisley-print housecoat over his silk shorts and tank top. He crossed to the sink and rinsed his cup. "Maybe the wife lied. After all, he *was* whoring around."

"Don't make him a killer. Wasn't around when Giovanni died, either. Besides, neighbors corroborated the wife's story." Morales sopped up sauce with his last corner of toast. "Damn, you can cook."

"Thanks. Always love to see a man satisfied."

Morales glanced up. Oz gave him a wink.

Morales dropped the toast and brushed his hands over the plate. "Got a watch on Rydell. Haven't heard from him, have you?"

"No." Probably wouldn't after I pounded and threatened him.

"Almost forgot." Morales tugged an envelope from his jacket pocket. "Special delivery."

I slid off the counter, took the letter and tore it open. "It's the subpoena."

"That attorney?" Oz asked.

"Parkston. He's giving me until next Friday to hand over my notes, list of sources, and documents related to the story. That's the prelim."

"Or what?" Oz saddled up beside me and peered over my shoulder. "What are you going to do?"

"Nothing." I tossed the subpoena on the table. "He'll have to take me to court."

In the meantime, I really *would* burn those documents.

I retrieved the envelope and turned it over. It was identical to the one the deputy handed Quint at the club, only mine had the Madera County seal in the corner. "When would a deputy serve someone living in the city?"

"When it comes from out of county and they got no address." Morales eyed me with suspicion. "How many suits you got against you?"

"Just the one." I carried my coffee to the table. "Any status on Ruth?"

"None."

"Did you arrest Quint?"

Morales shook his head. "Story checked out."

My hand trembled. Coffee spilled over the lace-trimmed mat. Oz tore the towel from the fridge handle and mopped up the mess.

Morales glanced at the spill and shrugged.

"Why have a watch on him if his story checks out?" I asked.

"Something stinks."

"Are you sure he's not involved?"

"Not completely. Said he was shopping for a suit between four and five. Clerk remembers him. Went home. That strange guy, Robin, said Quint was there until almost six. After that, you're his alibi. Didn't kill Giovanni. But he's hiding something."

I was still sloshing coffee. Oz took the mug from me and set it on the table.

"What about yesterday?" I asked, my tone dull and flat and I hardly recognized it as my own.

"Went to his uncle's in Fresno. Got the call from Grigsby on the way back. Checks out."

"The knife?"

"Volunteered to bring it in. Esteves swabbed the blade. No trace evidence. Guy's clean, or awfully damned slick."

I'd threatened him. Pounded him. Accused him of stabbing Dad. I poked my fingers beneath my glasses and rubbed my eyes. I'd gone numb inside and out. Even my brain didn't want to function. Frozen. Just like the computer.

Finally, I found my voice. "Any leads on who killed Claire?"

"Still checking. Detective who worked the case left the department. It's in the cold file. Quint was still in the service two years ago. Could have taken R&R, though. Like I said. Something stinks."

"I think the killer went to Borden High." Quint, Richard, Claire, me. School was the common denominator. "He wanted

Claire, couldn't have her. When Richard died, he pursued her again. But why wait so many years? Where was he?"

The military? Claire's brother said her boyfriend wore some kind of uniform. That tied to Quint, but his alibis when Giovanni was killed and when Dad and Ruth were attacked are solid.

"Can you check someone from Borden who was discharged from the service? Would have been two or three years ago. Between two and four."

Morales steepled his fingers and tapped his lips. "Something you want to tell me?"

"It's a idea, that's all. A lead?"

"How'd you come by it?"

"Oh." I bit my thumbnail. I'd forgotten to tell him about my talk with Claire's brother, and brief visit with De La Cruz's husband. I filled him in, hesitated when I came to the Sandmann, but gave him that information, too. "I think the same person who killed Claire killed De La Cruz and Pardini."

Morales sat there a long time, digesting everything along with the Eggs Benedict. "Rejection?" He shook his head. "Not the motive. This is too complex. Guy's playin' a game. Doesn't fit the profile."

"A method killer," I suggested.

"Huh?" Oz cocked his head.

"He's killing to bring about a specific outcome. He believes if he takes very specific steps—kills certain people—he'll get what he wants."

"What's that?" Morales asked.

I didn't know. I needed to figure out how the mirror came into play. If I were right in my theory of Hoffmann, the mirror would be woven into the opera. If I could make that connection, I might figure out who Sandmann is.

Chapter 27

Mid-afternoon sunlight streamed through slats nailed over dirt-caked windows and bathed Ruth Monakee in a burnt-orange wash. The air stirred with the passion of the *Barcarolle*, music that came alive in sweeping waves. Fast. Slow. Fast again, inching toward climax and sweet release. He loved how the music made him feel. Comforted. Powerful. *Alive.*

He propped Ruth against a rotted four-by-four support beam in the corner. Crouching before her, he stroked his finger against her cool, soft cheek. He lifted the syringe to the oil lamp's glow, flicked it, bringing bubbles to the top. Gently, he pressed the stopper until liquid seeped from the needle. Then he slowly inserted it into the vein in the crook of her elbow.

He depressed the plunger just as slowly. Drawing a deep, sharp breath, his body filled with a pleasant ache that grew more profound with each methodical step. He jerked the needle free and flung it across the room.

He curled up beside her, pressed his ear to her breast and closed his eyes, allowing himself a few moments to feel her closeness, her warm breath grazing his face.

He straightened, upsetting the crown of roses he'd placed on her head. He touched the flowers. Deep red, almost black. He'd taken them from her garden. Symbols of love and vengeance and eternity, all the makings of his quest.

Readjusting the crown, he pushed it down over her dark hair. Thorns pricked her temples. Thin lines of blood, just as dark as the roses, trickled down her creamy complexion.

He sat back on his heels and admired his handiwork. Something snapped in his mind, and his smile faded. Everything shifted. Not out of focus, but became sharper, like when his sinuses were plugged and suddenly cleared.

The switch. He hadn't flipped it. It just happened, the way someone barrels through a stop sign and crashes into another car. Unexpected. Out of control.

He felt himself pulled into that other world, sucked in like a thick milkshake through a narrow straw. The door started to close over him. He crammed his foot in the jamb, holding a five-inch gap. Through it, he stared at the woman almost as lifeless as those he'd left in the dumpsters. Light faded around him. Warmth faded with it, leaving him feeling frightened and alone.

He pushed the mind-door. Hinges screeched in protest. Pushed harder, and it opened enough for him to slip out. Before it could shut, he reached in and turned off the switch.

He didn't like that. Didn't like that door acting on its own, sucking him in whenever it wanted. *He* was in control. *No one and nothing else.*

He knelt, touched his gloved fingers to Ruth's neck and sighed. Alive. Good. He couldn't lose her. Not this one. She was special. She was his *muse.*

He'd spotted Nicklausse in time to stop her and now she couldn't mislead him, couldn't manipulate him, couldn't keep him from Stella.

Nicklausse would *become* Stella.

"One more," he whispered, and pressed his lips to Ruth's mouth, cold and unmoving. "One more and you'll become whole again."

She didn't respond, but that was okay. He could feel her essence reach out to him, yearning for the two fragments of Stella's soul that twisted and writhed inside him.

Chapter 28

Standing by the patio's French doors, I stared at the sun, watched it descend and light up the cloud's underbellies in shades of lavender and blood orange. This was the wettest Christmas season in more than twenty years, according to the Gazette. I wondered how much longer it could last.

Rain struck the windowpanes in sharp ticks. I rested my forehead against the cold glass. I'd shoved everything from my mind for the past hour, precious time I couldn't afford to lose. But I felt crippled beneath mental overload. Too much happening, way too fast. Too much to absorb. I couldn't shake the feeling there was a stronger connection to Richard than I realized. I would never believe he shot himself up with heroin. It looked more and more like someone may have jabbed that needle in his arm. Now, that person had taken our mother, stabbed our father, framed Richard's best friend and wanted me dead.

I'd spent most of the day with Dad. His condition was stable, but the doctors said it could be touch-and-go the next twenty-four hours. They promised to call if his prognosis changed.

There was one bright spot in my otherwise dreary world. I came home to a letter from Madera County Superior Court. The preliminary hearing had been rescheduled for February. That bought me a month to get rid of my notes.

I smoothed the curtains back in place, picked up the phone for what must have been the hundredth time and, for the hundredth time, set it down. What was I supposed to tell Quint? *I'm sorry?* That was like stretching a Band-Aid over a bullet

wound. I'd have to face him soon enough. The gala was slated for
nine.

I still had to figure out who Sandmann is. Above all, I wanted
to live through the night. One depended heavily on the other. I'd
have a better chance of living longer than the next twenty-plus
hours if I knew who wanted me dead.

Morales stretched out on the lavender La-Z-Boy and dozed.
He'd taken over babysitting duties from Badorini, and sent him
to the office to search military records, provided he could gain
access. Each time I crossed the room, Morales opened one eye
and watched me. Then closed it and resumed snoozing.

Oz had spent the last hour trying to unfreeze my computer. I
could have gone to the Gazette and used one there. But with
night closing in, I couldn't bring myself to step outside. When I
tried, hairs at the back of my neck prickled, my stomach knotted
up and I started trembling. Knowing Sandmann was watching
me, waiting to pluck out my eyes, chilled my blood.

I ran to the foot of the stairs. "Oz? Any luck with that
computer?"

"I'm an actor," he shouted back, "not a computer technician.
I called Clancy," he added, and I could imagine Oz blanch. "He's
walking me through some trouble-shooting thingies. But he said
it might be trashed and we'll have to reformat the hard drive."

"I don't have all the programs." I'd pirated Word. If he wiped
the drive clean, I'd lose my ability to work from home.

Morales came alive again, found the remote, flipped through
channels and settled on Showtime. *Die Hard*. He set the remote
aside, folded his arms behind his head and fixed on the movie.
Barefoot, glass raining around him, Bruce Willis dodged bullets
from an AK rifle. Ah, the magic of movies. Bullets of another
kind rained around me, and there wasn't anything I could do but
wait until one struck.

Shivering, I hugged myself and turned away from the television. Search and Rescue—headed by Quint—had broadened its focus to include surrounding neighborhoods, but so far, no sign of Ruth. Had he killed her? Was he now searching for a dumpster to drop her body into?

"They'll find her."

A tremor shot through me. I spun around and faced Morales, sprawled in the recliner. "Damn, don't scare me like that."

"Jumpy," he grumbled. "Gotta relax."

I brushed the obvious aside. "Will they find her alive?"

"Doin' all we can," Morales said.

I sat on the chair's arm and stared blankly at Bruce, who had ducked behind a wall to reload his weapon. If only my situation could resolve itself within two hours.

Morales slid his hand over my waist. I gave him a half-hearted smile at his attempt to console me. What I wanted was to crawl onto his lap, lay my head against his shoulder, and draw comfort from him. But he wasn't the *crawl-into-the-lap* kind of guy. He was more like Bruce—find a partition to hide behind while he prepared for the next battle. Instead, I kissed his forehead and stood.

The clock on the mantle read ten after five. Oz would have to leave soon to set up for the Gala. I jogged upstairs and found him with his cell cradled against his ear, fingers poised over the keyboard.

"Uh-huh. Been there done that, bitch. It's showing these blocks. There. It stopped." He glanced up, gritted his teeth, mouthed the word *Clancy* and rolled his eyes. "Oh yes. I got it."

He folded the cell and set it by the monitor.

"What's the verdict?" I asked.

"This thing needs to join your couch in landfill heaven. But," he added, "We got it working again. You've just got too much junk on here."

"Can you access the Internet?"

"Let's give it a try." He launched the browser, connected to NetZero and waited. The telephone icon flickered, the message below read *dialing*.

"You should be getting ready for the gala," I said.

"Don't worry about that, sweetie. The guild has everything under control."

"You're going, right?"

"I'm not leaving you alone with that brute of a cop. I've seen him snoozing. Huh-uh, girlfriend. I told you. Me and my stun gun are here for you."

"But you *are* going?" I sat on the corner of my rumpled bed. "You've worked so hard."

"I've worked hard to find a roommate I can actually get along with," he said. "Where would I be if I lost you? Alone and miserable, that's where. I have selfish motives."

Despite his earlier confession, I kissed his cheek.

"And yes, I'm going. We'll go together."

The connection finally solidified. A white box filled the screen. As though each frame, picture and emblem had to be retrieved separately through great distance, the box slowly filled in with the NetZero advertisement.

"Okay. We're in."

"Search Hoffmann."

"Hoff Man," he said as he typed.

"No. One word, two N's. *Hoffmann*."

"Don't get snippy. This is as good as this girlie-man gets." But he typed the name, just as I asked.

The box I'd gotten from Ruth's house was still by the bed. I pulled out Koontz's *Winter Moon* and flipped through the pages. Then, I pulled out the stack of envelopes. The red rubber band that bound them broke as I pulled one letter free. It had red, white and blue slashes like a barber pole around its edges. I turned it over and glanced at the return address: SFC Q. Rydell, followed by numbers and a Navel base in Florida. The letter, addressed to me, had a twelve-year-old postmark.

As if my heart hadn't had enough of a workout, it constricted, bound by grief and anger just as tightly as the half rotted rubber band had bundled the letters all these years.

"Oh, God." I shuffled through them. Eleven years ago, ten years, twelve and a half. Some of the dates were close together, some farther apart. He'd written from Florida, California, and Georgia. Twice weekly, once a week, then a couple times a month until finally, he'd given up. "He didn't walk away."

"How's that sweetie? Who didn't?"

"Quint—He didn't walk out on me." The onset of more tears tightened my throat, but I was all cried out. *"How could Ruth do this?"*

I showed Oz the letters. "Oh girlfriend. That's absolutely awful."

Part of me was furious with her, but most of me ached to find her. Regardless of what she'd done—for whatever reason—no one deserved to be in the hands of Sandmann.

All these years, I'd harbored anger toward Quint like a festering wound. And, all these years, that anger was unfounded. No wonder he acted so confused during dinner. We both were— me wondering how he could step back into my life, he wondering why I never responded to letters I didn't know existed.

I stared at the envelope, the printing so precise, neat and clean. I tried to imagine his words on the sheet of paper trapped inside. I was afraid to look.

"Don't tell me you're not going to read them," Oz said. "If you won't, I will."

I almost handed it to him, but gripped the age-yellowed envelope until my hand trembled. Looking at Oz for strength, I slipped my finger beneath the seal and pulled out the letter.

Dear Hannah,

I miss you. I can't believe I let Mom and Gramps talk me into this. I hate it here. No one talks they just yell.

I can't believe I'm here and you're there. That Rich is gone. How did the world go so crazy so fast?

I miss you a lot. Q.

This time tears flooded my vision, and cut hot trails down my cold cheeks. I glanced at the rest of his letters, wondering if I'd ever find the strength to read them.

"How could your mother do that?" Oz asked. "Oh, sweetie, that's so awful."

Yes, it was. But I knew, in her crippled manner, Ruth tried to protect me. She'd never cared for Quint, never thought he was good enough for Richard or me. No one was good enough, nor would they ever be. Even through the stone-cold barrier she'd placed between us, some small part of her cared. And I wasn't sure if not receiving the letters, or knowing Ruth had some place in her heart for me, hurt more.

"Hoffmann finally came through for us," Oz said, his singsong voice grating my nerves. "Which one first? Die Nacht— Oh forget it. German. Never mastered French, much less German. *The Night Pieces.* What do you say?"

"I say I've really screwed things up." Swiping tears from my face, I dropped the letters into the box and perched on the desk's edge. "What did you find?"

"A short story written by that Hoffmann guy, part of an anthology later adapted as the ballet, *Coppelia.*"

"A death dance, huh?" *Dance with the Devil.* I rubbed my arms against a sudden chill and read over Oz's shoulder. "Nathaniel, the gift of God, a narcissistic protagonist with a manic sense of mission."

"Sounds like your Sandmann. And look here." Oz tapped the screen. "Clara was Nathaniel's fiancée."

"Clara . . . Claire? And it says *Coppola* is Italian for eye cavities. He was a trader who Nathaniel saw as Fear."

Eye cavities—black, empty sockets from which he'd plucked green eyes. Coldness, icy as the rain outside, bled through me. I cupped my hand over my mouth, not sure if I wanted to scream or puke.

"Don't think I can do this." I touched my cheeks just below my eyes, wondering how long it would be before Sandmann cut them from my face.

"Of course you can," Oz said. "You've got guts, girl."

"Yeah, and I'd like to keep them inside my body."

"Oh, don't go there. Huh-uh, girlfriend." Oz wagged his finger at me. "Your guts, your body—*and your eyes*—are going to stay right where they are."

I hoped he was right. I nodded with resolve I really didn't feel, and again peered over his shoulder. "Okay. Let's do this."

"Look at this," Oz said and gave a visible shudder. "Olimpia. *She who comes from Olympus.* Like those scratches you saw on that toy."

"The robot De La Cruz took from his boy and stomped on," I muttered. "That must be what De La Cruz received with the rose, the equivalent to the mirror in my car. Olympia wasn't human, but a doll, and the reason for Nathaniel's madness. Doll. Model? Where do the mirror and rose come in?"

I read further. Nathaniel's father conducted alchemistic experiments with Fear who, in a metaphorical sense, was really the dark side of Nathaniel.

"Okay," I said. "But I still don't see anything about the mirror. Why would he smash mine?"

"Maybe he's afraid you'll see his reflection," Oz offered. "Oh girlfriend. What if he doesn't have one? That would be so *Goth*. What if he believes he's a vampire? They don't have reflections, right?"

I doubted Sandmann was a self-proclaimed Dracula. An image of Esteves, Kurkis and Tolson lifting the duffle bag from the dumpster the day before Christmas filled my mind. Somewhere was a blood-soaked trunk. I wished Morales could set up a checkpoint, search cars the way they searched for drunks. *License and registration please. And oh, yeah. Pop the trunk.*

"Hate to abandon you, sweetie, but I've got to get dinner going." He kissed my forehead. "Not so bad," he said and winked. "Just not the lips. Never the lips."

He sashayed out, leaving the door open. Light from the stairwell sliced across the carpet. Otherwise, the room was dark. I glanced around, half expecting to see someone crouched in the shadows. Then I crossed to the window overlooking the street below.

A block away, a street lamp flickered to life and cast a yellow sphere over the rain-slick asphalt. Just beyond that light, a silver Camaro idled, headlamps dark, a gray plume rising from the tailpipe. The same car I'd seen at the club three nights ago.

Chapter 29

I wanted to catch the bastard—he'd been so close—but the Camaro had driven off by the time I ran downstairs and alerted Morales. I wasn't surprised. Catching him would have been a stroke of pure luck, and Lady Luck was a bitch with a cast-iron heart.

After dinner, I showered, dressed in a black suit and silk fuchsia blouse. Jeans and sweater wouldn't do for a black-tie gala. But damned if I would wear a dress. Drumming in a dress was like running the Wharf-to-Wharf 10K in three-inch heels. Tonight wasn't about looking good, or even performing well. It was about living. More than anything, I wanted to wake up tomorrow. Alive. With another chance to catch the Sandmann, before he caught me.

I studied my reflection in the mirror. Skin pale. Dark circles around my eyes made them look sunken. Stress had taken its toll.

I started to braid my hair, and stopped. I'd gone so long not caring how I looked I'd fallen into a funk. I worked Bio Silk through my hair then dried the long strands to a silken shine. Almost as an afterthought, I touched mascara to my lashes, blush on my high cheekbones and a hint of mauve to my lips.

The rain had lessened to a drizzle. Black clouds clustered overhead in threat of another downpour. Toward the Sierra, flashes of lightning framed the mountains' jagged peaks in golden hues. I hoped the storm would hold off until after the gig. Sitting on stage surrounded by electrical equipment during a storm wasn't how I wanted to die, either.

After dinner, Morales drove me to the club. He claimed a table directly before the stage, a portable platform held together by hinges and two-by-four supports. The Hatfield room at the Madera County fairgrounds, reserved for vendors during the annual fair, had been transformed into a world of performing arts. Scenes of *Cats*, *Grease*, and *The Producers* were projected onto the walls, along with still shots of Mikhail Baryshnikov and Beverly Sills. The guild wanted to make sure everyone found something worth funding.

After depositing my purse with Morales, I climbed onstage. Quint tightened the nut on my ride cymbal. He glanced my way as I approached. Then he readjusted the stand, lowered the brass and did the same with the crash cymbal.

"Didn't expect you," he said by way of explanation.

"You were going to put Dobbs up here?" I shook my head. "Not going to happen. Besides, he's in custody."

"I heard." Quint motioned toward the throne. "Sit. I'll adjust this for you."

I slid onto the seat, rested my toes against the bass pedal, started to lean over and slide it closer when he knelt and did it for me.

At the table less than fifteen feet away, Morales fixed his gaze on me. He lifted his longneck, drank, and twirled the bottle between thumb and forefinger.

"I didn't hurt your parents." Quint brought the bass drum closer, loosed the toms on top and gave them more tilt. "I'd never hurt them."

"I know."

"I've got nothing to do with this." He crouched and pulled the floor toms toward me.

I touched the back of my hand to his cool cheek, freshly shaven, the scent of Noxzema cream and sandalwood soap wrapped the air around me. He looked up, and I snatched my hand away.

"Sorry," I whispered. "Quint, *I am so sorry*. It's just, I've been under—"

"A lot of stress," he finished for me. "I understand that. I don't understand your accusing me of something so horrible."

"You gave me reason." I tugged up my blazer's sleeves, exposing the bruises on my wrists. "What was I supposed to think?"

For a moment, he looked puzzled. Then his features went slack. "Ah shit, Babe."

"Want to explain this?" I really needed to understand.

"Told you. I was dreaming," he muttered.

"That I attacked you?" I uttered a sharp laugh. "Big Navy SEAL afraid of a hundred-pound woman?"

He propped his arms on his thighs and stared at the stage floor.

"Where'd you get the scar on your arm?"

"Okay." He nodded. "Fine. You really want to know?"

"Damned right I do."

"Five years ago. My unit was in Afghanistan." His voice dropped to a whisper. "We'd been tracking al-Qaeda operatives, took out a training camp earlier that day. I hadn't slept in more than a week," he added, and I got the impression he needed to justify something. He averted his gaze. "Didn't hear the fucker come up behind me. When I did, I spun around and he fired." He rubbed his bicep. "Hot lead. Any idea what that feels like? They say you don't feel getting shot, but that's bullshit."

Twelve years in the military, a war going on—It hadn't dawned on me that he'd seen action.

"What'd you do?" I asked.

He shrugged, noncommittal. But the hard set of his jaw told me there was nothing casual about his experience.

"Killed him," he finally said. "That night works into my sleep sometimes. I'm not used to sharing a bed, Babe."

"Better get used to it," I said, without thinking. Too late to take the words back. Did I want to? I touched his cool cheek again. No, I didn't.

A grin twitched his lips. "Guess so."

"Maybe you should talk to someone."

"A shrink?" He shook his head. "That's not gonna happen. I climbed until I thought I'd drop. That's how I cope."

"What if it happens again?" I asked.

"I don't make a mistake twice."

"Good. If you do, I'll bring up my knee. Hard." I cupped his cheek and leaned toward him. "Call it behavior modification."

"Damn. That's brutal, Babe." He winced, then raised his brows and nodded. "Remember that. If this fucker gets near you, *remember that.*" He fingered my hair away from my face, tucked the strands behind my ear. "You're a drummer, lots of strength in your arms and legs. You can take him down."

Maybe I could take down the Sandmann, but I didn't want to think about that right now. Didn't want to picture myself under his control, his blade inching closer to my eye. I shuddered, rubbed my arms through the suit coat's sleeves and tried to shove the image from my mind.

"As for suspecting you." I trailed my fingertips along his temple. It felt good to touch him. His absence left a sad, empty spot in my life. "I followed the leads."

"They led you in the wrong direction." He slid his hand around my waist and caressed my back. "Done and over?"

I smiled at the childhood saying, and nodded. "It's odd the way you showed up. Why now?"

"You've got enough to deal with." He gave me that cocky grin. "Tell you what. When they catch this freak, I'll confess everything."

"To me, or your priest?"

He laughed, abruptly stopped and raised his brows. "Damn. Probably both."

"I'm warning you. I'm a little obsessive."

"A little?" His grin returned. "You've changed a lot. Good ways. You've got guts."

"They're wearing thin." I scanned the crowd made up of about three hundred of Borden's upper and middle class. Women in evening gowns accompanied by men in black ties. "Sandmann's out there. I can *feel* him."

"Sand Man?"

"He takes their eyes," I said, and mine became watery. "I'm almost out of time."

"Haven't the cops found anything?"

"This guy's good. He leaves very little trace." A tear trickled down my cheek. Quint caught it on his thumb. "Richard's connected. You, Richard and Claire. Sandmann's playing a game, and I can't figure out where I fit in."

The mirror. Who was I to Hoffmann? In the opera, there was a muse who deceived Hoffmann. Is that who I am? The deceptive muse who disguised herself as a man so she could manipulate him? I stared out at the sea of faces. Somewhere, Sandmann was waiting for me. I only wished I knew if he'd take me tonight— after midnight—or tomorrow. I needed a few more hours to figure out who Richard and Quint went to school with that had focused his obsession on my family.

But all that would have to wait. Steve stepped onstage and picked up his guitar. Robin joined him, and fine-tuned his bass.

Showtime.

Chapter 30

We'd been commissioned to play show tunes, blended with our regular, classic rock numbers, and keep it low-keyed. Oz was afraid we'd overpower the black-tie gala. I promised him we'd turn down the amps so people could talk, exchange ideas and write checks. We struck our first number, the theme song from *Rent*.

"*How do you document real life when real life's getting more like fiction each day?*" Quint sang.

An hour later, he peered back at me, frowned and shook his head.

"We're taking a break," he announced.

"Wait—We always play an hour and half the first set," I protested.

He returned his attention to the crowd. "Check out the silent auction items, folks. Your money's going to a good cause. We'll be back in fifteen."

He set his Fender on its chrome stand.

Steve followed suit, and glared at me. "*What the fuck was that?*"

"Lay off." Wiggling his fingers, Quint motioned me to join him.

"Straight beat? Is that all you've got?" Steve asked. "Where's your soul?"

"*Stand down*," Quint said. "You've got fifteen. Make use of them."

Steve stepped off the platform and sank into darkness beyond the stage lights. I propped my sticks against my snare's rim.

"Am I that bad?" I asked, peering up at Quint.

"Nah," he said. "You're doing fine."

"Liar." I stood and stretched. "Steve's right. My heart isn't in it. I'm playing mechanically, locked in cruise control."

And while I played, every thread of the case wove through my mind. I may have a good idea of the killer's game plan, but I still didn't know who he was. And the feeling that Sandmann was watching unnerved me.

If Sandmann kept to his pattern, he wouldn't kill me until tomorrow. Wednesday, someone would find me in a dumpster. I fought to draw a deep breath, imaging my body lying among discarded chicken bones and potato peelings.

"Rum and Coke?" Quint asked.

"Sure. A couple of those, and maybe I'll relax enough to enjoy the gig."

"You really shouldn't be here," Quint said. "What if he's out there?"

"He is. But I can't sit home waiting for this creep to kill me. If he's going to do it then *damn-it, bring it on.*"

"You don't mean that."

"Oh, I do. If the coward would face me, I'd have a fighting chance. But he doesn't. He hides and watches and makes my life miserable. How am I supposed to fight that?"

"You don't have to fight alone." Quint reached toward me again, his fingers wiggling in that impatient manner. "I could stay with you. If you want."

I didn't know what I wanted. I took his hand, and followed him off stage. We joined Morales at the table, where a drink waited for me.

"Waitress, waiter, whatever the fuck. *He* brought it." Morales gestured toward one of the Carnegie group, a feminine-looking man in a French maid's outfit complete with ruffled bloomers, heels and fishnet stockings.

"Oz, you sweetheart." I drank. The rum warmed me. Instead of sipping, I swallowed a mouthful.

Quint fixed his attention on Morales. "Sergeant."

"Rydell." Morales tore a strip off his longneck Budweiser's label.

"Any closer to finding this guy?" Quint asked.

"Thought I had him. Not sure I didn't."

"Don't waste time. There isn't much, if this four-day pattern is right."

To me, Morales said, "This divorce. How bad is it?"

I scooped up some Chex Mix, picked out the light-colored squares and popped them into my mouth. "What are you implying?"

"Divorce can get ugly," he said. "Who filed?"

"Ruth."

"How'd your dad feel about that?"

"He accepted it. That's a dead end," I said. "Ruth wanted out. Dad wasn't going to hang on if she wouldn't."

"Ever been any violence?"

"Are there records of domestic calls?" I shook my head. "We've already covered this. Besides, you know better than that. Dad doesn't have a violent bone in his body."

"Called my cousin. Texas Ranger. Going to check if Ruth's out there."

"Aunt Lenore would have called," I said. "Ruth's still here. The Sandmann has her. I don't understand the connection to my family, but I believe this involves all of us. Richard, too."

Morales tore another strip off the Budweiser label, tossed it onto the table where curled beside the water-filled bowl with glassy stones and floating candle. He turned his attention to Quint. "Deputy served you papers Saturday night. What's that about?"

"Private matter." Quint motioned toward the waitperson and muttered, "Seven and seven."

"Divorce?" Morales asked.

"Nope."

"Paternity suit?"

Quint uttered a sharp laugh.

"Wrongful death?"

Quint's grin died. He combed his fingers through his hair and scanned the crowd.

"Quint?" I touched his arm.

"Running from the past is a bitch, ain't it?" Morales lifted the longneck and drank.

"I don't need your suspicious-cop bullshit." Quint pushed away from the table. "This has nothing to do with Hannah. You're wasting time."

"Am I?"

"That's enough." I'd never wanted to slap Morales, but I did now. With less than a day left, his focus should be on catching the killer, not locking into a macho death match over a piece of property: *Me.* Another reason we weren't together. I tugged Quint's hand, urging him to sit.

"You said his story checked out," I reminded Morales.

"Your boyfriend has something to say. Don't you?" Morales kept his attention glued to Quint as though interrogating a druggie. "How'd you get into the Navy? Didn't think they took people with a criminal history."

"Record was expunged." Quint settled in the chair. "My grandfather's an admiral."

"Don't leave me out of the loop," I said. "What record? Is this why you came back?"

"One reason." His Adam's apple bobbed nervously. He looked from Morales to me. His chest heaved. "Okay, fine. I fucked up. *Is that what you want to hear?* Dad had that heart attack. Mom was dying inside. He left her in bad shape and *I fucked up.*"

"That's when you went to work at the station with Dad, right?" I asked.

"Before that." The wait-staff set Quint's seven and seven on the table. He picked up the glass and glared at Morales. "Emma Langtry held the mortgage on Mom's house. She threatened to foreclose."

"The fur queen?" I slid my hand over his.

"Yeah. She was diversifying her holdings, bought property and notes all over the Central Valley." He drank, poked the ice cubes, dunking them in the amber liquid. "When she found out about Dad's death, and the financial mess Mom was in, she offered me three hundred bucks to drive a van from Sacramento to Bakersfield. I figured I could help."

"You were a kid," I said.

"Yeah, I know, dumb and naive. I didn't know three hundred wouldn't have covered the utilities, much less the back payments on the house. But, at the time it seemed like a lot of money." He shrugged, lifted the glass and took another swallow. "The next thing I knew, cops were all over the place. They hauled me in. The district attorney worked a deal. I testified against Emma in exchange for a reduced sentence. One year in CYA," he added, referring to the California Youth Authority prison for juveniles. "Mr. Langtry stepped in, took the rap, and Emma walked."

"The year you spent in Los Gatos." I'd never doubted his story. He said he was with his grandmother, and I believed him. I had no reason not to.

"Yeah." He glared at Morales, obviously pissed that the truth had been pulled from him.

"Now her husband's dead, and she's coming after you." I tucked my fingers against his palm.

He gently squeezed my hand. "My uncle has the paperwork. He'll handle it. She doesn't have a case."

Morales planted his elbows on the chair's arms, steepled his fingers and tapped his lips in that contemplating manner.

"You didn't know," I said.

"Do now."

"That's dirty, even for you."

"That's an interrogation." He pushed away from the table and stalked toward the bar.

Sneaky bastard. Turning to Quint, I asked, "What's the other reason?"

"Why I came back?" He folded his arms on the table and leaned toward me. "You can't stand not knowing, can you?"

"I warned you. I'm obsessive."

Steve strode by and jabbed toward the stage.

"Break's over." Quint gave me that cocky grin, and followed Steve.

I shoved away from the table and hurried after them. Damn-it. So close. But I'd get the reason out of Quint before the night was over.

Chapter 31

Second set. One more to go, and I wished this night were over. I could think of better uses for my time, like finding Ruth and digging up leads on Sandmann. Anything to stop him before he came for me. We struck up a *Guess Who* number from the Sixties, "These Eyes."

"Oh, these eyes," I muttered, settling into a standard, double-on-third beat: *bass, snare, bass-bass-snare.*

Green eyes.

Hollow eyes.

Dead eyes.

Cold dampness broke out across my forehead. The amber shells of my kit slid in and out of focus. I shook my head, tripped up, regained the beat and dropped a stick. Quickly, I pulled another from the leather bag and worked back into the rhythm.

My arms felt heavy. I lost the tempo. For a moment, we sounded like that old garage band we'd been years ago, struggling to find its niche. We wrapped up the number. The cold dampness turned to perspiration, which drizzled down my temples. I glanced at the water bottle: empty.

"Quint?" I said, but my voice fizzled out and he didn't hear me. I tossed my stick, striking him square between the shoulder blades. He spun around.

"Steve. Go solo." Quint pulled the Fender's strap over his head, set the guitar in its stand and came around my drums. He helped me off stage.

"Don't know what's wrong," I said.

"How much did you drink?"

"I didn't finish the one Oz sent. Feel like I'm going to fall." I could see clearly, understand what I saw, but viewed the world through a long, dark tunnel.

Quint lowered me into the chair beside Morales. "Why aren't you looking for this guy?"

"Because he's here." Morales tipped the longneck and drank.

"Christ, I told you it's not me."

"Know that." Morales drank again. "But he's here."

"Morales is right." I propped my elbows on the table and cradled my aching head. Every sensation seemed heightened. I could almost feel threads of air touch my face. I stared at the glass. Ice had melted. Dark strands of Coke wove through the water. "I think he drugged me."

"Babe—Your eyes," Quint said. "There dilated, I can barely see green. I'm taking you to the hospital."

"I'm not going anywhere." Again, the creepy feeling someone was watching washed over me. I glanced over my shoulder. "It'll wear off. And I'm in a room with more than three hundred people. I'm staying right here."

"Safety in numbers." Morales reached for the glass, hesitated, and glanced around the room. "Too many hands touched it. No way we'll get prints."

Maybe the waitperson knew where it came from. I started to voice my thoughts when Morales headed toward the bar.

As a waiter passed, Quint snagged a bottle of water off the tray. He slid the glass bowl aside, grabbed the cloth from underneath, soaked it and then stroked my forehead. Cold. God that felt good. Heat ebbed from my limbs. I took the cloth and ran it across the back of my neck. Quint scanned the room, and waved someone down. I followed his gaze. Tolson stood and hurried toward us.

"Let me take you home," Quint offered again. "I'll stay with you. No one will get you. I promise."

"Give me a few minutes. I'll be fine." I took the bottle from him, re-wet the cloth and bathed my throat. Cold water trickled into the valley between my breasts. "I'm not drinking anything that isn't sealed."

"Good plan." He stood as Tolson approached. "She's been drugged."

"What? How?" Tolson shifted his attention from Quint to me, and slid onto the seat Quint had abandoned. Gently gripping my chin, Tolson tilted my head toward the light spilling from the bar. Then he checked my pulse, which I already knew had weakened. "We should get you to the hospital."

"I agree," Quint said. "Come on. I'll drive you."

"Ladies room," I said. The room spun like a tilt-a-whirl, and I really wanted to get off.

"I'll help you," Tolson offered, and gripped my elbow. He led me toward the back of the building. Oz, sporting his snug-fitting tuxedo and pink satin bow tie, joined us and gestured toward the ladies room next to the bar.

"Sorry. Never been in here," Tolson said.

Quint and Morales jogged around tables and met us in the hall between *His* and *Hers*. Quint reached for me, but Oz slid his arm around my waist, placing himself between Quint and me.

"Oh no you don't, Buster. You're not going in there. Come on sweetie," he said, guiding me toward the ladies room. "Really, honey. You should take it easy on the hard stuff."

Inside the brightly lit room stuffed with cloying scents of roses, he helped me out of my blazer. Then he shoved me into a chair, dosed paper towels with cold water and ordered me to hang my head between my knees. I did, and dizziness washed over me.

"I'm not drunk," I insisted.

"It's okay, happens to the best of us. But really, girlfriend, save it for when you're not getting paid to play."

"Someone drugged me." I straightened too quickly, and almost slid off the chair. "Didn't even finish the one you sent."

"One what?"

"Rum and Coke."

"Oh sweetie, I didn't send you a drink." His hand fluttered to his throat. "You think it was the Sandmann?"

I nodded, slowly, not wanting to send my head into another spin.

"He's *here?* Oh—Oh, no." Oz shuffled like a toddler who needed to pee. "What are we going to do?"

"Calm down." I took the towels from him, and draped them over the back of my neck. "I knew he'd show up. Just wish the coward would let me know who he is."

"How did he drug you?"

"He knows I drink rum and Coke." I leaned my head against the wall and stared at the water-stained ceiling. "He seems to know a lot about me."

"Maybe we should get you to the hospital, get your stomach pumped out or something," Oz suggested. "That's what they do, isn't it?"

I waved the suggestion aside. "I'll get through tonight." Alive, I almost added. Time was running out. Sandmann's timeline dictated he would take me by daybreak, and kill me within twenty-four hours.

"I've got to figure this out." Right. How would I do that? Walk around and try to spot someone from high school almost thirteen years ago? Figure out who knew my family, Quint, and Claire? Hell, even I didn't look the same as I had in high school. I could walk right past someone from my gym class and never know it.

Morales had every cop on the force either searching for Ruth, guarding Dad, or right here, in and around the building. Maybe I should leave, alone, trust them to watch and follow and catch the bastard. Although it might work, the thought terrified me—what if he's someone so obvious they didn't suspect him and let him go?

"I gotta get back out there." I gripped the edge of the sink and stood.

"Sure you don't want me to take you someplace?"

"Positive."

Without Dobbs to fill in, the number—"*Pinball Wizard*" from *Tommy*—sounded flat. Quint and Morales met us in the hall. Tolson had returned to his table, now sat with his arm draped around Patty Newburg's bare shoulders.

Scanning the sea of black suits and high-dollar gowns, I caught a bright flash from our community reporter, Vi's metallic purple dress, cinched tightly around her ample waist. Matching feathers bobbed above her crown of tight, red curls. She sat at a table reserved for Gazette employees between her husband and Grigsby.

Grigsby pushed his empty glass against half a dozen others near the candle bowl. His wife, Diana, a blond-haired, blue-eyed beauty, reddened with embarrassment.

Two tables away, across from Patty and Tolson, Kurkis sat with his third wife. Or was it his forth? I couldn't keep track.

At the cop's table, Holmes hooked his finger inside his starched collar, tugged and shifted uncomfortably. Beside him, his mother chatted with Badorini's wife while the detective poured Mountain Dew over ice.

Carley, her black shimmering curls and trim fitting, cream-colored gown reflecting the red and blue lights, crossed to our table. I hadn't spoken to her since the day of Christina Pardini's autopsy.

"I have an answer to your question," she said, and I was grateful for her discretion. "Yes. Everything was *intact.*"

"Thanks, Carley." Although I knew Sandmann was watching me, anticipating the moment he would pluck out my eyes, a small measure of relief washed over me. The killer hadn't taken Richard's eyes.

"Always glad to help." She strolled back to a table near the silent auction items.

"What's that about?" Quint asked.

"A friend helping a friend," I said.

On stage, the band shifted gears and launched into a *Stones* hit from their Sticky Fingers album, *"Wild Horses."*

Quint brought more water. By the time the band took its next break I'd recovered for the most part. I still felt light headed, but it wouldn't keep me from finishing the gig.

Gripping my sticks, I kept to the standard rock beat. Kept it safe. Kept it simple so I wouldn't goof up again. The stage lights weren't so bright that I couldn't see most of the faces in the crowd. There were few I either didn't know or hadn't met. I stared at one, then another, willing them to make some move, look at me a certain way, anything that would mark them as a suspect. They laughed, talked, wrote checks, drank. So normal, so calm, I wanted to scream.

An hour later, we stopped for the countdown to midnight. I propped my sticks on the snare, stood and stretched—my body ached, no doubt a result of the drug. Quint looked at me with those soft, caramel-colored eyes. Giving me that cocky grin, he abandoned his guitar, came around my kit, pulled me against him and brushed his warm lips over mine.

"Gonna be a good year, Babe."

"Sure hope so," I whispered, and clung to him. Balloons, confetti and Juan's keyboard solo of *Auld Lang Syne* filled the air.

"It'll be over soon," Quint said, his lips inches from my ear.

Soon. Yes. I was hours from a different kind of count down, and wanted desperately to put an end to that one, too. I returned to my throne. We ran through a *Beatles* tune—*"Across the Universe"*— from the musical of the same name. By one o'clock, only a couple dozen people remained. Although we were commissioned to play until two, Oz let us off early.

An hour later, gear packed into the van, I slid my arms around Quint, propped my chin against his chest and peered up at him.

"You made it, Babe," he said.

"But it's after midnight. I've crossed into my last day."

"He won't get you." Quint pulled me closer, held me tightly. "Let me come home with you."

"Denny's?" Steve suggested.

Juan slid the van's door closed. "I'm in."

"You up for it?" Quint smoothed my hair.

"You go. Morales is taking me home." Beneath the security lamp's glow, he slouched against his Bronco.

"Come home with me," Quint suggested. "I'll stay awake tonight. No one will get near you."

"You're going to protect me?" I asked, and smiled up at him.

"I can't leave knowing this fuck is after you." He tightened his hold. I rested my head against his chest, listened to the steady rhythm of his heart.

"Morales is staying with me the next twenty-four hours," I said. "We have to catch this guy. This has to end."

"Christ," Quint muttered, and raked his fingers through his hair. He shifted his weight and glanced at Morales. "I'm not comfortable with that."

"Morales staying with me?"

"Not being there when this guy comes for you."

"Anyone around me is at risk," I said. "I'll sleep better knowing you're not a target."

"I'll sleep better knowing this guy's dead." Quint tilted my head back, and met my gaze. "I'll do whatever you want, Babe."

"Go home."

He nodded, but the tightness of his jaw told me he wasn't happy with my decision. "I'll stop by early tomorrow. We'll visit your dad."

"I'll be there," I whispered, hoping to God those words proved true. I cupped his cheek, kissed his lips, warm and tasting of whiskey. Then I joined Morales and headed home. Neither of us spoke. We both knew I'd run out of time.

Chapter 32

The mind-door shook on its hinges, slammed in its frame and made a series of small, explosive-like sounds. He clamped his hands over his ears, but that blocked the sound inside his head, making it louder.

The sensation—that the other world was trying to suck him in—returned. It pulled at him with hot cables of energy that bore into his gut. That burning in the pit of his stomach left him sick and more than a little scared. Frightened because he *wanted* to go back in there, click himself over, flip the switch.

But what if he couldn't get out?

He'd fuck up everything and miss his chance to get Hannah.

If he missed her again, he'd never bring Claire back.

His ear hurt. Tilting his head, he rubbed his ear against his shoulder. The clothes hanger that poked him didn't help. He shoved it further down the rack, and sat on a box. It sagged beneath his weight. The hem of a shirt brushed his shoulder. He clutched the material, brought it to his nose and breathed deeply. Fresh. Clean. Then he picked up her shoe, black with stiletto heel, and stroked the soft leather the way he imagined himself stroking her.

Setting the heel aside, he shifted against the back of the closet and peered through the narrow gap in the door. Only a quarter inch wide, too narrow for Hannah to notice.

It wouldn't be fair if he lost everything now. He'd worked so hard. He had to keep the mind door closed, keep the switch off just a little longer.

He spied the yearbook on the closet floor, picked it up and leafed through the glossy pages. This had been his junior year. Even then, Richard had captured all the attention. But he didn't care. Richard wasn't a threat anymore. He'd seen to that. He wouldn't fade into the background and go unnoticed like he had through high school. Wouldn't go unnoticed like he had in the service, either. Now, everyone would know him. Everyone would remember him. Everyone would see the miracle he'd performed.

It wasn't revenge. It was his *destiny*.

The thought of being so close to fulfilling that role sent a hot rush through his groin. All those years ago, when Mom played the music and told him the stories, he recognized his destiny. When he saw Claire in that short skirt, those perky breasts poking against the fabric of her Borden Crows uniform, he'd found that destiny.

Then Richard showed up.

It had taken awhile, but he'd fixed that spotlight-hogging bastard. Fixed him real good. Gave him a fix he'd never forget.

A grin split his face.

He shoved Richard from his mind, closed his eyes and focused on Claire. He could remember the first time he saw her in that uniform with her short skirt, and oh how he'd wanted to reach underneath it, rub his fingers inside her. Make her wet. Make her want him. Make her *scream*.

While on leave from the service, he found her again. Then, it wasn't a dream. She was real, so hot and soft. At first he'd had trouble maintaining an erection, but she didn't laugh at him like the others. She helped him, touched him, showed him she loved him and then he rode her all night.

He shifted uncomfortably. That's what he wanted. A hot, wild ride. He peeked through the gap in the closet door at the rumpled bed, the sweatpants and tank top thrown over the pillow.

Taking Hannah wouldn't be cheating. There was a part of Claire inside Hannah, the last fragment of her soul. He'd just close his eyes and pretend it was Claire.

One night. That wouldn't hurt anything. Just one hard fuck, and Hannah was a woman who needed fucking. Needed to be put in her place. Needed a man to show her she wasn't any better than her dead brother.

His jeans tightened around his crotch. He sucked in air, blew a hard stream, imagined his mind as a blackboard that had been wiped clean. No pictures. No words. Not a single streak of chalk.

"Dah, dah-dah, da dah-dah da dah, dah dee-dee-dee, dee dee-dum," he whispered, a full orchestra version of the *Barcarolle* filling his mind in waves so intense, it rocked his body.

My being is consumed with a sweet burning fire.

He'd left a message for Hannah. It was important she understood. She had to give up the last piece of Claire's soul willingly, just as the other women had once they understood. They hadn't exactly *said* they did, but he could see it in their eyes.

Green eyes. His favorite color.

In the distance, a car engine grew louder then died. A door opened, closed, followed by another. Then tumblers clanked in the deadbolt downstairs.

He set the yearbook aside, leaned back and stared at the bed.

*   *   *

Oz arrived shortly after Morales brought me home. Although we all knew it, no one mentioned the fact that Sandmann would come tonight. I wished I'd taken up Quint's offer to stay. But it was awkward at the club. It would be considerably worse if both he and Morales stayed in my home.

I rummaged in the fridge, found a bottle of Mocha Starbucks and twisted the cap. Oz must have opened it earlier, and changed his mind again: The plastic had been removed, and opening it lacked the usual popping sound.

Did I want coffee? Or did I want to sleep? I offered the Starbucks to Morales.

"Great. Can use some fuckin' caffeine." He took the bottle and retreated to the living room. "Gonna be a long night."

After prying off my shoes I joined him and unwound with a glass of Merlot. We watched thirty minutes of a movie I couldn't catch the gist of. At a quarter of three, I poured a second dose of wine and took it upstairs.

The computer screen cast ghostly light over the keyboard. I tossed my suit coat on the overstuffed chair, settled at the desk and pulled my foot onto the seat.

On the screen was Offenbach's *The Tales of Hoffmann: The Story of the Opera.*

Yawning, I grabbed a legal pad and found a pen. Then I read. The most famous piece from the opera was *Barcarolle,* performed in the third act.

I scrolled down to the prologue synopsis. Hoffmann's muse wanted to reconnect him with his gift of poetry. To do so, she turned herself into a man to guide him. But Hoffman was preoccupied over his lost love, Stella. A letter and key to the Prima Donna's dressing room, intended for Hoffman, were intercepted by the first of three incarnations of evil.

"That's right. I remember now." I flipped to the notes I'd made earlier. The elements of evil were really the dark side of Hoffman himself. *Is that who I'm up against? A man with three evil personalities?* I shivered and rubbed my arms. Then I scampered across the room and turned on the bedside lamp, wishing I'd had a light in the ceiling fan. The more light the better. The room's shadows unnerved me.

I returned to the computer, scanned the text and found Act One. My gaze locked on the name Olympia, who sang another of the opera's famous numbers, *Les Oiseaux Dans La Charmille*.

Sipping the wine, I let it pool on my tongue and continued reading. Evil, furious with Olympia's creator, tore her apart.

Chills rippled my spine. The feeling of being watched returned. I glanced around the room. *Calm down, girl. Getting the jitters.* But Olympia being torn apart too closely resembled De La Cruz in the duffel bag.

The robot. Crushed under Mr. De La Cruz's foot. The tiny scratches *OLYN*. Was the N an M? Were they the letters revealing that the robot—Olympia—was De La Cruz?

I sipped again, and set the glass on the phone book. Hoffman's second love, Antonia, was the opera singer like Christina. Carley's words rang hollow in my head—the bruises, severing Christina's voice forever. I absently stroked my neck.

In this act, Evil was a doctor with mystical powers who showed Antonia an image of her mother, inducing her to sing herself to death. The caduceus connection. But where was the mirror? Where did I fit in?

Grasping the wine glass' fragile stem, I stared at the words *Act Four*.

I reached to shut down the computer.

"Can't do that," I muttered. "Got to know. Only hours left before Sandmann's deadline, I need to know how to stop him."

On the screen, I caught a single word that suddenly seemed larger and darker than the others: *Mirror*.

"Evil bribed Giulietta with a diamond to steal Hoffmann's reflection, and trap it in a mirror." Which explained why he smashed mine.

Gripping the glass in both hands, I finished off the wine. It settled uneasily in my stomach. I realized I was gasping, and forced myself to take slow, deep breaths.

Finally, I looked back at the story. Out of love, Hoffmann willingly gave up his reflection only to discover Giulietta didn't love him at all. The Muse prepared poison to kill Evil, but Giulietta drank it and died in Hoffmann's arms.

The drink at the Gala. How did he think he'd get me out of there? Or didn't he realize cops would stake out the place? I shoved the thoughts aside and continued reading.

The three loves of Hoffman's life were all facets of Stella, as though she'd been fragmented. In the end, they all came together, in Stella, when she returned to Hoffmann.

I punched off the computer. The screen flickered and went dark. I hurried to the bathroom and flipped on the light, sending a rectangle patch of yellow across the bed. Now I knew what and why. But I still didn't know whom.

I twisted on the shower and let the water warm while I undressed and removed my contacts. I pulled sweat pants and a tank top from the dresser, tossed them on the bed and returned to the bathroom.

I stepped beneath the stinging spray. Heat seeped into my aching muscles. Steam clouded around me. Closing my eyes, I focused on the thrum of water beating against the tub. I scrubbed until the water ran cold.

Pushing back the curtain, I stepped from the tub and realized I'd forgotten to get a clean towel from the linen closet. I glanced at the damp one hanging from the rack, considered slipping into the hall, but Morales was on alert mode. I didn't want to get caught naked.

Damp would have to do. I grabbed the towel, mopped water from my body, tossed the cloth onto the floor and soaked up the trail I'd left on the linoleum.

Putting on my glasses, I glanced into the bedroom. Dark. I'd left the lamp on. Burned out? I searched my memory for when I'd last changed the bulb, and couldn't remember.

I padded across the carpet, slipped into my underwear and sweats, pulled the tank top over my head and tugged my wet hair from the neckline.

Behind me, a door slid in its track. I froze. Blood thrummed in my temples. I stepped toward the bedroom door, twisted the knob. The closet slid again, slowly, a faint hissing sound like air escaping a balloon.

Chapter 33

Sandmann was in my closet. I had to get downstairs and alert Morales. Perspiration dampened my skin. I opened my bedroom door and stepped into the hallway. I didn't want him chasing me. If I kept my cool, maybe he wouldn't realize I knew he was there.

If I kept my cool, I might get into Oz's room and grab the stun gun between his mattresses.

If. I. Kept. My. Cool.

My arm trembled as I pushed the door closed behind me. I darted into Oz's room, reached for the bed and stopped.

Bluish light streamed through the bedroom window. My baseball bat, wet and glistening, lay on the bedspread. The pillow beneath Oz's head had gone dark with blood.

Clamping my hand over my mouth, I choked back a scream. No, not Oz—*Please not Oz*. Where was Morales? Hadn't he heard Oz scream?

I hadn't. Maybe Oz didn't have time to cry out. I touched his neck to check his pulse. My fingers slid on the warm blood.

A slight click as my bedroom door opened. I jerked my hand away from Oz, and peered over my shoulder. Movement in the hallway behind me.

Kneeling, I rammed my hand between the mattresses, felt the metal prongs and yanked out the stun gun. A handheld device. I'd have to get close enough to lay it against Sandmann's skin, and I didn't want to get that close.

I gripped the gun and slowly turned around. A long shadow jittered in the hall, stretched across the wall by the stairs. He sank back into my room.

I had to reach Morales.

I considered screaming, but what if Sandmann got to me first? The only way out was downstairs, past my bedroom door.

I crossed the hall. The yawning black mouth of my doorway seemed to shift and stir with life. I inched past it and bolted downstairs. Once I reached the entryway, I let loose a long, shrill cry and dashed into the living room.

Morales lay on the recliner. The Starbucks bottle had slipped from his fingers, and now lay on the floor. A splotch darkened the carpet where coffee leaked out.

"Morales?" I gripped his shoulders, shook him, glanced at the staircase and shook him again. "Damn-it Morales, *wake up*."

His chest rose and fell with shallow breaths. I pried one eyelid open. Only a faint ring of brown circled his enlarged pupil. Drugged.

I stared at the empty coffee bottle, probably meant for me. Muffled steps pounded the floor. Raising the stun gun, I spun around.

A dark shape bolted toward me. I reached out, press the weapon's twin prongs against the man's chest, and depressed the button. Nothing. *Dead.*

"*No,*" I screamed.

Morales' gun. I reached for the Glock holstered at his side. The snap—*undo the snap, damn it*. I fumbled with the strip of leather securing the gun, and gripped the semi-automatic in both hands. I swung around.

The dark shape darted across the room. Arm raised, he caught me across the side of my head. White bolts of pain exploded

behind my eyes. I fired blindly, the deafening crack ringing
hollow in my ears.

Sharp steel bore into my arm. Heat spread through my
shoulder and neck. I sagged as my world went black.

*   *   *

He had drugged Hannah only enough to get her out of the
house without a struggle. Soon, she'd come around. He wanted
her lucid when he fucked her. Wouldn't be any fun unless she
knew what was going on.

That wild grin split his face. Cradling her to his chest, he
could feel life pulse inside her. Those warm, soft threads of life
enveloped him in a golden cocoon.

He stepped into the theater, pressed his lips to her temple,
kissed away the pain where he'd hit her. He hadn't wanted to.
He'd been forced to. He'd never intentionally hurt her. He loved
the part of her that was Claire.

The mind-door bulged in his brain. Pressure built up and
burst open. The other world reached out, grabbed him and swept
him inside.

The switch clicked on.

The music played. His world came alive with sounds of
Hoffmann's tales. Of his love, his desire to win over Stella, the
Prima Donna, the beautiful woman full of youth, music and
sensual desire.

Oh how he loved her.

The wooden stage, moments ago weathered and decayed,
shifted to a warm, polished shine. The moth-eaten curtains went
from drab to rich, heavy drapes. Rows of seats, threadbare and
with springs exposed, covered themselves over the way he

imagined flesh-eating bacteria would consume a body, only in reverse.

Soft, undulating sounds of *Barcarolle* drifted on the air. Candlelight flickered from gold-plated sconces high on the walls. Their glow cast Hannah in warm hues. Color returned to her cheeks.

He touched his lips to her cool flesh. Now, the life rushed through her and into him, burning his veins, heightening his senses like never before—his flesh tingled with the fresh scent of her soap, the dampness of her hair, and his mouth filled with the acrid taste of her fear.

Oh the power.

He breathed deeply. The air caressed his lungs like silk. It worked. He'd successfully brought her into his world.

He carried her across the pristine stage to the dressing room, no longer drab and with chunks of sheetrock missing. Everything had repaired itself. The reverse mitosis had sutured the walls and floor. Ancient fixtures cast amber light through the room.

The music touched him with luminous sparks of pure joy.

He laid her on the floor, and pushed her wet, tangled hair away from her face. An angry red mark ran from her temple to her chin, and he wondered where it had come from. He stretched out over her, slid his fingers beneath the waistband of her sweats and stroked her soft skin.

Chapter 34

The stench of stale urine mingled with odors of moldy wood. The air was dingy and thick with dampness. Nicotine-yellow light flickered through the room. The floor was spongy beneath me, and somewhere in my drug-fogged mind I knew he'd brought me to the opera house.

Fingers, like feet on a rat, scurried across my stomach, reached under my shirt, gripped my breast in a rough, impatient manner. A cold shudder ripped through me.

He pinned my arms above my head. I tried to roll away but only rocked and sagged back to the floor. The drug was wearing off, though. He must have given me a mild dose. Each time I tried, I could move with a bit more strength.

A glittery spark swayed before the dark shape of a man. I'd lost my glasses, so I squinted, forced my vision to focus. The spark solidified into a white-gold band suspended from a thin chain.

Music swelled around me, first soft, then deep. Repetitions of sound blended and grew louder, faster. Opera.

Then I remembered. *Barcarolle.*

And *Les Oiseaux Dans La Charmille.*

I stared at the ring. It swayed as the man shifted against me, reached down and fumbled with his belt. More words flowed through my head: *Pleure pour deux beaux yeux.*

Tolson. He said he'd come from Sacramento. Morales said Stockton.

Claire died in Stockton.

Tolson unbuckled his belt, unzipped his trousers with a ripping sound.

"Oh God." The words burned my throat. Hot adrenaline surged through me, and the drug-induced paralysis ebbed from my limbs. I bucked beneath Tolson. "Stop—No, *don't do this.*"

His weight bore down on me. He covered my mouth with his, hard, bruising my lips. A strangled cry bubbled in my throat. He pulled away and looked down at me. A crazed grin cracked his face. Then he dropped on me. His hot breath steamed against my neck.

I bucked again. I had to unbalance him, had to get him off, get him off of me, oh God, *"Get off of me."*

I saw him clearly then, and the madness in his eyes terrified me more than the thought of him raping me. Those eyes had gone stone cold and lifeless.

"Going to fuck you." He tightened his grip on my wrists. Pain burned through my arms. "Going to make you *scream.*"

Think, damn-it *think*. The opera house. A junkie's den. I frantically searched for anything I could use as a weapon. Then I saw someone leaning against the torn plasterboard, her eyes wide. Ruth.

"Help me," I pleaded. "Oh please Ruth—*Stop him.*"

She crawled into a shadowed corner and sagged to the floor. Black engulfed her eyes.

"She's next." He rammed his fist into my pants, forced his fingers between my thighs and rubbed. Hard. Even with the drugged-induced numbness that filled my body, I felt the pain tear through me.

Think—got to think—got to . . .

Enter his world.

Oh, God. His world was *crazy* and I couldn't go there. My head hurt and my mind felt sluggish, like a snail someone doused with salt.

Enter his world. Richard's presence, that ghost whisper I'd felt in this same room four days ago, filled my chest.

Oh, shut the hell up, I mentally screamed at Richard. *Shut up and get out of my head.*

But his voice wouldn't leave. He was right. I had to step into Tolson's world of madness, join him on the other side. Otherwise, I'd die.

Do it, just do it, just—

I clenched my teeth, and drew several deep breaths.

"Not like this," I shouted, breathing hard. My heart slammed against my ribs. "Not supposed to be like this." What was his name? *What the hell was his first name?* "Eddie. You loved me once, didn't you? And I loved you?"

Tolson froze. He pulled his hand free. I couldn't see his features clearly, but enough to know my reaction startled him.

"Don't f-*fuck me.*" I had to steady my voice, couldn't let him know my fear—steady— "*Make love to me.*"

"You're not—Not supposed to—" He leaned back, rose to his knees, and straddled my hips.

"I want to thank you for your reflection." I swallowed over the knot in my throat. "It was in the mirror, wasn't it? The one you left in my car?"

He tilted his head in confusion.

"Such a thoughtful gift. You wouldn't do that for anyone you didn't love."

"Claire?" He relaxed his grip.

"That's right, Eddie. It's me. Claire."

He shook his head. "You're not . . ."

"Yes I am." Softening my tone, I added, "I was wrong to leave you. I won't do it again." I glanced at the chain around his neck. "That's my wedding ring, isn't it?"

He fingered the white-gold band. Slowly, he nodded.

"May I have it?"

With a sharp tug, he broke the chain, let it slip through the ring and drop to the floor. He released my arms, pulled my left hand toward him and slid the band over my finger.

I brought up my knee, hard and fast, and caught Tolson in the crotch. His face, once filled with confusion, now tightened in pain and rage.

He clutched his balls and collapsed against me. Then he leaned his head back and roared; "Not supposed to do that— you're supposed to *scream*, bitch, *fucking scream*."

I shoved him off, rolled over, and struck the wall. Pain flared in my back. I rose to my hands and knees and looked at him, writhing on the floor. The litter of syringes, some still clinging to their needles, were pale yellowish lines in my crippled vision. I ran my hand across the floor. Something pricked my finger, and I yanked it away. I tried again, and slowly curled my hand around the hard plastic shaft. Then I flipped over, pushed up, stood on wobbly legs and froze.

Tolson had Ruth by her hair. He yanked her head back, exposing her neck. A thin cry escaped her, a sound that tore at my heart. He stroked her cheek with a scalpel, and then raised it to her eye.

"You fuck with me, I fuck with your mother."

"Oh no." A sob clenched my throat. "No, you don't want to do that, *please* don't."

The shelf behind him held three mason jars with black words on fruit-trimmed canning labels. Long ago I'd learned to recognize shapes of letters without my glasses, and the words I saw made my blood run cold: Olympia. Antonia. Giulietta.

Inside two jars, eyes—slightly flattened, milky and smaller than the size of a quarter—nestled against the bottom. The third jar was empty.

I dropped, which was easy given the sedative flowing through my veins. Dropped to my knees and stared at the knife clutched in Tolson's hand.

I wanted to lunge at him, but if I moved too quickly, if I startled him, he'd plunge that blade into Ruth's eye.

"Come away from her." My calm tone shocked me. I looked at Ruth, nothing more than a heap in the corner. I curled my fingers around the syringe. "She's not the one you need."

"I don't care which goes first. One will die. The other will stay with me forever. It doesn't matter."

"It does." I licked my lips, glanced at Ruth, and back at him. "She's worthless. What you're looking for isn't in her. It's here," I said, and poked my thumb to my chest. "What you're looking for is here."

He chuckled. "You're so much like him." The blade flicked closer to Ruth's eye, away, toward it again and touched her cheekbone. Blood darkened her creamy flesh. "He tried to talk his way out of it, too. But he had to die. Claire wasn't meant for him."

"Richard," I whispered.

Tolson's chuckle bubbled into laughter.

I couldn't breathe. My chest tightened, crushing the air from my lungs. "You killed Richard? Why? *Why did you take him from me?*"

Tolson raised a syringe filled with a murky fluid. On the exposed two-by-four, where sheetrock had rotted away, was a soft candle, globs of wax at its base, next to a spoon.

"Going to send you on a trip," he said. "Same trip I sent your brother on. Everybody loved him." Tolson waved the needle in the air. "Everybody. But not Claire. *She loved me.*"

When he killed Richard, he killed my family. He killed my best friend. My mind went numb. Then hot rage filled me and my body trembled.

I tightened my grip on the syringe. I had never wanted to kill anyone, didn't know what it felt like until now. And I didn't like the feeling. But if I didn't do something fast, he would kill Ruth. I couldn't let that happen.

If I could cripple Tolson long enough, maybe we could get away. But that thought nestled in my mind like a dirty secret. I'd have to do much more than hurt him. I had to kill him.

A drummer. Strong arms. Strong legs. And Quint's voice—*If he ever gets near you . . .*

I shot toward him and plunged the needle into his neck. His eyes widened. Growling noises escaped his throat. Then he shook with uncontrollable fury.

"*Bitch,*" he spat.

Before I could lean away he brought the blade up, sliced the tender flesh of my bicep. Stinging pain tore through my arm. Blood wove a hot trail over my elbow. I stumbled toward the bathroom, struck the doorframe. The knife whooshed through the air.

I backed into the cramped room, dropped and rolled beneath the sink. My head struck the rusty pipe, dislodging it from the wall. I yanked the pipe free. The curved part crumbled in my hands. I gripped the other half, still attached to the sink, and frantically worked it back and forth.

Tolson lurched into the bathroom and zeroed in on me. He raised the scalpel and sliced the air inches from my face. Then he reached below the sink, grabbed my leg, twisted and yanked. Bone snapped. Blinding hot agony flooded through me.

"Oh God," I screamed, and latched onto the pipe. The searing pain in my leg turned cold, like ice dumped into a pot of boiling water.

He grabbed my ankle and pulled me from under the sink.

The pipe broke free. The tension between us broke, too, sending Tolson careening backward. He struck the tub and flipped over the rim.

Swing, Richard screamed in my mind, *God-damn-it swing.*

I cracked the pipe over Tolson's head. The blade slipped from his fingers, clattered to the floor and skittered beneath the tub.

I dove for the knife.

Chapter 35

Movement behind me. I spun around, and saw Ruth just beyond the doorway. Frantically, I reached beneath the tub. The blade sliced my fingers. I jerked my hand back as Ruth stepped toward me.

"Get out of here," I screamed.

She gripped the doorframe. Her eyes widened in fear.

"*Get the hell out of here.*"

Fingers clutched my throat, cutting off my air. I searched for the knife, but couldn't reach it. Tolson grabbed my hair, slammed my head against the tub. Sparks exploded behind my tightly closed eyes.

Then he pulled me over the rim, into the basin, rammed his knee against my chest and pinned me down. Shifting his weight, he reached out, scratched the floor, searching for the blade.

As he leaned over, the pressure on my chest eased. One chance. I had only one chance, and please-oh-*please* let it count. If he found the knife, he'd kill me.

I planted my palms against the layer of rust and grime at the bottom of the tub, and used every ounce of strength I had to thrust upward, hoping to unbalance him enough to get away. He careened from the tub, stumbled back. His breath became a string of harsh growls.

I gripped the tub's rim, rolled over the edge and slammed to the floor. Pain burned through my leg. I bit my lip, trapping a scream inside. Reaching beneath the tub, my fingertips touched the scalpel.

Footfalls slapped the ground. I turned just as Tolson lunged at me.

I curled my hand around the blade, sat up and slashed blindly. The knife caught. A wet, black line spread across his neck. Thin at first. Then it grew thicker. The line of blood seemed to draw itself from below his left ear and across the front of his throat.

Fury drained from his face. He touched his neck and frowned. Then he growled, leaned his head back and unleashed a long, primal scream that chilled me to my very core. The gash in his neck widened. He sagged to his knees and stared at me with a pleading look that said I could stop this, I could make it all go away. His eyes glazed over and he crumbled in a heap.

My fingers locked on the scalpel. Faint light caught the smear of blood on its blade. My arm shook uncontrollably.

Ruth slid to her knees. Shifting her attention between Tolson and me, she crawled across the cracked linoleum. She wrapped her hands around mine, forced my fingers open. The scalpel fell and skittered back beneath the tub.

"Is he dead?" I asked.

"You did what you had to do," she said, her breath hitching. "Only what you had to do."

I stared at the blood on my hand. The numbness deepened, and I went cold inside. *"Is he dead?"*

"Yes." Her voice sounded tinny and far away.

"I killed him." My own voice touched my ears with a hollow, dead strangeness I couldn't recognize. "I killed . . ."

"You had to." She gripped my face and forced me to look at her. "Hannah. Listen to me. You had to."

She was right. And I'd be telling myself that every day for the rest of my life.

I yanked Tolson's ring from my finger and hurled it. The wedding band struck him, rolled down his chest and clinked to the floor. I clutched Ruth's blouse in both fists, buried my face against her shoulder and wept.

*   *   *

The cast from my knee down made it difficult to relax in the bath. Lying in the tub unnerved me, too—I'd much rather take a shower. But fiberglass and water didn't mix, and that casing held a bone together so it could mend. Every time I closed my eyes, I could feel Tolson's breath on my neck, his knee against my chest. I shivered despite the hot water.

I tottered on the cusp of depression; a black void where I felt numb and my thoughts stalled. I couldn't sleep without seeing Tolson, syringe clutched in his fist, come after me. Without seeing that bloody grin widen across his neck. I couldn't dream without feeling the dampness of the opera house close in on me. Maybe I'd stop by the station and visit Morales, go into the office although I'd been placed on three weeks medical leave. Work would make me feel normal again, help me move forward and help the memories fade.

From the hallway, voices rose in anger. Oz and Ruth battled over everything—how to do laundry, how to cook, how to dust properly. Now, they argued over what was best for me. I wished I'd thought to get my Walkman, plug in Petty and block them out. This had been going on for five days.

"She needs to get out of here," Oz said. "Fresh air, visit friends—Where is Quint? Why hasn't he come by to see her?"

"She needs rest," Ruth countered, and I imagined that authoritative tilt of her chin. "He may see her when she has regained her strength and her senses."

I closed my eyes. Hot water lapped against my ears as I sank lower in the tub. Scents of lavender rose on the steam. Water dripped, a steady ticking like a clock marking seconds that felt more like hours. I straightened, used my toes to flip the drain's lock, and wiggled out of the tub. Oz was right. I needed to get out of here.

*   *   *

An hour later, the windshield of my Corsica had fogged over and isolated me from the world outside. Cold air, heavy with musty odors of damp earth, seeped through the gap I'd left in the window. I set the letter down and tore open another envelope. This one, Quint had written while training in Georgia.

Rubbing the glass, I cleared a hole in the condensation and stared across the cemetery. The rain had stopped, the sun peeked through the clouds, and drops glimmered on the grass. I set the letter on the passenger seat, dumped the weekend edition of the *Gazette* out of its plastic and pulled it over the cast on my left leg. The elastic ankle band on my sweats, bunched at my knee, held the bag in place. I shoved the door open, worked the crutches out, and slid from the car.

Quint's Mustang wove along the cemetery's narrow road and stopped a few feet away. He climbed out and ambled toward me.

"Thought I might find you here."

"Where have you been?" I asked.

"Ruth's running interference. Every time I stopped by, you were sleeping. Every time I called, you were in the tub—You take a lot of baths." He flashed me a grin. "She's at your dad's now, so I finally got Oz."

"She's good at that." I motioned through my car's open door.

Quint glanced inside. His jaw went slack. "My letters? You never read them?"

"I thought you just walked away." Wind blew my hair across my face. Before I could finger the strands back, he tucked them behind my ear.

"I would never do that." He cupped my cheek, stroked his thumb over my lips and kissed me. "I shouldn't have left you the other night."

"If you hadn't, you might be dead."

"Went to Denny's with the guys, but something didn't feel right. I went by your house, and the lights were off. I found this." He reached into his shirt pocket, pulled out Richard's Celtic knot ring, and rolled it against his thumb. Then he gently took my right hand, slid the ring onto my middle finger and kissed my palm. "I went inside, found Morales and called the cops." He squeezed his eyes shut, wrapped his arms around me and pressed his cheek, rough with stubble, against mine. "Christ, Monkey. I though you were dead."

I thought so, too, and now life never felt sweeter. I absorbed the moment, his closeness, the scent of sandalwood and the warmth of his cheek against mine.

"I never want to lose you," he whispered, his voice muffled against my hair. "You want to know why I came back?" He chuckled, leaned away and met my gaze. "You're like a disease. All those years, I couldn't get you out of my head even though I thought you ignored my letters and phone calls. You infected me, Babe."

"Better than the flu," I offered.

He laughed. "Nope. I would've recovered from the flu."

For the first time since finding the rose on my car's dashboard, I felt happy. I tried to rise on my toes, but the cast kept me grounded. As though he knew what I intended, Quint bent toward me and touched his lips to mine. I latched onto him, needing the comfort of his embrace. He wrapped his arms around me, tightly, as though letting go would somehow sever our lives.

I leaned back, and smiled at the warm, caramel shade of his eyes.

"I want to visit Richard."

"Yeah, me too." He kissed me again, and then released his hold.

I readjusted the crutches beneath my arms. Quint crept along beside me as I made my way among the row of headstones. Seventh from the street, beneath the shadow of bare willow branches, the flat, granite marker looked more weather-aged than it had Christmas Eve, less than two weeks ago. *Richard Thomas Monakee.*

I wanted to kneel, clear the debris from the inscription as I usually did, but the cast on my leg was too bulky to maneuver. As though reading my thoughts, Quint crouched down and brushed wet leaves off the marker.

"I don't remember Tolson at all," Quint said. "I understand he was a year ahead of Rich and me. How could Tolson be so obsessed over Rich's life, and no one knew the guy existed?"

"How does the kid's who's bullied go unnoticed until he comes to school with a shotgun?" I shrugged. "They seem normal, hide their psychosis until something snaps and someone dies."

Quint nodded thoughtfully. "The car Tolson was driving? Morales said it *was* Rich's. Tolson found it at an auction. He'd gone AWOL from the Coast Guard, moved to Stockton where he probably killed Claire, according to Morales."

"You and Morales are getting chummy?" I never thought that'd happen.

"No," Quint said, shaking his head for emphasis. "He and I had a few things to straighten out, like him getting off my back." Then he switched subjects: "Hear about Dobbs?"

"He's on parole."

"Yeah, but his parole agent agreed to transfer his case here. With the prison overcrowding problems, the state's hesitant to send people back. Guess they figured he wasn't a threat. We're gonna need him, too," Quint added, motioning toward my cast. "That's too bulky for a high-hat pedal."

"Steve will be happy. He keeps trying to edge me out."

"That's not gonna happen. The judge sent Jimbo up for three years, so I'll be around a while. And Steve? It's not you. He's pissed off because Della kicked him out."

"Oh?" Maybe Della finally wised up.

"Guy's got a problem at the tables, lost three grand up at Chukchansi. She'd had enough. I tried to help," Quint said, and stood. "Gave him the plan."

"What was that?"

"You know, buy her something sexy," he said, and my mind flashed back to Carley's comment on seeing Quint purchase a pink lace negligee. "But he didn't follow through."

"And the rest of the plan?" I shifted the crutch to my other side, leaned against him and slipped my arm around his waist.

"Dinner. Bottle of wine. You know. Mood stuff."

"Entrapment?"

"Yeah." He gave me that cocky grin. "Worked on you, didn't it?"

Yep. It sure did.

ACKNOWLEDGEMENTS

Thank you to all of the following, I couldn't have gotten here without you: Doris Booth of Authorlink Literary Agency for believing in my work and me. A great agent, and even greater friend; my dear friend Roy Sollenberger for the wonderful title page art and the years of encouragement and support; my sons, Aaron and Adam Sanders, for their support and encouragement; the members of the Central Valley Writers' Workshop, particularly Barbara Mohler, Sharon Morningstar, Larry Patten, Bill Moal, Mark Johnson, Lee McKay, Monica McClanahan; Madera Police Department officers Sergeant Robert Salas, retired Sergeant Ken Alley, Officer Brian Esteves and all those detectives and officers who treated me like one of their own and read the manuscript for crime-related accuracy—because of you, Morales rings true as a detective; Detective Brad Stevens of the Fresno Police Department and my Crime Stoppers contact; Lieutenant Bill Ward, Sgt. Tyson Pogue, Sheriff John Anderson, PIO Erica Stuart of Madera County Sheriff's Department; former District Attorney Ernest LiCalsi, the deputy D.A.s and investigators for Madera County; members of The Writerie Kat Goldring, Shirley McKee, Roy "Rocky" Hatley, and Jane Ostrander; Gary Price for his knowledge of paramedics; all those who read the entire manuscript and provided the viewpoint of the reading public including Tina Amendola, Roy Sollenberger, Lee Modin, Rhonda Cargill, Lorraine Best, Cal Tatum, Robert Jarvis, Tami Jo Nix, Paul Sanford, Bradley Phillips; Madera Tribune publisher Charles Doud; retired librarian Karen Esteves; members of the DFW Writers' Workshop; my father Donald Jarvis who always told me "never give up"; and all those who encouraged me over the years while I learned, wrote, and strived to accomplish my goal. The list of those who have believed in and supported me would equal in size to a novel.

ABOUT THE AUTHOR

GLENNA JARVIS spent 15 years as a journalist in Cleburne, Texas (*Cleburne Eagle News*), Newport, Maine (*Rolling Thunder Express*), and most recently Madera, California (*The Madera Tribune*) where she served as managing editor, news editor and covered the crime beat. Founder of the Central Valley Writers' Workshop, Glenna has conducted numerous classes on the art of writing, and has learned as much from her fellow authors as she has taught them. She lives in Central California with her Border collie, Penny Lane, and cat, Sadie.

The author may be contacted by leaving a comment at www.glennajarvis.com or emailing Glenna@glennajarvis.com.